BLUNT FORCE MAGIC

THE MONSTERS AND MEN TRILOGY

BOOK ONE

LAWRENCE DAVIS

WILDBLUE
PRESS
WWW.WILDBLUEPRESS.COM

BLUNT FORCE MAGIC published by:
WILDBLUE PRESS
P.O. Box 102440
Denver, Colorado 80250

WILDBLUE PRESS is registered at the U.S. Patent and Trademark Offices.

ISBN 978-1-947290-10-5   Trade Paperback
ISBN 978-1-947290-11-2   eBook

Interior Formatting/Book Cover Design by Elijah Toten
www.totencreative.com

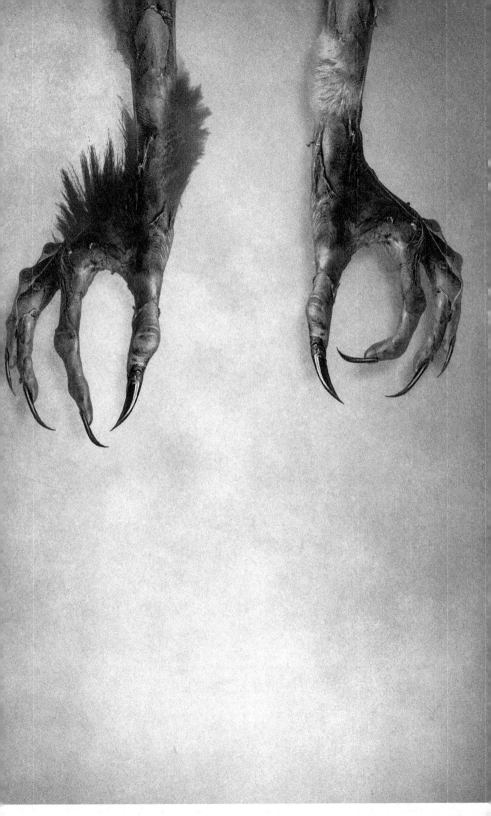

This book is dedicated to Patrick James Marinazzo

My best friend, a man who lived like a legend and loved like a saint, you are greatly missed.

Always forward.

I would also like to specially thank and acknowledge my mother, Deborah Davis; my biggest fan, greatest supporter and the person responsible for introducing me to the wonderful world of science fiction and fantasy.

CHAPTER 1

For a month and a half straight I'd been staring stupidly at this door.

Correction: for a month and a half straight I'd been staring at the green insignia carved *beside* the door with the same blank, dumbstruck face my father use to hate so much when I was a kid. Once a week I dropped a package from a fancy meal kit company on the welcome mat and just gawked. The symbol resonated with the life I used to live. It was an emblem of some kind, but who could say?

Most people imagined that when a ragtag group led by a hero was combing through tomes and scrolls, they usually happened upon whatever they were looking to find. In reality, that could take a *long* time. People and civilization were older than our concept of time, older than written language. Finding context for an archaic hieroglyph was tough work, I know; I used to be part of a merry band thumbing through those endless stacks of books. The search was maddening; you had to force-feed yourself so much information that you ended up brain-dumping half the lore you'd learned almost immediately after assimilating it once you were confident it wasn't what you were looking for.

Anyway.

For a month and a half straight I dropped the package down, stared, reflected, and usually just shrugged before leaving. It didn't just bother me because I couldn't place it; there was something about the insignia that didn't *fit*. Not my business anymore, though. I was an aging vagabond working a dead-end job because the benefits package was respectable and I could usually get through my entire day with only a few exchanged niceties as shallow as my faked smile.

Today wasn't any different, aside from the fact that I closed down the bar the night before and was suffering the consequences. At least it shouldn't have been. Package deposited, I gave myself the usual span of time to scrutinize the symbol. This time, I entertained the notion that it may have had some kind of localized Pagan origin. This area had an extensive and rich history, and, as I wasn't really an expert in it, maybe that was why it was such a mystery to me. I was about to return to my asinine, uneventful life, when I felt *it*.

When you've consorted with evil—and I'm not talking about a rambunctious frat boy or some hyper-aggressive meathead who's heavy-handed with a girlfriend, but actual evil: you feel it coming. It has a distinctive, suffocating presence. We all experience it differently, but the effect and impression are universal.

So, there I was, half a decade removed from a life I'd left behind, when everything went to absolute shit. Whatever the governing power behind timing was must have hated me. Once a week for a month and a half I'd spent no more than a minute on this doorstep. The disparity between the time spent there compared to the time spent everywhere else had to be astronomical, and yet there I was.

The hairs on my arms had just about fully risen when the door I was staring at exploded open. I was fast, but not supernaturally so. I'd spent more time in the thick of violence than I cared to admit or recall, and that alone saved me from getting a face-full of splintering wood. I spun out of the way just in time to see the guy who'd just wrecked his own door with a Spartan kick follow that up by leveling an old school, pump-action shotgun at the very quaint fence I'd just walked past to get here. There was a life-threatening fear in his old eyes, his hands shook as he aimed the barrel of the gun past me and toward the gate in his front yard. I turned to see what could possibly have driven so seemingly sane a man out of his mind.

That's when I saw it. That was when everything started to come together.

This isn't a world of make-believe, yet we still seek what we know to be impossible—from the wild extravagance seen in filmmaking to the outlandish lore built into any science-fiction series. It has a way of speaking to us, an escape from a reality that's grown stale or unforgiving. All of us have daydreamed about it, growing pensive while we wonder what it would be like to be surrounded by such wonder.

It's not everything you think it is. Walking in a winter wonderland is a cold, scathing trek.

Routine has a way of bastardizing normalcy which makes it seem so unremarkable that we strive for something completely outside of our understanding: fantasy.

The problem with fantasy is that we've largely relegated it to the *happily ever after* genre. It doesn't work that way, in real life. We're afraid of the dark because a cultivated sixth sense is warning us away from it. Our instincts were honed over countless centuries, a direct line to our subconscious protecting us from something. Man built fire not only for warmth, but to ward off the shadow that was eager to swallow us whole; it's why the Bible begins with the creation of light to divorce us from the darkness, that separation is foundational to our species. Over time we've lost that fear, the limelight of our neon paradise making us immune to it. You should know that there is an ugliness just beyond our understanding that if we invite it, if we consider it too long, if we happen upon it, will strike. It might flirt with us, all coy and suggestive, but like every arrogant predator, that's just it toying with a meal before devouring it whole.

I know, I'd been eaten alive. And here I was, in the middle of it again. They say the path to hell is paved with good intentions, and they couldn't be more right.

***

The shotgun thundered, the sound reverberated through my eardrum and it felt like half my head went numb. It snapped me back to the present. If you've never had the distinct pleasure of standing beside a powerful weapon when it's gone off, it wasn't everything Hollywood had made it out to be. It was deafeningly loud and incredibly angry.

The guy who'd just come out like a suburban Rambo had a mix of madness and betrayal in his stare; before he could fire again I slapped a hand beneath the barrel and directed it toward the porch roof. "Stop," I hissed with as much calmness as I could muster. "Get. Inside. Now." I was trying to stay calm even as adrenaline tore through me quick as a lightning strike.

The thing he had shot at was an abomination. Humanoid in shape, but warped by something insidious. Its fingers were spindled and long; halfway down each was a bloody opening where its claws started. Its knees were snapped backward like a bird and its legs ended with six-toed feet, gnarled and lethally clawed as well. Claws so sharp they cut back into its own body, leaving its hands and feet filthy with dried black blood. Literally rending the very flesh they sprouted from.

All of that didn't compare to its face. Night-black eyes glittered in sunken slits, the suffocating void in them a direct reflection of their indifference to dealing out so much death. An exaggerated mouth was not quite canine but in that cast, as if its maker couldn't decide what kind of monster this would be. The beast's teeth were several rows deep like the jaw of a shark, elongated, razor-sharp, and capable of biting clean through a person. Its arms were so long they nearly dragged those clawed fingers on the ground, which made it easier to sink down to all four limbs and prepare to pounce.

I had only ever read about this abomination, only seen estimations of its likeness inked on parchment, but it all came flooding back. It was an ancient enemy of mankind, a conjured creature with more names than I cared to cite. In most circles they called them Stalkers, as they were used to hunt down someone who was notoriously hard to find and even harder to capture or kill. Here's the breakdown: first, in order to bring one of those things to this reality, you had to be powerful—powerful enough to alter the future of mankind. The second part was that they were a perfect predator: fearless, nearly indestructible, and singular in their focus to obtain their prey. They tipped the scale somewhere between three and four hundred pounds, moved too fast to register with human eyesight, and they topped off at just beneath seven feet. We were desperately outmatched and wasting ammo was going to get us all killed.

I wasn't easing my grip on the gun, and the old man's shocked look turned into full-fledged panic. I'd had very little time to understand what was happening and less to react, and because this was just a banner day when the man started trying to hurriedly explain what was happening he was speaking in Spanish.

Perfect.

It wasn't all his fault. My complexion led a lot of people believe I was of Hispanic descent. I was short and stocky, five-seven if we're being honest, five-nine if it's a dating website. A fan of a good workout but also guilty of frequenting dive bars and burger joints so it wasn't like I was going to win any shirtless competitions. I had the everyday-guy thing going for me, though if the girl is desperate enough I think I passed as handsome in the right light. The confusion was caused by my jet-black hair and standard issue brown eyes that seemed to come stock to my tan skin and with that people assumed I was a card-carrying member of the Spanish-speaking community. I wasn't.

So, while he was yelling in Spanish, I had a major-league bad ass dropping to all fours—the telltale sign it was about to burst across the whole lawn and start ripping me to shreds—and five years of rust to contend with. You know, another Tuesday afternoon.

***

In the life before this one I was a budding Artificer. Now, the internet dictionary will tell you that's a skilled inventor or craftsmen. Beneath that there will be a description from Dungeons and Dragons. Don't believe me? Check it out, I'll wait. The idea was that I would become something between the two. The truth was that my mentor was an Artificer and I was a promising student who'd had all the right stuff to be one myself but couldn't quite put it together. That's how it is in this life. Hell, life in general—a quarterback with every tool and physical advantage who just can't step up in the big game, a wizard from the most esteemed family line unable to bring together the simplest spell. The optimist in me kept at it for as long as I could until the work I started to produce was actually becoming less helpful and more a liability, so eventually the pragmatist in me won out. Still, I had an ace or two up the old sleeve and a treasure trove of trinkets handed down to me when the old man, my mentor, was killed with the rest of our merry band of do-gooders.

It's like I said though, this life isn't an ideal escape into joyous adventure. This life also just had a way of finding you.

Even with the tragedy, hardship, and let-down that came with having to play second fiddle to the people I loved and respected most, I was never much of a quitter. If I was going to punch my ticket for that big ride in the sky, I would rather do it in the thick of a fight. Going gently into the night just wasn't my style.

***

A mix of adrenaline, youth, and momentum helped me wrest the shotgun clean out of what I assumed was the homeowner's grasp as I used my other hand to shove him back through the dangling door he'd just kicked almost clean off the hinges. I was trying to control the cadence of my breath and stifle the rise of fear, even with the incessant cries going on behind me. I could distinctly make out the old man and another voice. I had some modicum of success with gulping down the desire to run for my life. This creature was full of enough self-preservation to be wary when faced with someone who won't turn and run the second they laid eyes on it.

I imagined that this was what a gunslinger felt like when faced with an even bigger and badder opponent while being without a revolver to draw. This game was going to be based on a bluff, which was hard enough when my attention was undivided. Right now I was worried about whoever was yelling in the house, what this thing was doing here, and this nagging feeling about the pagan symbol next to the door. I fed the monster a smirk, playing my utter lack of hand with this all-in gambit for what it was worth.

That is when I heard it. *Maria.* That was the name the old man called the female voice inside. Apparently, the name got the mud-stuck wheels in my hungover head going because the symbol I had been wrestling with trying to figure suddenly leapt out at me. *The Morrigan.* The Irish goddess of witches and about everything else. That was what bothered me. The symbol guarding the door was wrong, which was a pretty common thing when trying to decipher an ancient text that was based off another, even older text and translated into a foreign language that hadn't even been invented yet. The stalemate on the lawn was ending fast, the beast was either growing too restless to give a damn about the fact I hadn't backed down or it simply had seen through my guise of worthy guardian. It gave a stilted sniff that drew in the still air between us for a taste. The action somehow came off as a kind of snide cackle to me.

There it was: the calm. The calm right before the storm.

Those powerful, twisted haunches flexed and both it and I exploded into motion. It crossed twenty feet with one incredible leap, bounding right for me. Me? I slapped the broken door as hard as I could, the familiar sensation of pain lanced through my hand and down my forearm. One of the fractured shards of wood cut into my hand producing an ugly cut that bled freely, but I didn't slow. Slowing down would get me killed. I turned to the symbol that I had stared at for a minute a week for six weeks and finally solved at least one mystery before an untimely death.

Dipping my free hand fingers into my cupped one where the blood from my laceration was pooling, I drew one last line above the circular singlet decoration just outside the door frame, crossing a lone line that rose from above the oval that the symbol was held inside of. That last bit was the missing piece to complete the circle of power. It didn't require blood or anything so dramatic, but I was out a pen (packages are signed for with a digital pen now) and it wasn't as if I had a lot of time to work with. Plus, with the language barrier between me and the owner of the house, it wasn't as if I could convey what I needed quickly enough. Still, blood has power in it too. Magic is a funny thing, anyway. Belief in something can empower it.

The Stalker was so close that I swear I could feel that *thing* breathing down my neck. It hit the invisible barrier like the force of nature it was, shaking the entire foundation of the house and sending a literal *whoosh* of air washing over me. I could smell its acrid breath and taste the sheer foulness of it. I was half in the door and half on the small porch when a very human urge came over me. Despite knowing better, I turned back around to get a real good look at this old, ancient evil. For a long time we took measure of one another. They say it's dangerous to stare into the abyss because it will eventually notice you. There was a cold intelligence in these wild eyes and I knew it had marked me, from the way it was glaring to the deep draw of breath that was thick with my scent. In a heartbeat I'd made mortal enemies with the most powerful thing I'd ever had the distinct displeasure of crossing.

And it wasn't even three o'clock yet.

Skip over the part where an impossible Hunter from another reality was here, or the fact that the panicked man knew to immediately open fire at it, and of course the botched symbol of an old, powerful goddess revered by witches, and we still had a guy in khaki shorts and a puffy coat (me) from a brand name parcel service stumbling into a living room with two wide-eyed strangers staring slack-jawed at me. From the outside looking in, what I'd done was impressive. I'd smirked at a monster before cutting my own hand open, repaired their protection emblem, and raised a field of invisible power that stone-cold stopped a freight training monster midway into a crazed rush.

"Hi," I winced foolishly, trying to gather myself from a wave of emotion that I couldn't even begin to streamline into any kind of coherent thought. "*Hola?*"

"I speak English," the girl countered irritably. I had a way of annoying people almost instantly and judging from her disposition it seemed that my run of bad luck with women was going to hold strong. "Who are you?" There was something off about her, but, given the fact there is an age-old Evil stalking a barrier I'd just whipped up on the fly and the still-talking old man is serving as a soundtrack to our strained conversation, I was having a tough time placing it. She quieted the shotgun-wielding lunatic with a reassuring word or two, but before I could think how I was going to answer, she was looking at me again with those gorgeous brown eyes.

Gorgeous? *Dammit.*

"Janzen," I dumbly pointed at the badge that proudly displayed my name across it. "Janzen Robinson."

"Maria," she said curtly, clearly disinterested in spending any more time on formalities. "How did you do that?" An up-nod from an elegantly shaped chin directed my attention back to the barrier. I wasn't really empathetic to the worlds beyond the In-Between, but I've enough sense to discern that the Stalker was gone.

"You didn't draw the symbol correctly, but it was close enough to do most of what it's designed to do. Precision is pretty important with this stuff, almost as much as the belief that'll fuel it." I don't know why I only realized at that moment, but I had my hands up. I was either clutch under pressure or an utter mess. Demonic monster? Bring it on. Pretty girl? Catastrophe.

I put my hands down with a half shrug. It looked perfectly ridiculous since I still had the shotgun. Exchanging a look with the father, I awkwardly handed the spent weapon over to him and he, being just as embarrassed, muttered his thanks.

"We got lucky," I answered honestly. "I assumed someone in the house believed in Morrigan, the old Irish goddess of witches. Since I was right, when I completed the insignia it amped up the protection spell. Before, it probably kept someone from aiming a tracking spell at you or maybe scrying, but it wasn't going to be able to ward off something like that unless done properly."

She murmured in Spanish to her father, translating everything that had been said. The blast of the shotgun in this Pleasantville-esque neighborhood was going to be problematic and, with as colorful as my history was and a job I was barely skirting by at,

I really didn't want to be here when the police stopped by. "That thing is pretty heavy stuff, Maria." It was taking everything in me not to start humming the main song from *West Side Story*. I was a mess. "Nobody sends something that bad after a newcomer."

The newcomer bit touched a nerve judging from the prideful squaring of her shoulders. She was gorgeous. The kind of gorgeous that kept you from thinking straight. Five foot nothing but with curves most women fight a lifetime for, and her modest makeup only emphasized her natural allure. Probably just into her twenties. There was some old scarring on her cheeks and the photos on the walls showed a girl whose expression said that she preferred there not to be photographic evidence of her teenage years. I'd guess she was an ugly duckling type, the kind of kid who got picked on in high school and turned to the strange and occult for some semblance of acceptance. Most of the time people cruised through that phase without running afoul with any kind of issue, but once in awhile someone stumbled over something real enough, and that was when all the worst kind of bad would come crawling out. What should have been a gimmick book was actually an old journal of a real conjurer, or maybe an authentic how-to for summoning dark spirits and demons. It was worse if they had a natural inclination or talent, and even though she hadn't smoothed over all those rough edges, Maria was brimming with raw power.

Get a young kid who was ostracized by community and peers, compounded by the tragedy of a missing or dead parent—a snapshot judgement I was making about her based off the fact that there wasn't a mother in any of the pictures decorating the house and the father was still wearing a wedding band—and bam, we have a renegade in our midst. "Renegade" was slang in our world for someone who not only happened upon all this stuff on their own, without guidance or help, but had a real potential to tap into some pretty considerable force. They were the equivalent of giving an eight-year-old an Uzi. I couldn't remember the last time the term "renegade" came to mind, or any of the old colloquialisms from my past life for that matter, but I could feel the memories stirring.

"I know what I'm doing." There's the wail of a siren, the hallmark of an authority figure who was not going to buy the whole illegal-discharge-of-a-weapon-because-a-demon-dog-was-chasing-us excuse. "Plus, wh—"

"That thing is going to follow you to the end of the Earth." Interrupting wasn't usually my style, but the small window of time was fast closing and this girl had attitude written all over her, even if she was scared half to death. "You need my help, and if you want me to help, you have exactly..." I paused, more for effect than anything else to pull back my sleeve and stare at my old, rickety timepiece. "One minute. Otherwise? They get my statement, you get a smile, my job gets to fire me and I get to be at the bar before happy hour is over. Do you even know what the hell that thing out there was? Because either you're the strongest practitioner in the city by a long shot or you have no idea what the hell you're doing and you're trying to save face right now. That thing out there? That's an apex predator, a great white shark; it's as old as time and has remained at the top of the food chain since the dawn of it."

"Why do you even think it's after me?" she asked heatedly, and gestured toward her father. His frustrated rambling had become a kind of white noise to all that was happening. "My father has been losing sleep for a week, saying he's seen a Devil after him." I knew she didn't believe it had been set after him, I could tell by the look that washed over her picture-perfect face.

"You've got an emblem of your belief on you somewhere?"

She gave a hurried nod, pulling a necklace out with a pendant that represented a faction of witches of Gaelic origin.

"It probably used him to find you; that probably shielded you. I don't really have time to give you a whole breakdown of this stuff right now." Another cry of a racing cop car stressed my point for me. "Why the hell would something like that be after you?"

There was something incredibly cute about the way she deliberated on whether or not to tell me. That was also a sure sign that this was going to become a complication I couldn't afford on a laundry list of stuff already well out of my price range. In short, a pretty woman was going to make an impossible situation more difficult. With an indignant huff of air and nod she relented.

"I did a spell for a client about two months ago," she said, tucking a wild strand of sun-kissed brown hair behind her ear— dammit, *focus*. "It was just a tracking spell. I don't know who the guy was but he paid in cash." The way she bit her lip told me there was a whole lot more to why she accepted, but judging from what I'd heard about the economy going to hell and the hardship of middle America, it wasn't hard to guess why it was she'd take a shady, back alley deal in a crunch. "All I had to do was use a piece of what he was looking for and perform the ritual. That was it, I swear. My coven recommended me to him."

I believed her. Well, I was an idiot with women and I was always going off believing them, but between the confusion of her father, the wailing siren and the adrenaline starting to wear off from staring down a literal nightmare I didn't think she had enough in her to lie.

"And no name?" I asked. I expected the shake of her head. "Anything you remember at all?" We were pressed for time and to make it worse, I had to coach them through some kind of fake alibi for when the cavalry did arrive. "Tell me everything, even stuff you think is insignificant."

***

Usually I'd throw myself in front of the investigation to try and stall, but time was of the essence and there wasn't a lot I could do from behind bars. We cooked up a story about a would-be robber trying to get the drop on me and her father coming to my rescue. Of course, that meant I had to get a black eye to sell it, which didn't take as much convincing as I would have liked. An old friend once told me I had a punchable face, but I owed him money so I took that opinion with a grain of salt.

I'd written down every detail she told me about the man who'd hired her and, after making her review those notes a second and third time, I instructed her to stay in the house until I could contact her with more information. The sigil wasn't going to hold very long but it was the only place I knew for her to weather the proverbial storm. The symbol, now correct, wasn't going to hold because of the quality, forget the mind-numbing attention to detail necessary to perfectly replicate the painstaking intricacy required for each rune to work, the base wasn't facing the right direction, the circle wasn't chiseled, the networking of lines that started every symbol and ultimately decided just how powerful it would be would have taken me a week to get down and that's a rush job. There wasn't enough time to perfect the sigil, but for the day it would hold. It's not just about an obstinate, uncompromising eye for detail but belief, too. I hoped that the Stalker would lie low for a while so the shoddy work wouldn't be so big a risk. Not to mention there was something about the way it looked at me that told me in no uncertain terms that it may have a keen interest to rip me limb-from-limb first.

Small victories. Hooray.

CHAPTER 2

RE-INITIATION

I went home. I lived in a cheap, generic one-one apartment. My dog was rowdy and poorly trained, but he was the only creature not pissed off at the sight of my face so I tended to let him get away with a lot. Max was a fawn and white pitbull, somewhere between a brawny fifty to seventy pounds, depending on the weather and depression (I ordered a lot of pizza when I was down and he was good at getting the crust), and an absolute lover. The breed was misunderstood and I could relate to that, so adopting one only seemed natural. I kept all of my old equipment in the back closet of my modestly sized bedroom and, for someone who was only twenty-five, it was a lot tougher than it should have been to kneel down and pull the big cardboard box from out of the back. Duct tape robbed me of any attempt to look dignified in my nostalgia while fighting to get to my stuff. Each artifact rifled through was like shotgunning a whole bottle of booze, that flooding fire of unease stoked by embers of melancholia. I guess in the end it was just a painful experience, digging through a past I wasn't satisfied with.

I'd cut my teeth as a two-timing hustler, a pauper prince trying to become some kind of concrete king. The city I came up in was a cesspool of violence and crime. I love Cleveland, but it's a rough town. It'll unapologetically eat you up and spit you out if you're not up to snuff. It was even tougher if you were in the lifestyle. That meant anyone who couldn't carry their weight was bound to find themselves in a shallow grave at an early age. I'd had an affinity for addictive behavior, the best kind of bad was my vice: whenever I came across some cold hard cash I doled it out to whoever had the fix of the week.

That changed when I tried to pick the pocket of someone who had a hand twice as fast as mine, which at the time was saying something. I didn't live a lavish lifestyle, but between a forgivable smile and some charming quick-talk, I could escape most of the trouble I stepped in.

At sixteen I ended up working as the help in a second-hand store owned by the guy who had caught me trying to pick his pocket. The store was a front for a kind of trafficking I'd never imagined. The whole sordid history isn't important, but suffice it to say I got to look behind the curtain: that thing going bump in the night is very aware you're looking for it and no matter how far we've come as a species, we'll forever be a staple in its diet. The man who took me in owned an antiques store with a makeshift cafe attached to the side of it. Our clientele was what made the place unique. We didn't cater to renovating housewives; we instead made our coin bartering with the unbelievable. Witches and wizards were the steadiest customers, but we got it all. It took me a while to believe, but seeing is believing and while I only got a glimpse in the beginning, it was enough to sway me. I was a trickster, so when I tell you they sold me, they sold me.

Still, it didn't take long for me to get burned out on that life and, after losing pretty much everyone I'd come to care for, I got out as best I could. Dead mentor, estranged parents, and a nonexistent social circle don't add up to a very cheerful holiday season.

I had to get away from any piece of good in my old life. I couldn't handle this new world. The impossible came with an equal price to pay for it; nobody died clean here and that's how it ended for all of us. Facedown in a nameless alley killed by some dark piece of modern day walking macabre.

I'd never been a promising pupil, and I fancied myself something of an anti-hero, so after getting my ass handed to me countless times, I finally curbed the headlining act and relegated myself to the background. The guy who took me in didn't mind; he used to prattle on about how the biggest difference is made by the smallest influence, but now that I'm on the late side of my twenties and the wrong side of fate, I thought it was best to try and move on.

After shrugging into an old jacket, boots, and hat, I set aside a belt and continued my search. The shoebox I was looking for was secured in the farthest corner and by the time I got to it, I'd had more than enough time to realize how bad of an idea this was. The problem was that there wasn't anyone left in this town to take up this fight. They'd died half a decade ago. Better men and women than me. They died and left all the innocence in a sinful city without a champion.

I shook my head while trying to shake off those thoughts. Opening the shoebox revealed my old life, and I was quick to stow it away in a series of pockets all over my person. It was bittersweet, the feeling of that old weight in my jacket was a cold comfort and yet again I was ushered back to a time much better than this one. Notebook and pencil, two bracelets, a necklace with a pendant that was less a symbol and more a bunch of intersecting metal, a small bag of marbles, a broken watch to replace my slow one, and finally a leather wrist band. You know those really awful ones that got popular for a little while? Yeah. When you create a tool, don't disguise it in something that's a fad. Rookie mistake, but I was young then.

I didn't carry a gun. It wasn't that they weren't effective or that I was against them, but me, personally? I was an awful shot and it'd end up being a liability instead of an asset. Still, a twelve-gauge slug will knock the stuffing out of a lot of things, so I never discouraged someone from picking one up. Sunglasses were the last bit of the ensemble, and once again I was a victim of youth because they were more fitting of a highway patrolman or a cocky fighter pilot. Unfortunately for me it was tough to craft an item and without my mentor being there to walk me through it, I didn't have the talent to construct anything of worth.

So, I was stuck with the classics. The jacket, leather band, excessive trinkets, wristwatch, and sunglasses all banded together to make a perfectly ridiculous outfit. I spent a little extra time feeding my dog, then left a voicemail to the closest thing I had in the way of a friend to be on alert that I may need him to stop by and take care of the mutt.

It was a cold night. The chill was going to remind me that I was in a leather jacket for most of the day, and already the leather of that comically out-of-style band was irritating my skin. It was closing in on nightfall by the time I poured into the beat up pickup truck I tooled around in. My first stop was the Last Love, a swanky little bar with a nightclub ambiance. They stuck to postmodern blues at the insistence of the owner. Not my scene. My scene was a rom-com on the couch while devouring take-out and having a one-sided conversation with my dog while he gave me very tolerating, humoring looks in between gazing at my food. This was the only thing that might help me get on the right track, though. It was a kind of unofficial gathering for all of those who are in the know. Even I couldn't help from frequenting it once in awhile.

It was run and operated by a woman named Gale, no last name. She was the bartender; she didn't take orders. She'd pour you whatever she was feeling up to making, and she was a profoundly frightening woman. In a world where most of the unbelievable like to name-drop and posture, she was incredibly secretive—even by our standards—and it seemed that nobody ever had any interest in making trouble at her establishment. There was no neutrality banner, no ceasefire agreement; the peace was kept by the threat of Gale and the doorman alone.

I got there just before dark. The horizon was broken shards of fire combatting the calming black of night. The skyline was made sharper by the contrasted lighting, inspiring a gothic feeling when staring at it. That, or I had just read too much noir.

The doorman was big. Uncomfortably so. Dead between six and seven foot, he had the frame of a truck to match. A Stetson sharply cut over half his face and yet somehow he was able to make it work. Dressed in loose flannel and denim that was faded and torn by work and wear, not styling, he was a cowboy, down to the tanned leather skin and hide boots. Muscle strained against the fabric, enough to make someone wonder why he wasn't pile-driving quarterbacks into turf for millions of dollars a year instead of standing idly beside a small club door. Well, the everyday patron might wonder, but we didn't. They called him a lot of names, but best I could tell the real one was Xander—and big-bodied Xander was looking quite comfortable despite being perched on so small a stool. In fact, I was almost convinced he was dead asleep, a mistake many people had made in the past.

Beside him was a smaller fellow, one dutifully asking for identification and quickly scanning it. He was a studious looking man with a stare so keen and sharp it cut clean through you. He wore generic clothing that was tailored to him, despite being cheaply made. There was no hint of personality or care in that listless stare, he just mechanically went about the job he'd been tasked with. I hadn't seen him before and thought I'd do the courtesy of introducing myself.

"Hey, I'm—"

"Janzen Robinson," the small one said.

"Uh, yeah—"

He interrupted me a second time, except this time it was with a finger signaling for me to pause instead of that monotone voice. It was annoying, I decided just then, but I had to choose: me or my ego. "She'll see you after the first set."

I must have watched a dozen people walk in before me and not one got checked, and yet when I moved to enter I ended up colliding with a wall of scratchy, bourbon smelling mass. I didn't get a thorough pat down; instead, the doorman leaned into my personal space to take an intrusive sniff. It was a none-too-pleasant reminder of the Stalker I had just tangled with. Between what I'd heard about this man and the spellbinding color of his stare, I wondered whether or not he was wholly human. His eyes were decidedly reptilian, a kind of brown and gold agglomeration that dimmed and brightened based on temperament. His rough face may not have given anything away, but those damn eyes did.

"Nice bracelet." He was posturing, although making fun of my excess of jewelry and the leather band I was wearing was certainly warranted.

"Yeah? Well your hat is stupid."

That earned a chortle from the small sidekick, and while I felt as if I'd effectively signed my own death warrant, I tried to keep my stare steady and my smile smug. They exchanged a look after the short one seemed to hear something the rest of us couldn't; whatever passed between them garnered me entrance. Before I could make it all the way through, the doorman and I checked shoulders. I saw it coming, so I put every bit of my two-hundred-pound frame into it.

I stumbled through the door feeling like an asshole who just tried to tackle a brick wall.

Inside was spacious and dimly lit with the kind of atmosphere that would be ideal after a long week. The music was magnificent, even though I wasn't a jazz guy. Give me alternative any day, you know, wayward revolutionaries and misguided angst. That was me. I sidled up at the bar and waited patiently. From here I was able to watch the dozen or so nobodies populating the place. Everyone was giving the talent on stage his proper respect, and while quite a few of the glasses were empty, not a single complaint was being voiced. From here I could see Gale's back. She was leggy, lost between a well-lived forty or a hard-partying twenty. She had a kind of realistic ageless quality, really, because no matter where the truth lay, she was still impossibly lovely. Her auburn hair flowed freely down to a wasp waist; the curved line of her body continued down into toned legs crossing one another. I'd speak on what a great ass she's got, but I like to think myself better than that.

I sat. I listened. I replayed a very full day over in my head.

"You gained weight," she said. Judging by the slight and the annoyed look plastered over her incredibly beautiful face, it was obvious to me that this wasn't the first thing she'd said. I daydreamed hard, it was kind of a curse. She'd made me a drink already. As I said, Gale didn't take orders, she simply gave you a cursory once-over and would make you a drink. Take or leave it. "And you're aging terribly."

I feigned a sunny disposition that was ripe with sarcasm, took my drink and lifted it in a makeshift salute. "Thanks, Gale. Nothing like a good solid kick when you're down."

She had a feline grace amplified by a Cheshire grin as she bowed down to meet me eye-to-eye. Hers were a powerful collaboration of green and sea blue swimming together in concert. They moved like a living constellation, and I was again reminded that I was walking in a world of giants while very much a man.

My fear must have been palpable, and she sated by it, because Gale shifted from her predatory mannerism to something mercifully softer. I daresay it was an attempt to comfort me. I was about to dive into the proverbial deep end while wearing cement shoes and she knew it.

We sat in a companionable silence; the music started again and while I expected her to return to the perch at the end of the bar to regain a front row seat to the show, she stayed with me. Whatever fruity concoction she had cooked up was pure magic, smooth and yet with enough bite on the ass end to remind me I was still numbing all my worries, if only for a small while.

"I did not expect to see you here again, Janzen. What's it been, a year?"

"Makes both of us, but I kind of fell into something and wasn't sure where else to start. And yeah," I mumbled distractedly while the music took me away. "About that."

While Gale was a frightening thing, if you knew what it was you were looking at, there was a kind of comfort in the fact that she was not looking on me with pity. "Are you really waiting for me to spur you on?"

I barked a laugh. "I was doing deliveries—"

"—Deliveries?" she interjected, disapprovingly.

"Hey, it's a job. Anyway, deliveries, and I come across this house. As luck would have it, I get to this place just as it's being attacked." I wouldn't bring up a run of the mill mugging or breaking and entering to her and she knew as much. This was something different, the pause I had purposely timed when retelling this story is clueing her into as much and now I had her undivided attention. "...By a Stalker. An Ancient, one of the *Cura*—"

"Do not speak that name here," she snapped with an unremitting authority that made my mouth audibly *click* it shut so fast. "And one of those haven't come into the realm of man in centuries, Janzen. Centuries." Another spell of silence, this one less agreeable, was shared between us. "Swear it."

I'd heard from many that once you attached your name to something it carried a different kind of weight, that there was a power in it. "I do," I said. Now, this whole anchoring your name to a statement was new to me, so I clumsily did a crisscross over my heart. "It couldn't have been more than a few miles from the bar. Now, what I need to know is who has the kind of reach to not only call one of those up from the Abyss and get it through the In-Between, but leash it as well."

The implication of her being one of those suspects was hopefully nullified by the fact that I came to her about this very issue and, truthfully, while I knew Gale was a power, I wasn't sure if even she had the reach to bring one of those over and make it do her bidding. Bidding. *Christ*, I felt so corny just thinking it.

"That's not a simple task, Janzen, but you may not be looking for so big a power as you think." I was missing something, and judging by the very expectant look written across her face it was evident that it should be fairly obvious.

"I don't know," I said, hesitantly. "That's some major power."

"There are only two types of people who would do something of this magnitude," she said. One long, elegant finger ticked off from a fist. "A master..." she was baiting me, now. Waiting until I filled in the elongated silence drifting between us.

It took me longer than I would have hoped, but not as long as it might have for some; the epiphany dawned on me as if a physical blow. All this time I had immediately jumped to the worst case, I wasn't breaking this down from every vantage point and seeing clearly. I was afraid and dealing with my own doubt, fixated on my own insignificance that I hadn't even entertained that this could be so some rank amateur in way over their head, or some precocious punk aiming too high too fast. "...Or a fool."

CHAPTER 3

CONTACT

Outside greeted me with a rush of air colder than expected and for once I was glad to be in this patchwork leather blazer that had obviously been tailored for someone taller than me. The lifeline of the city lay within cold slabs of man-made stone, and the people walking listlessly across it were its blood. At the heart of the city was downtown, an impressive series of skyscrapers reaching for the indifferent stars. Walking in the city centered me, reminded me how small and trivial I was in the grand scheme of all of this magnificence. It sounded bleak, but it gave me perspective. People in our world liked to play it close to the vest, it could be maddening. They spoke riddles in cryptic dialogue; sometimes I wondered if I should have some kind of an interpreter. Made getting a lead on anything a pain in the ass. Nonetheless, I'd at least gotten the beginning of a scent. Either some big-time influence was after Maria, which if that was the case I might as well call this a suicide run and start churning through my bucket list, or somebody in the same weight class as her was pissed enough to go nuclear.

I spent the next hour or so just kicking around theories, but none of them gained a lot of traction. I liked the nameless client theory at first, but if they knew who and where she was there were easier ways to kill her. Coincidence was usually a red flag but that one just seemed like a case of timing rather than motive. Try as I might, I never really had the mind for this, and to make it worse, while I was aware of some of the happenings going on behind the curtain, it was hard for me to accurately place it all. My knowledge was left wanting when compared to people like Gale, the doorman, hell, probably most of the people in the bar I just walked out of.

"Behind the curtain" was a turn of phrase used by the community to describe something that could directly affect us in our day-to-day lives, but was still a well-kept secret from those who lived normal lives. The most you'd get was a flash in the news about a wild dog attack, brutal mugging or missing persons report.

For instance, vampires weren't smooth talking sophisticates that wanted to seduce you. They were vicious, top-tier predators that ravaged their prey. They hunted them down, broke them into submission, harvested them for food by keeping them alive for as long as possible. Behind the curtain was ugly as hell.

Speaking of ugly, I suddenly caught a distinct, pungent scent, one that made me cringe; while my original thought was to chalk it up to bad sewage, my fight-or-flight instinct was starting to signal me. That was something else; our sixth sense was something I've mentioned before and for good reason: listen to it. It was the product of millennia after millennia of sharpened instinct; it was evolution trying to communicate something to your addled brain that you weren't consciously aware of.

Deduction was swift: since my rent was actually paid this month and I hadn't pissed the doorman off so bad that he'd make it personal, that only left the Stalker. I knew what I needed to do. Steel the mind and wipe it clean. Move from the panic of being hunted to the lines of cold, hard logic that could help me figure a way out of this. While I hadn't immediately recognized it, I was slowing down, so I faked giving my upper half a pat down before pretending to be satisfied that I felt something in my breast pocket and kept right on. I finished selling my casually walking production by starting to hum *Hips Don't Lie* by Shakira. I was scared shitless and it was the only thing I could think up. Not my proudest moment.

Lore was tricky; as I've mentioned with the romanticized bastardization of vampires and the poring over centuries of text, a lot of it was hearsay and exaggeration written down as if gospel. Stuck between wanting to run and knowing I wasn't fast enough, while ducking into a residence would no doubt endanger anyone inside and maybe worse wasn't an option... I was about as bad off as I could get.

I was tough. Self-deprecating humor and a bad sense of my own value had a way of making me come across as a push-over, but the truth was I was anything but. If I could steer this to a main street where the attention of the masses could be an issue, it was likely I could limp out of this. Even the boogeyman wanted to stay out of the spotlight, and it was a general rule of thumb among all of us in the lifestyle that we kept it quiet or something even bigger and badder would end up retiring us.

Slumping over as if warding off the cold and concealing my hands, I hung a right onto a street one over from the main drag—but, as luck would have it, this block was currently doing its best impression of a ghost town.

These things killed before Cain and Abel, they were as smart as they were ferocious, and once it had gotten hip to what I was doing it, was on the move. I'd spent a lifetime outsmarting people more intelligent than me; the trick was to play off hubris, whether that was constantly praising the person you were pitted against or maintaining a dim-witted facade. This was no different. I caught a blur of movement to my right, so I whipped abruptly around to face it. The Stalker was more cunning than rabid, and they were notorious for strategy and deception. This move to the right was just to draw my attention, to put my back to where it was really intending to strike.

That was when I heard an annoyed howl and those twisted knife feet scraping excruciatingly off the cement behind me. A moment earlier, the surreptitious creature was soundlessly bounding for my exposed back, ready to rip me limb from limb and rend my throat wide open. Now it was trying to skate over a few dozen marbles, their translucence blending into the asphalt.

I was coming back around, full circle; my arm with the broken wristwatch whipped with all the momentum built up from the pivot, the force of my weight behind it and the know-how of a kid who spent his entire life fistfighting. Plant the leg, twist the hip, throw six inches behind the target. Normally a punch to the face of the demon-dog would have been an idiotic move, their leathery flesh was shield enough from most physical blows and the fact that they are a clear head taller than most of the tallest men made them immune to melee.

But my broken watch with its etched sigils came to life, snaking over my whole hand. The roughed metal slithered over exposed flesh, concealing my human hand and replacing it with an iron gauntlet with two protruding spikes across a bar of steel that protected my knuckles. I hit the thing and the sigils hissed with a soundless explosion, something felt rather than heard. The off-balance beast was sent careening, firing off like a bullet into the car parked across the street. The watch was made of steel (which is why it didn't work) and for those that hailed from the Abyss, it was a cancer just like iron was for anything from the Veil.

Think Heaven and Hell minus any clear cut bad or good guy. Most of the Pure, what they call a creature born of those realms, are all just about impossible to kill—but iron and steel hurt them like a son of a bitch.

Now, as the fire rushed through my veins, the hammering of my heart deafening me to the ambient noise outside the howl of pain from the Stalker and the crumpled metal and glass from the car I sent it into...I'd love to say I took the moment in, cried victory and was generally a badass, but the hard truth was that hit was more a byproduct of veteran savvy and luck. It wasn't nearly enough to put this thing down for any respectable period of time and in point of fact, those bladed fingers were screeching across the battered metal of the car door to get itself upright. As if I didn't have enough problems, that screeching sounded like nails on a chalkboard.

I took off running, pumping my legs for everything they were worth and was suddenly reminded I had not kept up with my fitness as much as I had intended to over the last year or two… or five. As an Artificer, I was less a force of nature like the Stalker hot on my tail, and more a clever survivor. The Stalker was more of a great white shark to my rodent. We'd both survived as far back as can be recalled, but while one survived because it was a paramount hunter at the top of the food chain, my reason was just a general resistance and resilience. Turning my focus inward, I managed to descale my arm, the metal slipping like living plates into itself and coiling back around my wrist for a snug fit. I needed to get to a more populated area.

The street was fifty feet away.

Forty feet.

I thought about enacting the power of the old shoes I was wearing, but the truth was I had imbued them with a talent that tended to hurt the wearer more than help. It was a last-ditch option, given every test run had been a monumental failure.

No matter. Thirty feet.

That nagging fear was totally quiet, muted by a kind of wary optimism that was walking hand-in-hand with budding confidence. I'd really jacked that thing in the jaw, cleaned it up good.

Twenty feet.

Cars whizzed by in a steady hum that was downright musical; I'd made it, and not only was I feeling better about my general circumstance in this mess, I had knocked this mythical monster down a few pegs which was going to make dealing with it a lot easier. Hell, maybe I should actually pump the brakes and go deal with this son of a bitch now?

Ten feet.

That was the last thing I remembered. I faintly recalled being hit by a mass that blacked out the ethereal, moonlit glow of the sky, the bone-jarring feeling of having all my momentum not just ceased but brutally reversed and sent me back down the road I'd just sprinted up. Very much in the fashion I had just done to the Stalker.

There was a dull burn, a gnawing bite of wounds rubbed raw by the unforgiving asphalt, wounds earned as I tumbled a clean twenty feet end over end.

Thirty feet.

Fifty feet. Fifty feet might as well have been a mile, and suddenly the only sucker involved in my turnaround haymaker was me. Ego was a tricky thing and it had been the downfall of better men, as I tried to demand strength to return to my wobbly arms. There was that weird drumbeat of darkness fraying the edge of my sight as my body battled with my brain's desire to shut down. Or maybe the other way around. My saving grace was the still-cautious Stalker, circling me as if waiting for me to employ another trick. I had a few up my now-torn sleeve, but with an inability to string together conscious thought, I was sure it was growing more emboldened by the second.

Slunk down on all fours, my pitiful portrait was contrasted sharply by the vicious-looking hellhound. Spindled limbs crept it soundlessly closer, stalking just a few feet in front of me. I was down and, even before this started, I was punching out of my weight class.

One thing I had over every innately gifted practitioner, every well-bred and better trained warrior and anyone else in all this mess, was that I was tough. I don't mean to say they weren't, but it was different. Monsters such as this spent so long as a domineering alpha that they forgot that not everything was just going to lay down and die for them. A lot of the spell-casting types got such an insurmountable amount of training and wielded an equally impressive array of power that they never really had to face down an actual challenge.

I'd been hungry. Stomach rumbling, fear of dying, dumpster-diving hungry. I'd been hurt. Body broken, ribs kicked in, eyes puffy and swollen shut. There was no doubt that living this life was a surefire way to an early grave. Hell, I had only stepped back in it for a few hours and I was already being hunted down by an evil beastie so old some people call it an Ancient.

However, I wasn't going to die on my knees.

I waited until it was right on me, until that foul breath washed over me and those beady, soulless black eyes fixated on my prone body. I smashed a flat hand to the concrete, shattering the marble into it. I growled through the sudden explosion of pain, a savage snarl on my face when I heard it, too, howl out in agony.

The marble's shattered, serrated pieces sliced into my palm and the eruption of heat was enough to make me rethink the whole sanity of this scheme. The marbles were a cheap trick. I had drawn a sigil on them, a magical insignia that absorbed ambient energy. Leave one in front of a fan it doesn't do much, but leave one in front of a dozen fans for a week and suddenly you've a gust strong enough to lift a car. In a freezer for a month and you've got something with enough cold in it to slick a whole street.

Leave one in a fire...

Well, you get the idea.

There was a geyser eruption of fire. It sprung to life between us and like a starved monster moving up and out to eat all the excess oxygen. It wasn't the heat but the light that I was after. When I first came across the Stalker I was too stunned to try and make sense why it was so weird—aside from, you know, a seven-foot demon-wolf being on our side of the world.

It was the daylight. They didn't like light and they outright abhorred the sun, it had a type of sapping quality on their strength. It was only after the wash of adrenaline and panic that I had settled down enough to see that. It was important to replay any major event over in the aftermath when emotion wasn't hampering perception, a good lesson learned from my old teacher. Meditation wasn't really my thing and I wouldn't quite call my process that, but it's in the same ballpark.

With the Stalker giving out a shriek so piercing my skin crawled, I found my feet and roared back, denying every ache in my body, rejecting every bit of fear trying to paralyze it, and I charged. Normally this thing would have tossed me around like a rag-doll, but with a face masked in second degree burns and eyes seeing spots, I was able to drop a shoulder into a surprisingly svelte waist and drive it into the far side of the street. I ricocheted off it the minute we hit the side of a van. The kind of van that I wouldn't want to see next to a playground, but now was not the time for inappropriate jokes. I ran my focus back to the broken watch and the gauntlet grew around my arm again, spikes protruding at the knuckles. Instead of push an offensive immediately, which was outright suicidal, I actually threw my back at the thing and tried my best to shrug out of my out-of-style leather jacket. One of the Stalker's long arms was shielding its newly vulnerable countenance, the smell of burnt flesh a darkly satisfying addition to the beast's pungent aroma, while the other limb was blindly lashing out for me. I reached across my body and nested my fist beside my hip, and with a silent command one of the protruding spikes fired through my jacket like a railgun.

An artificer has to make all their own equipment, usually. There were of course exceptions to the rule, tools that were built more for general use rather than for a custom purpose. We did our own stuff, which is why none of mine were particularly stunning. Our work was most effective when reflecting our own person. I wasn't full of finesse, I wasn't meticulous, I couldn't do stylish or suave. My mentor was a master at his craft, and while I wasn't destined to follow suit there were a lot of ways to be effective. I couldn't emulate his craft, but I could produce stuff that was a better reflection of who I was.

Gritty, tough, sneaky, and fucking violent.

Painfully arching my arm back to reach my hip on the same side, which isn't easy when you're out of shape and wearing leather, the second spike fired off. The jacket was now stapled to the van, an arresting makeshift belt on the beast. I lunged forward and did a very bad combat roll to both keep momentum high and my head low, away from a clumsy swing from the bastard that would have still taken my head clean off.

Normally, a jacket would be a shitty thing to try to bind a low-rent beast with, let alone one of the more renowned powers from the Abyss—but this wasn't an ordinary jacket. It was why I endured all the Billy Idol jokes. The enchantment on it upped the durability of the material a hundredfold, so instead of a thick, resilient layer of leather, it was the equivalent of wearing a hundred. Good enough for a few bullets, though they'd still leave a nice softball-sized bruise. Anyway, before I could gauge just how good it was holding, I took off as best as my unsteady legs could carry me. Being short wasn't the worst—while I couldn't go for distance, in small spurts I could move pretty well.

Fifty feet. That thing could shriek, it was milk-curdling, skin-crawling awful; I wished it would just shut up.

Forty feet. It went quiet. Not just quiet, but eerie, hear your blood pumping silent. I wished that thing would have kept the rancorous shrieking up.

Thirty feet. I'd either hurt it, or done enough to sap some of that considerable strength because I could actually hear those caustic claws digging into the road, that shrill scratching setting my teeth on edge.

Twenty feet. This felt all too familiar, except now there was a limp and I was so tired it was less my contracting muscles carrying me and more the rattle of bones collapsing on one another. I felt sluggish and I knew it wasn't all in my fear-addled brain.

Ten feet. Where it would all go to hell. This thing even when wounded was half terror and half asshole. I realized now that with the kind of speed I saw it exhibit that it should have been on me in an actual instant, this thing moved at a blur and had actually crossed an entire yard in the blink of an eye. It was still toying with me. This kind of arrogance was infuriating, and yet...I should have expected it.

Abruptly I threw all my weight to my right, just in time to feel the *whoosh* of a clawed arm violently coming down for me. That same cockiness that kept the Stalker from executing the final blow until the last minute as a point of torment was betraying it, those beady, abysmal eyes went wide and it lost its precious balance. The Stalker tumbled headlong into the street, where luck—who must not be a lady, because women hate me (rightfully so)—was breaking my way. One of those douchebag Hummers was barreling down the road, at least twenty miles per hour over the speed limit. The crunch of steel and flesh was unmistakable, and to me it was a sweet, sweet serenading sound. No matter how ancient, evil, or magic immune, two tons going sixty miles per hour was going to fuck you up.

I threw my arms up in exultant triumph. "HAHA! FUCK YOOOOOOUUUU!"

I must have cut quite the picture, stumbling to my feet jacketless, covered in a patchwork of road rash, blood gushing down my face, while manically laughing and flipping off the now wrecked Hummer. The better half of me wanted to check out the people driving, but the worse half of me assumed that since they drove that truck they had it coming a little bit. It was canary yellow and the rims still spun even though it was firmly planted into a streetlamp.

Of course, a siren crooned over the low-lit street and that hallmark chirping sound of a cop car alerted me that there was a new arrival. While I should have tried to keep my composure, I couldn't keep from half-collapsing on the hood of the Hummer. It gave me some semblance of dignity, as I didn't face plant into the very street I had just crawled off of.

My concussion-rattled brain was about to try and conjure up some kind of worthwhile excuse as to why I was looking like an extra in a B-movie horror flick, even entertaining the thought of claiming I was drunk and seeing if I couldn't get a sound night of sleep in the drunk tank at jail, when I heard it.

That fucking *thing*. Shouldering off a hunk of debris, the Stalker's one good arm cast aside road and metal from the collision while gathering itself. Hobbled leg, bloody maw, horribly disfigured arm and yet it was still coming. Now there was no pretense of arrogance, nothing in it of cautiousness; it was pissed and ready to blood-let me while slowly picking the flesh from off my bones.

If the imagery is specific, it was because this monster was projecting the image into my brain, and it suddenly dawned on me how far out of my weight class I was punching. It was a startling epiphany, and my fear compounded when I heard the cop getting out of the car. There was no time to placate the cop and soothe what I was guessing was paralyzing fear, which meant there was no time for another hail Mary trick to save the day. To be honest, my broken body was so exhausted I could barely keep my feet.

That's when I heard something else.

Click. I'd played enough first person shooters to recognize the sound of a bullet sliding into the chamber, and I was savvy enough about police from my days of being cross with them to know they didn't have to load their sidearm. While it was a distinct, unnerving sound, I never was so relieved in all my life to have a piercing ringing immediately echo through my already buzzing ears.

The cop wasn't frozen in fear, that motherfucker had taken one look at this preternatural beast, an impossible monster come to life limping its bloodied body down the street, and instead of demanding an answer, panicking or just outright leaving, he'd gone and retrieved his semi-automatic rifle and let loose a barrage of bullets.

"GET IN THE CAR!"

This guy was putting it together faster than I would have been able to explain even if I had been prepared for this shitshow. I resisted this weird, automatic urge to try to explain what was going on; instead I half ambled, half crawled to the passenger side and collapsed inside. Normally a gun wasn't ideal, but given that I managed to throw a fine beating into this beast, it was the tipping of the scale we needed. It only took a few bullets for the bastard Stalker to understand that it wasn't up for this, and before it could decide on a sounder course of action the cop was in the driver's seat, throwing the squad car into reverse, and the screeching tires sent us off in the opposite direction. With all the frantic, violent motion, my swimming head, the blurring lights and the brutal ringing still reverberating in my ears, I shouldn't have had the wherewithal that I did. Yet somehow, I couldn't keep from staring at the Stalker. It didn't give chase; it was off to lick those superficial wounds that would undoubtedly heal supernaturally fast. It abruptly whipped the mangled arm away from itself, and the violent breaks that sent jarring bone fragment through flesh set themselves in front of my own eyes, the mutilated flesh knitting itself back to prime condition.

Life was so unfair.

We held one another in our glare for as long as we possibly could. In my circle, they said it was a bad move to stare demons in the face, that these kinds of things could imprint upon you, that if they caught your sight they had a way to track you by some mysterious method we had yet to decipher.

So what. I was pissed. I was pissed, headstrong, and, in that moment, fearless. I'd spent half a decade in a heavily repressed monotony, working a dead-end job because I was afraid of this very type of evil. Afraid that without my surrogate family I wasn't good enough to square off with what was out there. Afraid I wasn't worthy to take up their mantle, that I didn't deserve to be in this fight. I had been afraid for so long, but after tonight, even if I was on the losing end of an ugly brawl, I wasn't going to be scared any longer.

I was going to be angry.

That anger carried me another half a block before everything went dark.

CHAPTER 4

UNLIKELY ALLIES

I came to in a foreign room. Small, neat. I would even go so far as to say excessively tidy. The spartan decor was explained when I saw a neatly folded flag encased in glass, a traditional keepsake for a fallen soldier. My guess was the cop was military himself. Despite what you might think, police only qualify at the range a few times a year, if that, so they aren't always as accurate as we'd like. This kid had incredible grouping—all the shots hit the same, very small area—and even though I had seen the rising swell of panic and confusion, the gun had a kind of calming effect on him. That was a byproduct of coming to rely on it many times before. Most street cops didn't have to use their weapon but once or twice in their whole twenty-plus year career, but a veteran had probably seen more than his share of shit. That rifle had become an extension of him, and when he started letting off rounds it was with the natural focus of a battle-tested warrior. In a way, it centered him.

I was hyper-observant, but only on reflection; as I said before it was kind of a poor man's meditative state.

I was bandaged up. Not with the proficiency of a doctor maybe, but it was obvious they knew enough about the little stuff. I couldn't guess the hour, and while I knew the right thing to do was thank my host and presumptive savior, I knew that was going to come with the stipulation of fielding a lot of questions that would be hard received even after what's been seen. So, I just sat in the darkness, alone.

There was solace in solitude.

These last five years, I'd really played the outcast role to perfection: a shanty apartment in a mediocre part of town with an unremarkable job that allowed me to stay beneath the radar. While that might have been pathetic, it was also familiar, so whenever I was alone there was a kind of habitual comfort that eased me. Testing each limb, I discovered that nothing was broken and I was surprised to feel how easy my breathing was. The road rash had a dull burn that clued me into the fact there were still chunks of debris and asphalt in it, meaning that in a little bit I'd have to stop by the hospital so they could use that metal cheese grater to peel a layer of flesh off to prevent infection.

Couldn't say that I'd missed this.

The bottom half of my clothing was still on, and given the state of disarray my now-stylishly torn-up jeans are in, I'd guess there hadn't been an inclination to strip me naked. While not shy, I won't lie that I was not thankful. A lady had to keep some decorum, dammit. Seriously though, if I'd had to go explain to some random guy that the world he's living in is half a lie and that all the stuff they told us to fear in bad cinema was in fact real, AND he'd seen me naked?

A guy can only take so much and this dude had already saved the day.

Stealth took a backseat when I groaned all the way to my feet. Apparently, my initial appraisal was not as accurate as I had hoped, and every muscle screamed out in agony when I tried to employ them. I saved face by not landing on it because I seized the nightstand where all my gear had been neatly strewn about, just as the door creaked open to reveal the very cop who'd played hero.

He was young, not yet thirty and probably only halfway into twenty. Fit, too. Broad shouldered and thick armed, but not bulky. He had the kind of build that lent itself to functionality and overall fitness rather than aesthetic. Definitely a soldier. Ladies probably loved him; he had that Captain America jawline and traditional good looks that made me want to punch him square in his perfect nose despite the fact he'd saved my life. We shared an episode of silence that wasn't quite uncomfortable, but flirted with it. Without a word, he shoved the door the rest of the way open, he turned, and I heard him walk down the hall. Taking the hint, I dug out a shirt which was probably a size too small and followed suit.

"You know they make these in none-skin tight sizes, right?" I tugged on the black undershirt clinging to my chunky stomach like a second skin; the ill-timed joke didn't hit home as I joined the stone-faced cop at the small table beside the kitchen. While young, there was an inherent seriousness about the guy that won him more of my already considerable respect. He pushed a box of cereal over to me—that high fiber, wheat-y kind. Personally, I was more of a Count Chocula guy, but he was young and I couldn't expect everyone to be as sophisticated as me. I went about making a bowl of cereal for myself, and since he'd adopted such a stoic silence I decided to mirror it. I didn't mind pushing a conversation, but pushing, maintaining, and directing a conversation is a whole different thing.

I held off on shattering the silence for a minute, though it felt like a freaking hour, and then I broke. "So, you just going to play strong and silent type this whole time?"

Annoyance flashed over the face of the officer, an annoyance I was quickly coming to share.

"Alright, so why didn't you take me in? You seem to be okay with going all hush-hush on this whole debacle and for that matter, you're handling it really damn well."

I couldn't say why, but the hush-hush part seemed to push him from annoyance to anger and with a huff he shoved off from the table. He grabbed a pen and paper, and stood there, his attention given completely to a long series of quick scratching. He was writing angrily, I knew because no matter the bridge of communication I had a talent for making people cross it pissed off.

The pad dropped in front of me on the table.

I'm deaf, asshole.

I didn't take you in because I am not a cop, it's citizen patrol.

Now, I spent the majority of my life feeling like an absolute asshole. This was one of those monumental moments that would be inducted into my personal hall-of-fame of assholery. I groaned as my hand met my face. "But, I heard...you speak?"

"I can still talk, dipshit."

It was strained in the way we've come to expect of deaf people, stilted and a little too loud which might be why they were so reluctant to do so. The citizen patrol thing made sense; judging from the pictures, he'd been a fairly long tenured soldier, I would guess straight out of high school. All the encased moments seemed to be from overseas and in filthy uniforms. Men like this, men made to serve, didn't know how to stop. If I had to keep guessing I would piece together that the rifle in the car was illegal, since I was pretty sure most of the people who volunteered weren't supposed to carry a weapon.

"Right," I said. Whether I was grimacing from pain or embarrassment was hard to say, and I hadn't completely ruled out that it was a combination of the two. We ate in a shared silence that was a vivid reminder of a youth I was inclined to forget. After a spell, I looked up again and met his eyes. "Well, thanks."

What else was there to say? This guy had dragged me from the mouth of Hell, cleaned me up after and now put a meal in me. Not a great one, I mean this was, after all, skim milk. Skim milk is disgusting. It's flavored water. Badly flavored water. Then again, this kid was probably less than ten percent body fat and I was stretching his medium shirt out so bad it was kicking my self-consciousness into a whole other gear. I was a worse guest than he was a host, so I stiffly reached for my bowl. I figured to drop it off in the kitchen and hit the road, but when I met the cold gaze of the hard-eyed kid I stalled.

One of those *a-ha!* moments hit me, and because I had become so accustomed to the life despite being out of it for a spell, I forgot how shell-shocking that must have been for someone else. Usually, they were in a full-blown state of mania by now. He was made of tougher stuff, though. I think I allowed myself to forget because of how little he was actually pushing the subject. With the impression that he'd never been much of a talker, I gave a nod as my still-swimming head was only now starting to make sense of it.

"It was a monster." I waited for the statement to hit home, the gravity I put in every utterance wasn't because I have a penchant for theatrics, but because it was important for someone who faced down evil to know the seriousness of it. "From the umbrage, the darkness, out of our worst nightmare kind of monster. You get it?"

People struggled with the impossible when they saw a sliver of it, a premonition or suspect silhouette out of the corner of your eye were easy to shake off over time. People, though, are dumb *en masse,* but not so much on an individual basis. This guy had stared right at this thing, watched it gurgle blood and play chicken with a Hummer, and still keep moving forward. My guess was he'd dropped an entire magazine of bullets without much in the way of an effect, and, gauging his steely stare and the array of awards hung all around the quaint apartment, I would wager he was a hell of a marksman and each shot was a precise one.

One-on-one was manageable. "I am going to spare you the whole *there's more than you know* speech. You know bad shit is in this world," I let his gaze follow mine, acknowledging the impressive scatter of pictures and awards for a second time. "But there's different types of it. You weren't supposed to see what you saw today, and believe me, we're lucky we got out of there alive."

I dug into my pocket, my bruised knuckles protesting the tight fit, before fishing out my wallet and tossing over a card. It was my business card, and judging by the surprise that walked over his practiced stoicism, I was guessing he didn't expect me to be a parcel courier.

"What's your name?" I asked.

"Grove," he answered, more murmured than stated, staring at the card while recalling the events we'd just survived. I knew he was doing that because it was the most rational thing to do. This kid screamed pragmatism.

I thought it weird that he hadn't asked for my name. He didn't ask for my name because he can read, a fact that dawned on me so late it told me I might be dealing with an actual concussion. I had to admit, he was taking this in stride and I was a little thrown by how little he was asking.

"Grove, I've got to get to it, man. That thing isn't down long and there's someone in trouble. It's not after me; it's after an innocent girl." The cynical part of me resisted the urge to make some kind of snide caveat to the phrase *innocent girl*. I managed. Barely. "Plus, if I don't feed my dog he's going to feast on my furniture."

"Calling that stuff furniture is a little generous," he said.

Narrowing eyes asked a question so I didn't have to.

"Wallet," The soldier said while producing it from his pocket, throwing it over to me. "Thought it would be smart to check out the unconscious guy in my guest bedroom. I fed and walked the dog."

"You're lucky, usually he's vicious."

"He didn't even stand up when I walked inside."

"He's very economical with his movement." Snark was my default but after getting it out of my system I felt obliged to offer up some sort of thanks. "I owe you. If I live through this, use that number. I'll dock your express payment on your next package or something." Smiling, despite myself and the circumstances, I struggled to my feet.

Grove mirrored me, though a lot smoother. He was literally in perfect shape, and Hollywood handsome; kid saved my life and I just wanted to kick him in the groin. Quizzically lifting a brow, I invited him to explain, but just by looking at him I picked up that he was wearing a gun on his hip and another holstered beneath his non-dominant arm.

"You're fucking kidding me." My aching head had sluggishly trudged through the deduction process, but I'd finally caught up enough to realize what it was he was intending. "Kid, no. *Fuck* no."

By now it was clear he could read my lips, and while stone-cold staring at them he shrugged into his jacket. That look was one that wasn't lost on me. I'd seen it before. It was gritty determination. Dour-faced, hard-bodied, and unafraid wasn't a bad set of traits to have when you were in the business of battling monsters, but I would be a real bastard if I dragged him into this.

"Monster. Do you get that? This thing comes from a world we call the *Abyss* for Chrissakes, because anything spit from that hellhole is an all-consuming death machine."

His keys made a distinct singsong jingle as he scooped them up. As an afterthought, I noticed him take up a tablet, more shove it into my chest than hand it to me, and check something on his phone.

I would have made fun of him for being a card-carrying member of the Eagle Scouts, but this guy didn't seem to flinch about that kind of thing. At the door, he was messing with the phone, then turned an expectant gaze on me.

The tablet *dinged*.

Evil triumphs when good men stand idle.

I knew the look. I knew the type. Worse, I needed the help. Exasperated, I threw my arms up and coughed out a dramatic sigh that let me know in no uncertain terms that I did, in fact, have a penchant for theatrics.

"You start quoting scripture or any of that shit and you're out." I emphasized the threat with a hard shoulder check that did nothing to him but damn near spun me all the way around in the hall of his apartment. 0 for 2. I wasn't too keen on walking someone through this complicated world of madness, but I was playing out of my league and while he was also out of his depth, maybe the pair of us could somehow survive this without drowning to death. Plus, while I was making a conscious effort to ignore it, something about this felt very right. It fit. Scrambling back to the room where I'd comfortably slipped into a mini-coma I collect my effects; gear, watch, jacket before meeting him at the apartment door. We walked in silence to the garage. He was driving a newer model SUV that was nicer than anything I'd ever owned, though to be fair anything nice I'd ever owned I usually made a mess out of in record time, so I stopped buying decent stuff a long time ago. That had less to do with bad luck and more that I'd had really bad periods of just deplorable laziness.

I resisted the urge to make a Batman joke, as the black truck had black interior, black seats, black tint, and all of it matched the black jacket and boots he was in. He reached over me to open the glove box; there was a rattle that dropped my eyes to the hilt of a gun. I waved the offer off and closed it myself. "I can't shoot," I explained with a shrug. "And I know how dangerous these can be when aiming at a moving target."

You can lie to yourself all you want. You can lie to everyone around you, too. It'll have repercussions, and while we like to bank on karma, a lot of times a career liar will just get better at it over time. Nonetheless, that was a game with an expiration date. Eventually you drew yourself into a corner you couldn't escape except by telling the truth. Truth was both liberating and inevitable. In this line of work, if you lied to yourself it didn't get you killed. It got someone else killed. Now, when I assessed myself, I did so with an unflinching honesty that did a number on my confidence but ensured that I didn't go into anything disillusioned.

A shrug was the only response I got and when the car was coaxed to life it awoke with a nasty grunt and rumble. Not nasty as in unhealthy, but this thing was a powerhouse and even knowing nothing about automobiles I could tell as much. It took me longer than I cared to admit to realize we didn't move because there wasn't any direction given, so I punched an address into the tablet he'd given me and settled it on the console between us.

We moved out of the working district, through the industrial and onto the highway with nothing between us. No looks, sounds, or even awkward attempts at conversation. My brain had finally gained enough of the lost higher function back to realize that music would be kind of a moot point and that, while I was vehemently against bringing someone else into this, I needed help. If pressed I couldn't have explained it, but that ride was as easy-going a ride as I'd ever had in all my life, and for whatever reason I knew in that moment I had gained a friend. The first since I began my self-imposed banishment. Weird as that was, I not only felt that way but I suspected that he felt the same.

People with disabilities got a lot of shit; even in the stuff we tried to pawn off as niceties, they were constantly reminded of the perceived shortcoming they were having to overcome or cope with. I didn't know if it was because I was a prick or that I just could relate on some level, but I didn't offer a lot in the way of sympathy. It could be off putting, sure, yet I couldn't help but theorize that he was grateful. Plus, when a warrior was taken from the fight, they were devastated. Especially if they believed they had one last battle in them.

This kid wasn't done. Down, forgotten, but far from finished. I could relate.

When we got to the address, I got a curious look. It was a good neighborhood though we were on the outskirts of it so there were more working class folks here than high society. The fence was in disarray, torn from yesterday afternoon and my first encounter with the Stalker. The door was crudely boarded up and all the windows are slammed shut. I say slammed shut because they were sealed with something that was preventing the blinds from even shifting, and if I had to guess the other side of the window panel had some kind of shoddy barricade behind it.

"Come on," I said. Pausing before we exited the car, I signaled with my own jacket to have him conceal the holstered weapon on his hip. He gave a nod and exited the car smoothly, then joined me at the curb. We fell into step, and I reached out and knocked on the door that started this all.

Maria cracked the door open and my thoughts were immediately hijacked when I saw her again. She had the kind of body women paid a small fortune for and, even in her modesty, it was hard to hide just how perfectly every inch of her curved. Her attention shifted from me to Grove; the glance to him gave her pause, and her appreciation for such a good-looking kid was impossible to hide. It was the third or fourth time I wanted to punch him in his perfect face. To his credit, the guy seemed none the wiser. I suspected he was in full-blown soldier mode, scanning the area. Hearing was crucial for a soldier, and it was still occurring to me how hard it must have been for him to lose it. Outside of a musician, I couldn't imagine anyone who relied on it more.

"Come in," she said, struggling to move the broken door for us.

"No. It's not safe here, we have to go." I tried to make sure there was no room for argument in my tone.

She hesitated at the threshold, her uncertainty palpable while she glanced between me and Grove. I knew that concerns for her father were keeping her tethered, and while I was trying my best to be sympathetic of that fact—something that did not come easily—we didn't have much in the way of time. That thing had me dead-to-rights, and if we weren't moving, in a crowded area or a protected space, we were in danger.

"If you stay, it'll kill him too." I couldn't wear kid gloves here. Her expression hardened; she wasn't going to allow for that eventuality. "No bag," I continued. "No phone. We have to go, right now."

I could tell the phone part threw her, and while I wasn't in a sharing mood I also wasn't trying to be a total asshole about it, so I elaborated. "I don't know what's tracking you." Before she can jump on that, I pushed through. "I mean who—I know *what* is tracking you, but as powerful as they are they are usually leashed. This one is, for certain. They aren't so focused, they are rabid, mindless killing machines and if this wasn't here for a purpose it would have just continued to rampage on down the street."

The last shreds of her hesitation fell away when she stared back at me and really looked at the state I was in. Bloodied bandages, favoring my right side, and running only on the sleep I got when I had passed out. Suffice it to say that I looked like a bag of badly beaten shit and my smell might fall in line with my juvenile metaphor.

"I have to get you somewhere safe, and Maria? I'm not asking."

Apparently, that worked. She nodded, and said quietly, "I have to tell my father." She stepped away from the door for less than a minute. I could hear through the cracked door an exchange in Spanish that sounded strained with love and fear, but Maria was firm in her resolve, and she came through the doorway shortly after. I had the rare decency not to make a quip.

She fell into step between the two of us. Grove was sticking to his soldier stereotype and kept the questioning looks to a minimum, instead dutifully scanning the road. We got to the truck without incident, and I let her have the front after inputting the location of where we were going next. I wasn't a religious man but it felt like the Christian thing to do, and she'd had a rough go of it. Not to mention the only person who would believe her and help is me, and that was punishment enough.

In keeping with the appearance of a hardened badass, I immediately passed out.

I was shaken awake violently. "Wake up!" Maria insisted, twisted around in her seat.

"Huhwha? Fire?" I had no way of gauging how long I'd been asleep, but when I glanced out the window it still looked like her neighborhood.

"Where are we going?" she asked. "Your friend isn't talking to me."

"Oh, that's Grove, he's deaf." She looked at me like I was a world-class jerk, and to be fair, I felt like one for not introducing them before abandoning them alone in the front seat while I escaped to sleep. "We're going to a friend's. Last one I got. They can keep you safe while I try and sort all this out."

"What is there to sort out? And why aren't I coming? I can do magic, I'm not just some ditzy damsel in distress." Her perfect eyebrows were furrowed. This was going well.

I sighed. "I know, just look, you gotta trust—"

"You? Trust you? You won't even tell me what's happening, you aren't showing any trust in me and I don't even know you."

"I'm Janzen." I tried flashing a smile to see if it would defuse the situation.

"Don't be a smartass."

I opened my mouth but she cut me off with a raised finger so fast that I stupidly held it that way during our duration of challenging silence.

"Don't." Her narrowing eyes drove home the very fiery warning.

"Okay. It's a Stalker. They have a lot of equally creepy names but that one does a good job of conveying the point. They're usually the right hand of something big and bad when they aren't busy being that big and bad thing. One just roaming around Cleveland isn't exactly a common occurrence."

"How do you know about them?" she asked. Luckily, she was softening, looking at me in a searching light. Mysteries had a way of digging inside of someone and taking hold. Even if she was annoyed at the way I was going about everything, I suspected two things: one, I was the only person she'd spoken to who seemed to have any real answers, and two, she hadn't expected all this to come from her local delivery guy.

"I used to work for someone who was part of a kind of group that... well, would handle something like this." I don't think I had spoken aloud about my old mentor for five years, at least not to anyone outside of my own circle.

"Will they help us?" she asked.

"No."

"What? Why, did you piss someone off?" She was starting to have an unflattering read on me.

"They're dead." My answer stopped her cold with a look that was probably just as frigid. "And you'll be well on your way if you don't just shut up and let me think and figure this all out."

If ever there was a doubt about my other-worldly power of pissing people off, one need only look at her now-soured face as she turned around. I laid back down, but sleep couldn't find me, not now, not with my mind running blind through a forest of memories I had avoided for all this time.

The car jerked to a stop. Apparently, my treatment of Maria had managed to isolate Grove, too. That was fine, this wasn't the time for half measures, and they would need thicker skin than that if they wanted to see this all through.

The shop we were at was a magic shop. Seriously. Now, this was all gimmicky stuff. People who were going to host a birthday party, or trying to enter a local talent show stopped by. A few of the serious types who turned the hobby into a struggling career were mainstays, but by now it was empty. To the fledgling community of actual practitioners something like this gimmicky store was an affront to their craft. Ironically, this place had the best stuff in the city in a room secreted away beneath the main store. The places they frequented, with dangling crystals and special scented candles that sold for twenty bucks a pop, tended to be the fakes. It was a traditional growing pain to learn this on your own. We all had to go through our own petty version of hazing.

"Stay in the car," I told her. I waved for the tablet. "I'll zap you on this thing when it's safe to come in." I waved it haphazardly in the rearview mirror, earning me a narrow-eyed scowl that I can't lie, tickled me. I had a feeling, or maybe it was a hope, that this might end up being a common interaction of ours. Now that Maria was aware that Grove was deaf, and, of course, because she was this perfect belle of beauty and compassion, she was signing to him. The crafty-eyed veteran watched me as I struggled out of the vehicle, my interrupted sleep making my movement uncoordinated. That, or the concussion. I patted my hip just before closing the door behind me, a none-too-subtle sign that he should maintain vigil. Of course, he already had been, almost robotically scanning every nook and cranny of the road while politely signing back to Maria whenever the occasion demanded as much.

Good kid. Solid oak.

I walked inside the magic shop. Above the door, a bell chimed, pretty standard stuff, except I knew the bell very well. The chime's pitch was dictated by just who and what you were, and the proprietor also claimed it could distinguish intent. I learned long ago not to doubt anything she said. There was a kind of living energy about the entrance that made me aware of every trinket and keepsake I had, anything magical momentarily hummed as if announcing itself. The interior of the shop was one spacious room, large enough to show you that it was constructed like a gigantic circle. Well-spaced rows gave ample room for several people to wander down each aisle and at the end of the aisle was another looping one that could take you back to the front of the store or to the back, where the owner busied herself behind a big sprawling desk.

Kaycee was my oldest friend in the city. She was less a friend and more an older sister, in truth. She was pretty, if a bit heavy. There was a gaggle of children responsible for that, although she didn't make any kind of fuss about the matter. The woman might have lived in a world of make-believe, but she was the realest person I had ever met. Her cherubic face flashed with concern; apparently, the rumor mill was already churning, because she seemed to follow it with some kind of slow waking realization. Our eyes locked, and then immediately broke as I stepped on a discarded LEGO brick on my way over to her; karma was a comical thing as it was a piece from one of the toys I had bought for one of the kids last Christmas.

"You come out of it to go toe-to-toe with a *Stalker*? Boy, you was never all that good at this to begin with." She was speaking while walking, and despite her size there was an undeniable grace in her gait. Less walking and more floating. It was almost hypnotic, and more importantly soundless.

She wrapped me up in a hug and I'd be a liar if I didn't say it was a big relief, a momentary reprieve from a world set square on top of me and growing heavier by the minute. I may have been an asshole, but I tended to be an honest one. The hug felt great and I returned it thankfully. "Hey, mamabear."

As if she were my own proud parent, those deceptively powerful hands arrested each arm and pushed me back so that she could get a better look at me, doing a sweeping once-over. "Well, you're standing and, for going against that thing twice, that's a hell of an accomplishment, kid. Hell of an accomplishment." I knew she was trying to cajole some of this rot that was infecting every bit of my being out of me, and, while knowing should make me resistant to it, it didn't. She was right. I had taken two good, square shots to the jaw and was still standing.

"Does me good to see you," she said. I saw it coming a moment too late, and before I could react there was a stinging slap right on my hurt arm. She didn't know it was hurt, what with the bandaging and the shirt still holding for dear life covering those bandages but it was likely she wouldn't have cared, either. "And that's for not coming around sooner. It's been damn near a year now; I gotta order one of them dang overnight things just to get you to stop by. Ain't right." She affixed me with a scolding gaze from behind an accusatory finger, and when she was sure I'd received the message, she dropped her hand away. "Anyway, you didn't come on account of socializing."

My scrunched look was enough to merit an ear-to-ear smile.

"I'm almost hundred, Janzen, you don't break habit when you're a creature of one. Half the town is locking themselves away and the other is going on and on about some thick-skulled boy wonder going tit-for-tat with an Ancient. Plus, it's past noon and coming at this hour risks waking the little ones and you *know* that rule."

I couldn't help it, I laughed. A good laugh, too. The kind which started from your belly and got your whole body involved. The one which kneaded out some of the enervating tension twisting every inch of me vice tight. The rule? If you woke a kid up, you stayed with them until they fell back asleep. They took afternoon nap time serious around here. Kaycee was fearless, and not in a *she's got moxie and spirit* way, either.

"Spit it out."

She led me to a table that was for children, stacked with puzzles and small trinkets, and while I recounted all that was happening, I am ashamed to say I tried each one out. Several times. One could go so far as to say I was playing with them, and I don't know if I would have much in the way of a defense for that accusation. Kaycee took the time to clean up while listening, bringing me some kind of tea and generally looking disinterested.

I didn't take offense, she had an incredible mind that could juggle several things at once.

Kaycee was half elf, so she was a natural practitioner of magic, and although they were similar to us, she had a very different type of thought process. It was best to respect that and allow her to conduct herself accordingly, especially since she was probably the most powerful caster in the city. Elves were long lived, typically five or six times longer than us, which had an effect on the way they saw time and prioritized things.

"Best you bring her in, then, so we can get to the bottom of this."

I could tell by the way she was looking at me and the emphasis of her tone that she'd been trying to get my attention for a little bit. I snapped back to the present and wore a smile for the sake of civility.

"Sure."

I pushed outside, the bell sang my song and at the car I told everyone to move inside. Grove tucked another weapon inside of some cleverly concealed compartment and followed suit, leading our ragtag charge. The bell rang, the octave a pitch lower but probably because of the wariness in the soldier. The third time the bell chimed for me was identical to the first two.

Maria passed through the doorway silently; the magical bell didn't chime at all, not even mundanely. It was mute.

We're all made up of energy. Magic was just another expression of energy, harnessed and cultivated to do what the modern world would insist was impossible, but at the very core of it? Energy. Magic was energy, and while science and magic seemed as if they were natural enemies, you'd be shocked to find how far from the truth that thought was. The bell absorbed ambient magic and, for lack of a better word, expressed that energy signal in the form of a sound. Our mere presence gave off energy. Call it a soul, call it whatever you want, but that was just a fact. Energy had to go somewhere. The fact that the bell didn't sound when she entered wasn't just unusual.

It was impossible.

Kaycee, with eyes as vibrant as an exploding star, kept her stare firmly locked on the slip of a woman I'd subconsciously roped behind me during the ongoing revelation. *"Interesting,"* she said with a crooked smile.

CHAPTER 5

OLD FRIENDS, NEW FRIENDS

"An elf?" Maria balked, though she immediately seemed embarrassed by her reaction.

"Half," I corrected nonchalantly. I was halfway across the room, digging into a veritable treasure trove of junk set in the big chest in the corner of the room. The rest of them were sitting at a circular table, facing each other uncomfortably. Well, Kaycee wasn't, that woman was hard to unnerve. I'd seen steel give before she'd even blink. Grove was quietly sipping his tea, acting natural although his posture and systematically roving gaze told me that he had considered every exit and avenue of escape a dozen times. He'd even chosen a seat with his back to the wall so he could watch the shop's front windows. In front of him were both his phone and tablet ready with the writing application he'd used to communicate with me earlier. The guy was almost mechanical, and it wasn't the first time I was thankful that our paths had crossed.

Maria shifted in her seat. "Aren't..." she cleared her throat, doing her best not to stare at the fact that Kaycee wasn't some petite waif of a creature.

"If I asked you if you were a maid, because you're Hispanic, would you be offended? 'Cause every two-bit sitcom I have seen has told me that's pretty accurate." Only she could throw out an insult and make it sound kind of like a compliment to your reasoning ability. Pointing out the hypocrisy of predisposed bias was important; there were a criminal number of inaccuracies about the supernatural that held as if gospel because of how widespread the belief was. Stories, fairy tales and lore usually only got a single aspect of something right and the rest was just a centuries-old game of telephone.

I could tell by the quick succession of expressions that Maria swallowed a knee-jerk reaction; she quickly settled on the point of the example and not the sentiment. Kaycee was an amazing teacher and had a way of cutting to the heart of something. People as a rule are visceral, we react almost immediately when it's a matter of pride.

I was no different.

Something passed between Maria and Kaycee and, while I wasn't one to pry, if I had to guess I would have called it respect, or at the very least acceptance.

"How do you two know each other?" Maria asked.

I just now realized how long it had been since I'd said anything. I looked up from the trunk in the back; the small pile of stuff I'd assembled beside me would look perfectly strange to anyone except for me and Kaycee. A chisel, some medieval-looking bracers, and a wooden baseball bat laid beside an aluminum one. I was chewing on how to answer the question, but while I was deliberating Kaycee forged ahead. She might not hold the same concept of time that we did, but she was polite and astute enough to know when I was uncomfortable.

We went back a long time.

"Janzen used to come into my store and try to steal some of the magic trinkets," she said, smiling fondly despite the thievery. "A few times I let him get away with it. He was a neighborhood kid, and a good one." Kaycee paused, tilting her head as she thought back on my youth. "Relatively speaking."

I didn't grimace at the last bit, she was right and I wasn't going to try and sell myself as something I wasn't. My knuckles were callused twenty years before their time because of how often I used to fight, half the teeth I had were twisted or chipped, and there was a criminal record out there about five pages longer than it should have been because of my pigheadedness.

"There's more to the story," Maria said, trying to walk the line of politeness and insistence on being included. Kaycee had the decency to check with me and I acquiesced with a shrug of feigned indifference.

I dropped the bats down on the round table, took a seat, and started adjusting the bracers on each forearm. I was too tired to care how ridiculous I must have looked, I was a little bit annoyed by having to fight with the tight restraint of the too-small t-shirt cutting off my circulation.

"His mentor was once my student," Kaycee said, puncturing the silence which had stood longer than I'd been comfortable with. "And so, as is the way with our practice, I kind of inherited Janzen as well. I actually was the one to recommend him to Zachariah." She was watching me with a softened look, and though the others might have mistaken it for nostalgia or affection, I knew what it really was.

Sympathy.

My old mentor was dead and so was the group of friends I called family that I used to do this very thing with. I didn't look up from my work, I just honed the chisel on the strap of leather while blinking away the wetness that had thankfully not spilled over. I drove the point into the wood. The baseball bat had a few sigils in it, but they were old and hadn't been touched in years. I was the last to touch them.

"So, the little boy who used to try and steal my magic came here to learn it instead." Shifting to sit upright, Kaycee continued. "Speaking of magic, Maria, I am told that you're some kind of practitioner?"

Maria hesitated a bit; the pride she once had in being a caster seemed a bit more cumbersome now. Letting Kaycee dictate the direction of the conversation wasn't a mistake, she and I had designed this to be an introduction into the world that Maria had stepped in. Well, more leapt in. Usually we bread crumbed people into this stuff, showed them a magical light show, talked to them about incantation and some lore. It was no different than a real education, but Maria—and Grove—had gone from finger painting to quantum physics overnight.

"I… dabble," Maria said reluctantly. She seemed to fully grasp her position now, that what she knew was a fraction of what we were involved in, and cast a glance at me like she was asking for me to throw a life ring.

"Hey, don't look at me. We're all in this now," I said. I used the chisel to point to myself, Kaycee, and even the stoic soldier who was so at ease in this fast-changing lifestyle that I had a mix of envy and contempt for him. "You gotta help us put some of this stuff together, though."

Kaycee's shift was less about comfort and more an attempt to get the full of Maria's attention. "Maria, do you even know what it is that's after you?" she asked pointedly. I didn't know how, but from anyone else that would have come across as condescending. Kaycee was a mother, and I felt like it had less to do with power and more to do with her maternal instinct. No matter how old you were, when faced with something irrevocably bad there was a small piece of you that wished you could just go home. To that first home. Where the thing under your bed cowered at the threat of your father, where your mother was there to whisper away any illness and there was absolutely nothing that could get through the sheet you used to hide your head under.

She wasn't chiding Maria or even coming down on her, she was trying to cajole a very scared, very young lady into our circle. Maria spent a long time looking around the room as if it might offer up some kind of explanation or aid. When her lip curled from the incessant chewing, I knew she hadn't realized how hard she'd been biting it. The sigh did more than take the air out of her, for a second it took the fight from her, too. She shook her head, admitting her ignorance.

"Janzen, get that junk off my table," Kaycee snapped, bringing with it some much needed levity. Grove chuckled and Maria couldn't stave off a smile and, to play the routine, I even exaggerated a wounded ego, muttering to myself while casting everything off the table. "Grove, Maria, if you would kindly lift your things. Go on." She thanked me with a look for understanding what she was attempting to do; easing Maria was important, and I was never against being the comic relief. It was why I was so uncomfortable standing at the forefront of this whole thing, the spotlight wasn't exactly my specialty. Plus, I delivered stuff for a living. People berated me every day as if it was my damn fault that their box was dented or delayed.

I grabbed the edge of the table and lifted the entire top off, then turned it over and set it back on the base upside down. The wooden countenance revealed beneath it an old, well-kept map. It was a map of the world. Not sprawled out, but contained in a circle. Layered around it in another series of circles, spaced about three or four inches each, were three layers.

In-Between.

Veil.

Abyss.

The old map of the world didn't show any divisions of mankind's devising, no country lines or borders. Instead, it was made up of a weird crisscross of lines. Green, blue, and black. Wherever those seemingly random lines intersected were the only things designated on the map. Usually it was a city, though there was the Bermuda Triangle, a point that was supposedly Atlantis, and some other legendarily weird stuff. On our part of the map there was just as much going on, but it was only where the three lines meet that were important. Miami, Chicago, the wilderness on the Canadian and Washington border, Las Vegas, and our little blotch—Cleveland. While I understood the implication, I figured it was best if this was a history lesson given by someone who had a more authoritative station. Plus, while I understood all this in theory, I was a little hazy on the details when put in the application of practice.

"What's after you has many, many names," she started, settling back at her seat. "Ancient. Stalker. *Cura'sha.*"

The last given name was new to Maria and she responded by looking at Kaycee and me to see if it was significant. When

Kaycee didn't elaborate, I realized that she wanted me to chime in. She was inviting me to play adult.

"We call it a Stalker mostly because it's such a popular word but a good description of it, this way we don't have to say the true name of it. Saying the true name of something bad is... well... bad." I was eloquence personified. If ever you wondered why we didn't like to speak the true name of something so awful, it was because they could hear it. They couldn't use it to pinpoint your exact location, they couldn't even really get your scent, but if you said it often enough, it'd leave a trail. This was of course where superstitions like Bloody Mary originated. Emotion was a powerful amplifier to any magic, and the more potent the emotion the more powerful the magic can become. Stuff like fear, hate, lust, just about any sin, can be really powerful stuff. You stand in a dark room, chanting a name you shouldn't? Well, you're basically inviting that evil entity into your life and if you're frightened enough, you might just give it the bridge of power it would need to cross over.

Magic was tricky though; while I understood that there could be serious consequences associated with naming things, I wasn't sure why a name itself could be so powerful. I really didn't know if anyone knew how that worked. I'd been surprised by how much had remained a mystery, even by those who'd been around a long, long time. You could read *Cura'sha* over and over again. There was a city that was pronounced just like it, though the spelling was slightly different and it would seem there had been no repercussions. People who knew as much as we collectively knew about magic would have had an easier time explaining to you what they didn't know or understand rather than what they did know, and I wasn't anywhere near a subject matter expert on magic. In fact, anything resembling a hierarchy of magic users would have me at the bottom. If I was a ditch digger, Kaycee was an architect; and when it came to big picture even she was just a dot on the map.

Kaycee reached toward the map. "They come from the Abyss," she said, her tone subdued. Of the three layers around the world, her finger paused on the black one, which bled into the world through Las Vegas and seemed to spider web out from that location. "Those of the Abyss are starved, voracious, usually mindless killers. They are gluttony and violence. That's why it's so odd a Stalker is after you. If they get out, they don't fixate on any one thing. They just massacre until they're sated, until whatever is holding them to our world is killed or they themselves are killed."

"It's a rabid dog in more than just appearance." If I wasn't going to be articulate, I could at least simplify some stuff, help drive it home.

Kaycee nodded. "That's a common theme for stuff coming out of the Abyss. Vampires, for instance." I shuddered at the thought of a vampire, but Maria and Grove were enthralled. Their attention was rapt and undivided as Kaycee continued. "Of all the realms, the Abyss is the one we know the least about. It's impenetrable darkness, just a vast realm of seemingly nothing where monsters prey on each other constantly. Something like a Stalker isn't supposed to be able to come over, and if it does, it's not supposed to be able to stay long." Half-bred stuff fared better, since it already had one foot in the door, so to speak. Vampires were said to be bastard cousins of the *Cura'sha*, something I couldn't think on long for fear of turning my stomach. "To beckon a Stalker and control it would take a huge amount of energy and effort. Keeping it tethered to this world as long as it's been here is impressive enough without even taking that other stuff into consideration."

"Why me?" Maria finally asked. She had been absorbing the map in a fashion I would expect a fledgling practitioner to. Wide-eyed, with barely checked amazement. Grove was staying true to form as well, seeming more meticulous and calm, committing a lot to memory.

"I don't know," Kaycee lied. I knew she lied because I used to lie all the time. I lied for no reason, I lied when the truth was perfectly sufficient. I lied to people who, when lied to, knew without any reservation or doubt that I was lying. When you were a career liar, reformed, the only good that really came from that dishonest period in your life was that you cultivated an incredible knack for knowing when someone else was lying.

"Could you bring one of these over and anchor it to you?" Maria probed.

Kaycee wasn't big on promoting the fact that she wasn't just a capable caster, she was arguably the best in the city. When her disposition shifted to a contemplative one I knew we had some time on our hands. When someone who was a hundred years old and destined to probably live two, maybe three more hundred years took a moment to consider something? Well, we had time.

I butted in while Kaycee considered her answer. "Do a lot of people know you practice?"

Maria seemed a bit unsure whether or not to answer me while our host was thinking, but again, I had known Kaycee the better part of twenty years and knew she was less in the conversation and more in a meditative state. She was going to review what it would take to conjure up a portal, construct a Walk—a bridge from the Abyss to our world—and whatever else was pertinent to turn one of these death-dealing machines to heel.

After giving Kaycee a moment but finding no signs of return to the conversation, Maria glanced back at me and sighed. "A few, I do remedies and minor tracking stuff. I have a group I go to twice a month to discuss... Just, well, what we've learned and what we're doing." She folded her hands under her chin and cast her glance back down at the table, looking very much in over her head.

A group. That was it right there, a concrete piece of information I could actually use to run down anything that might resemble a lead. My revelation from my conversation with Gale kept turning over in my thoughts like a mantra.

... *Or a fool.*

"Are you dating anyone?" I blurted out, my suspicion finding form, and before the startled girl who looked a gorgeous mix of offended and confused at the question could even answer Kaycee snapped back to the present.

"Yes." Kaycee's timing was splendid, being such that it left me and Maria at our most awkward interaction to date. Of course, when she claimed to be capable of this kind of magic, that certainly got my attention. Apparently, nobody was above suspicion to me. "I could do it. It would take all I had, though. I would have to use blood magic, it's the only way I could think to keep that kind of power going through two different worlds."

I hissed. Blood magic sounded bad because it was.

"What?" said Maria, trying and mostly failing to not sound distressed.

"Certain magic works in this world, certain magic doesn't. Some things in the Veil or Abyss can't pass through. There's a barrier that keeps all of them from bleeding into one another. We call it the In-Between. If someone was going to pull something from the Abyss, for instance, they need a kind of conduit. You can do it through your body, you can do it with water, you can use a lot of channels with varying degree of success. The best, but most dangerous, is blood. Using the blood of someone else, you can keep an open channel to that world. Bad juju. If you ain't on team asshole, using that once or twice will convert you pretty quickly. Still, it's a good clue." Kaycee leaned back in her chair, folding her arms across her body.

Maria still looked half-lost, so I picked up where Kaycee had left off. "If this was a heavy hitter, they would stay away from blood magic. All magic is like a drug, but this is like heroin. It was bound to use you up before you could do the same to it. It was a quick fix. Serious people in the know stayed away from that stuff. It was messy and dangerous, especially to the user. If Kaycee could bring one of these over and hold it, we know it's possible for those who fall under the serious category. Blood magic is the kind of thing that can give you just enough juice to kind of play above your pay grade. It's actually how I closed your protection circle."

While Maria just gave a solemn nod, Kaycee shifted a look at me. I shrugged helplessly. I knew better, and while I could lay it out for her, the truth was it was a do-or-die situation and if I had to I would do it again.

I'd be lying if I said I hadn't seen just how effective a little blood could be to a spell and thought on it a few more times, myself. Stuff was dangerous.

Between wrestling with that troubling thought and Grove being so statue-still, when he moved it actually startled me. He typed away on it for a moment before handing the tablet over to me.

I nodded. "Yes, it's likely someone new and the fact they picked the Abyss is telling, too."

Kaycee wasn't going to help me explain and while I knew it was to instill more confidence in me so that the two of them would trust me, I also knew she was curious to see my own development and thought process on the matter.

"The Veil and even the In-Between have a lot to offer in the way of doing this kind of work, but both of them tend to have denizens who are crafty. The Abyss is stronger but a lot less cunning. This person didn't want someone who could two-time them, so they opted for something much more dangerous than clever. They are new and if I had to guess pretty unsure of themselves. There's more—if they picked something from the In-Between, for instance, and it was working the way it is, they would most likely be appealing to reason, so there would be a solid line of logic we could follow. The In-Between is neutral, they only usually get involved if it's to restore a disrupted balance. The Veil, well, they would be the choice of someone who was really practiced and confident in their craft."

The Veil boasted some of the greatest tricksters to ever live. They could play on a phrase or even a word so well that by the end of it you were the one on the losing side of a deal made all for your benefit. That's why in all the old lore regarding genies, people had to be explicit and careful in what it was they asked for. The In-Between wasn't as slippery, but since they could be so literal it was much the same. If you didn't specify to an almost obscene degree it could backfire. Plus, while we knew where the

Veil and Abyss are, the In-Between was another thing entirely. It was the least well-kept secret that somehow remained secret. Nobody knew where it was.

Getting a hold of something tangible was elating. I dragged my fingers through my hair as I untangled myself from my thoughts, and realized that I had missed Maria, sick with concern, ask for help directly from Kaycee. I'd been too wrapped up to catch the exact way she'd phrased it, but Kaycee just shook her head with an empathetic, somber expression.

"Kaycee is half-elf," I said quietly. "She can't get involved. She is considered an ambassador from the Veil to us. She has to maintain a certain neutrality."

"Oh." And there it was. The shattering of my heart. Splintered into a thousand pieces all over the damn floor. The girl was hanging on by a thread and when she found out that Kaycee, this indomitable, motherly figure couldn't step in and make it all go away she seemed to just crumble. Her face dropped and the slump in her shoulder could have all but spelled out her resignation.

"Maria," Kaycee said, smiling with a touch of light that if pressed I would say was preternatural. "This is the beginning of a story, not the end. Think of it like this, you have a mailman—"

"Delivery specialist," I interjected, laying it on heavy.

"Who is at your house, what, once, twice a week? For no more than a minute or two?"

I hadn't told her about my thought process on this, but this was not the first time I wondered just how expansive Kaycee breadth of power really is.

"A *delivery specialist*," she said with heavy sarcasm, casting a smirk my way, "who was once the most promising young Artificer I had ever known, was at your doorstep the day a demon came for you. An Artificer who agreed to help you out against a fiend he's no match for, and, when cornered by it, beaten by it, along came a cop."

"Citizen patrol," I clucked, earning a narrow-eyed scowl from the elf. The first interruption was cute, the second was bordering on rude, and while she was a good sport about enduring my bravado, there was a point being made and I was derailing it. I surrendered, hands up, and allowed her to continue unimpeded.

"A man who bore witness to something so vile, so repugnant that the sheer sight of it broke most men and without blinking fought. Instead of having the courage ripped out of him, he stood side-by-side with Janzen, for you; even if they didn't know it yet. A fearless citizen patrol officer and a delivery specialist who ended up being an Artificer. My darling, we are compounding a lot of coincidences here, aren't we?" There was a lyrical hum to her voice that could hypnotize when she so had the desire, and right now Maria was spellbound. "So, you see, if I was to guess, you're already being helped, and in my experience, people who are being helped in such a fashion usually see through to the end of it."

The trance was broken with an abrupt clap that sharply echoed throughout the dimly lit room. I appreciated the calming effect it had on Maria and yet at the same time, the novice practitioner in me wondered why it seemed to resonate with my deaf friend, too. For the second time in as many moments I couldn't help but wonder just how deep the well of her power ran. She was deceptive in her perpetual calm, disarming in her kindness. Still waters ran the deepest, did they not? Knowing what I knew of the craft, I had often recognized that anyone who crossed her and walked away unscathed did so at Kaycee's discretion and decree, not their own.

***

It was well past midnight when Kaycee found me back downstairs at the very table where we'd all been speaking. Grove and Maria had fallen asleep long before, the soldier trying to stay dutifully beside me and so taking up residence on the couch. Maria got the luxury of an actual bed beside the kids room, which was well deserved. Grove I wasn't worried about, the kid was corded steel in body and resolve. Maria probably felt safe for the first time in a long time and she was almost asleep before her head hit the pillow. Probably didn't hurt that Grove was at the foot of the bed, sleeping on the floor without anything in the form of a complaint. Half pit bull and half Brad Pitt.

Kaycee had been good enough to offer us refuge for the night without making me suffer the indignity of having to ask, barter or beg. Sanctuary in a fight was an essential; no matter how battle-hardened someone was, they could get war weary—and quickly. I had just finished working on the wooden bat before switching to the aluminum. She picked up the one I completed to examine my work; the fondness of her smile was tough to read since she seemed to delight equally in praise and chastisement.

"You were so much better than you ever realized," she said.

I cringed at that. "I find that hard to believe based off what you two used to tell me."

Taking my attitude in a tempered stride as only a mother could, she continued, "You were precocious, Janzen. Precocious, cocky and headstrong. That's great material but tough to build with. Plus, you're quick to forget, Zachariah was very young, too. Maybe you were as hard on him as he was you?"

My mentor. Zachariah. Young wasn't the word I would have used for him, given that he'd been on the back end of his forties. Still, in this world, stuff could be very long lived, and as I stated time and time again, Kaycee had a different relationship with time than we did. Zachariah belonged in the pages of an old epic, not on the city streets of Cleveland. Worldly, funny, confident and yet so approachable. We clashed a lot because I was an insolent, strong-willed prick who was just relentless. Pushing boundaries, defying structure and teachings, forgetting my place in almost every social setting. Despite all of that, Zachariah loved me. He fed me, clothed me, and continued to direct my tutelage despite my obstinance.

"This is good work." She interrupted my pensive stupor with a soft utterance. I had a bad penchant for zoning out and at times it cast me in a rude light, which is one I am quite capable of casting myself in. Falling into such a rude episode of awkward silence wasn't helping my cause.

"It's basic stuff."

I half expected the same encouragement I got from the old man, but instead she agreed. "Yes, very basic. Almost elementary." She rotated the bat in her grip carefully. "Clever, though. Artificery is magic, whether you like it or not, and the best magic is made when it's a part of who you are. When you stop fighting who you are and allow that to be reflected in your craft is when you'll really understand what it is to stand on your own." Her hand smoothed over the tapered line of the bat, down to the handle. "Rough, but clever." She secured her hand on the grip, giving her free hand a nice slap. "Ugly, but effective."

She kissed me atop my head, the warmth of her embrace enough to stall my workings on the other bat if only for a second.

"Reminds me of you." She kept her hand on mine for as long as possible before disappearing upstairs.

***

"Here's a list of names."

I took the paper from a disheveled-looking Maria. She'd overslept badly and I was glad for it. I woke up a little after eight and inhaled a monstrous breakfast. Home cooking was a rarity for me, so I decided I'd splurge. Grove I think was up before the sun, probably made everyone's beds, cleaned his weapons, and ran ten miles. I was coming downstairs just as he was returning from a run.

Instead of prying about her love life or making an ass of myself by outright asking about it, I just made a mental note of every guy on the list. The names belonged to those in the group she met with. Some of them from the occult, some are more pagan. I knew Maria's involvement was of some Wiccan origin, though I hadn't bothered to ask.

She asked us if we could check on her father if possible, though she had called and explained to him what was happening. Even though she'd gotten some sleep, she seemed withdrawn and disinterested in any more banter between friends and she went downstairs to the real magic part of the store to read. I called out of work, which, say what you want about working unions, but those mandatory sick days came in handy when you were moonlighting as a champion for righteousness.

The first thing I learned when apprenticing as an Artificer wasn't magical sigils, cryptic insignia, or dead languages, but actual craftsmanship. I fastened the new makeshift leather belt on my waist, as well as a rig I designed for my chest. I could cinch one bat to my hip and the other across my back, though I wasn't insane enough to do that in broad daylight in downtown Cleveland. With the broken watch and leather bracer I was almost ready, though I felt a bit naked without my old, ratty jacket.

"I saw you working so hard last night, I decided to restock you myself." I hadn't heard Kaycee's footsteps, but as she got closer, there was a distinct sound, a kind of stifled jiggling.

"My marbles!" I'd love to tell you I was playing along with a joke and my excitement was not genuine, but that would be an outright lie. Kaycee stood there expectantly, and with the sun pouring through the shop window soaking up all the darkness that was clouding my mind and life, she was just an old friend again. Mother of three, with a hardworking husband and a smile that could lighten any load. I took the small leather satchel graciously and attached it to my hip as if it were some kind of low-slung six shooter. She had even divided them up inside the bag, somehow understanding both my concept and philosophy about which pouch inside the satchel held what, without ever having to ask.

Grove, the champion of stoicism and looking like a badass, was stifling a reluctant smile at the fact that I erupted in euphoria about a bag of marbles. The quizzical look aimed my way was largely ignored, and I hoped that he was going to think I was just insane and never have to find out why an adult was so excited to be handed a satchel of marbles.

We were at the end of winter but it was cold enough to justify the heavy coat he was in. Better to conceal the pistol on his hip, the revolver at the low of his back, and one beneath the arm. Usually I would reprimand someone for being so gun-crazed, but given he emptied an entire magazine into this thing and all it did was piss it off, I could understand why he was throwing caution to the wind.

Just as I was about to turn and leave, a thick *ahem* seized me in place. I pivoted back from my half-turn to the door and allowed a cartoonishly high eyebrow to do my talking for me. An expectant hand was held out at me, and I couldn't help but grin.

Grove, who had been through hell and back unfazed, finally gave me a puzzled look as though to ask what else I could be smug about after a bag of marbles, but I fished out my wallet and laid a dollar bill in her palm.

"Neutrality," I explained. "Nothing's free."

Understanding dawned on my new friend's face and I couldn't help but like this guy more and more. Don't be deceived by someone with a big, broad set of shoulders. Unless they were a natural, there was a lot of know-how involved in building that kind of body. Before I could get my wallet put back away my old friend snatched it out of my hand, emptying it of its meager contents. I would have felt slighted, but there was a whole seven dollars in there.

Dramatically sighing, she murmured, "It'll have to do," and then vanished into the back room...

She returned with an old rifle, one of those that you had to rack the bottom trigger guard to feed in a round. You saw them in the western style movies all the time. At the bottom of it, instead of something like a railing system or bi-pod legs was a blade. Not like a bayonet at the spire of the barrel, this was at the bottom. It was spaced so you could put a hand around the snout of the gun still, and if all else failed it would make a fine melee weapon. An axe gun.

I was intensely jealous.

"It's silver; that might not make sense to you now, darling, but trust me." Kaycee extended the gun to Grove.

With the graciousness of an old knight, my silent friend took the gun with a healthy dose of reverence, signing a *thank you* before examining the weight of it. "Don't use those bullets unless you have to," she warned sternly, and I was glad to find that not even Grove was above some motherly reproach. Hiding a snicker, my friend said, "Thank you, ma'am," aloud before carefully tucking the weapon beneath the layers of his jacket.

Obnoxiously, I shook out and squared my shoulders with a shit-eating grin spread all across my almost handsome face. We fell into a standoff. She was pretending like she didn't know why I seemed so damned pleased, and I was not letting anything get in the way of my self-satisfaction.

She relented. "Fine. Get over here."

Resigned in the face of my insufferable optimism, we both dropped our charade and shared a secretive smile. She took my arm, the one with that awful leather band, and clipped a small silver token to the top of it. At the center were two people farming, and surrounding this image were several smaller depictions of everyday tasks. While I was not quite sure of the significance, I recognized where it was from and nodded. It was Greek lore. The pendant itself was actually silver, as well, which would be incredibly useful in the coming days. It was a small gesture, but one which carried with it a profound amount of gratitude.

We exchanged hugs. It was very organic between me and her, and while Grove was a little stiff, Kaycee was more than happy to make up with it on her end, hugging him as if he was one of her own. At the door, she yelled my name one last time, and suddenly I realized this was penance for all the times I interrupted her last night. I didn't get a chance to show her how exasperated I was at her antics because by the time I'd turned to face her I got a face full of leather.

It smelled like sweat and sadness, and before I could curse I realized what it was. My old Billy Idol jacket, the one I thought I'd lost in the fight with the Stalker not two nights earlier. Both my respect and thankfulness amplified tenfold for the woman, and when I aimed to ask how she'd gotten it back and mended all the tears, I could see in her face that she was keeping that secret.

I know I looked downright ridiculous in my leather band and 80s jacket, but I happily slid into it and shuffled around like a proud peacock. Grove, not only confused but a little sad for me, just cocked a wave at Kaycee and pushed out into the world. I stayed for a moment longer, hoping my stare imparted just how glad I was to still have her in my life after what an absolute shit I'd been. I owed her money, woken her up with midnight drunk dials, left her worried for me for months on end when I couldn't get over my own despair, and now I just dropped in and asked the world of her.

And she delivered.

I stepped onto the sidewalk with a rejuvenated sense of self, purpose, and dare I say hope.

CHAPTER 6

BOOK CLUB

At this point if I kept pointing out that we rode in silence I was just being an asshole.

We did. Just me whistling to myself. My constant fidgeting was caught by way of Grove's peripheral vision and, thankfully, the merciful mute switched the radio on. I hadn't for fear of being rude, which was rare for me, but between saving my life, feeding me, clothing me, tolerating me, and now staying with me while I went ahead and actively sought out the very beast that could kill me with incredible ease, I owed the guy. I wasn't really up to speed on what constituted rudeness, and while our dynamic was surprisingly organic, I didn't want to compromise that by doing something that would come across as an intended offense. I'd offend all day by way of my own nature, something I couldn't bring myself to be overly apologetic about, but if it was a pointed offense and I delivered it as such, then I was just being a jerk.

Music helped me think. Since I was scatterbrained as hell if I was doing busywork, music usually quieted the white noise enough for me to see a line of thought all the way through. Mind-numbing games on my phone, people watching, or massacring the lyrics of whatever top-forty song radio syndicate was basically force-feeding us by repeating it every other track.

Earlier this morning I'd used the list Maria gave me to text the de facto leader of the group to call an emergency meeting. Using a different pretense was important since, by my way of thinking, one of them was the most likely culprit. I spun a story about her coming across an errant delivery boy who'd had the misfortune of drinking a love potion and now was fawning obsessively over his own reflection.

The best lies were grounded in truth.

We were there well before noon. We pulled up to a Norman Rockwell house: white picket fence in a good-to-great neighborhood. Children weren't afraid to leave a bicycle in the front yard and half the garages were open. I didn't even know what weekday it was, I realized as an afterthought. Envy crawled up from inside of me, giving voice to the part of myself that I hated.

I entertained the notion of leaving them all to their own devices; when this Stalker finally fractured, the shitty spell leashing it to an undeserving master, it was bound to turn the tide and seek revenge on the person that brought it over. I basked in the ugliness of that thought for a while. Used to be, thinking something like that would throw me into a tailspin, questioning my own morality and ethical standing for having even considered it. Now, I better understood my own nature and the nature of man.

A thought didn't define me, action did.

Grove looked at me after we'd parked, his face neutral. "You're taking this really well," I told him, over exaggerating my mouth to make sure there was no mistake, since I seemed to be the only person in middle-America who hadn't taken the time to learn ASL. "The down time is the worst, and that's when I usually lose people."

That was a lie, but I'd heard it said by a man I respected. He'd made a kind of career out of heroics and I admired the way those around him felt inspired yet aware. Nobody was fooled about what it was they were doing, but they seemed ready. Courage could be contagious.

Sadly, all I had was sarcasm.

Grove chewed on that for a while. Not only was the guy quiet—and not just because of the disability—he also took time to consider what he was intending to say. Grove wasn't a social pariah, maybe a bit awkward; if I had to guess, the man deliberated carefully before speaking even before the loss of his hearing. Men like him put a lot of weight into what they said, a kind of dignity lost on me since I'd fill just about any void by talking a mile a minute.

War is like that, he wrote.

Whether it was because I wasn't keen on going inside or I'd have liked a little more insight into the man I was very likely going to die beside, I waited, expectantly. It was a trick I learned from watching the women last night, and while I failed at putting on airs, I was sure the fact that I'd managed to keep quiet was clue enough. Grove set back to typing.

95 percent waiting, 5 percent action. The anticipation can be the worst part, almost as bad as the complacency that can come from a long period of nothing.

I wasn't a genius and luckily it wouldn't take one to guess that there had been a friend or two lost by way of the very thing he was speaking about. I realized that was the common thread between us. Not that we both had fought a fight that would break better men, not that we lost a lot of people, but the fact that we both felt alone.

There was solace in solitude.

And while I knew the urge to point out how contradicting this would sound was going to be fierce, I was enjoying sharing the solace of that solitude with another weary soul.

I turned off the radio and sunk back into the well-kept leather of the truck we rumbled up in. As I thought of my mentor and the motley crew of do-gooders that he'd assembled to fight back any umbrage that tried to hurt the innocent, and where my life had now taken me, I was aware of the fact that the soldier was doing the same.

"You ready?" To make sure my mouth was shaped right, I was speaking louder than I would at any other time, to which Grove replied with his own voice instead of the tablet.

"You make me glad I'm deaf."

We were quite the pair. Model-handsome fit guy beside a gentleman in aviator glasses, a bloody shirt a size too small, and a biker jacket that a crossdresser would think was overdoing it. On the other side of the door was a mousy-looking woman. I was bad with age but I'd guess she was around thirty? It was hard to tell, since she was behind the biggest pair of black rimmed glasses I'd ever seen and the sweater she was wearing was big enough for someone twice her size.

"We're here on behalf of Maria," I said. She looked at me apprehensively—to be fair, I had gathered them under false pretenses. "I need to talk to the group."

Her darting eyes leapt from me to Grove—of course giving him the respect due by lingering up and down once—and back to me. I got a once-over too, but it wasn't to appreciate an Adonis frame or my unbrushed hair. Her gaze paused on and assessed my wrist, feet, my satchel that suddenly felt outlandish, and my watch.

"You're a seer," I said.

She suspended her investigation of my person in order to lock eyes with me.

"You can sense magic. It's why you opened the door." I only played a dumb guy on television; once I was working with a cup of coffee in me and was a full day removed from being banged upside the head, I was pretty quick. Case in point, I didn't mention that I was aware those thick glasses framing her small face were actually a charade, a tool that amplified her gift. A good seer could succinctly guess magic, race, and even see through a good glamour. She was a living bell, so to speak.

"Please, we need to come in. It's not safe out here and we have to talk to everyone," I said, aiming for a tone that was polite but authoritative. Being trapped at the threshold was problematic. I didn't want to clue anyone in the group that the best hope for a suspect was among them. My suspicion would become evident fairly quickly, so I wanted to get a good look at these people before they got savvy to what I thought. I also didn't want to sit outside. Although it was sunny out and I know we weren't exactly cannon fodder, the Stalker had a thick hide that was notoriously quick-healing, and if I was ignoring my already-bruised ego at the moment I would guess my best punch did little more than piss it off. "They're in danger."

She vanished behind the door and guided it open for our entry. None of my gear would set off an alarm, really. Mostly it registered as minor incantations and the work was shoddy. With glasses like that, I bet she could count the hairs on my arms, so she'd probably seen enough to convince herself that I wasn't much in the way of a threat. Grove, on the other hand, might have been the one to hold the whole proceeding up. Magic types tended to get a little too snotty for their own good. Power had a way of inflating an already bloated sense of self. People of smaller, more humble origins weren't as bad when it came to looking down their nose at someone who fit under the category of normal, but they weren't innocent of it either.

Personally, I'd been beside godling and lowlife, and at the end of the day I knew better than to underestimate either of them. Men, such as Grove, with the proper amount of conviction and enough knowhow could be as dangerous as any monster living beneath the labyrinth of pages that made up old-timey tales.

Watch the men.

One thing I'd learned was that, while the fact my new partner did have some setbacks, there were a few advantages I hadn't yet explored. Such as being able to mouth damn near anything to him and he'd be able to decipher it.

Watch the men, I mouthed again. I probably needed to work on phrasing, honestly. I winced, but lucky for me the former soldier wasn't as juvenile as I was, so he was able to pick up what I was trying to get at once we go t inside.

Grove and I didn't cut an imposing figure; neither of us inspired intimidation, and yet the whole of the room looked like a still frame, they were so perfectly frozen. This was an assembly of low-tier types who were quick to scare and, judging from the wide-eyed expression each of them was wearing, it was hard not to imagine that if any of my movements came too suddenly that they'd just scatter.

My arms were up again and I couldn't help but wonder where this habit formed. I hadn't been arrested all that often as a kid. Maybe my subconscious just assumed it was nonthreatening, which I wanted to convey to the crowd. Occasionally my hotheadedness was troublesome.

Somebody in this room was most likely culprit for setting this shitstorm at my feet. It vexed me, but I wasn't going to win any insight with a prickly demeanor.

Maria was the one on a supernatural variant of death-row, but I was the headstrong idiot determined to set myself between her and that ugly end.

"He says we're in danger." There was a haughtiness in the voice of the empath and it was by no means subtle. In fact, the word haughty came to mind because it felt like that old school, regal kind of arrogance rather than just some bitey disposition.

I shared my best scowl that was every bit as heavy handed as her tone. "Somebody set a *Cura'sha* after Maria."

Saying the name of it took the air out of the room which, in an ugly way, it delighted me to see several of them jump to their feet. Rumor was born by exaggeration, and while speaking the name wasn't ideal, saying it once wasn't going to have immediate repercussions. It did, however, have a way of gaining immediate attention; the ones who knew were terrified, and the ones like Maria who were still new or uneducated, were immediately alarmed by their friends' reactions.

Since this group based their belief system on the ritualistic, they tended to lean a lot on the myth of a thing rather than any firsthand experience. From my cursory inspection, there were probably a dozen of them, four men and eight women, a baker's dozen if we included the hosting seer. I could tell she was the host because of the decor, the sense... and there were a few pictures of her with cats scattered all about.

A regular Sherlock: that's me.

Grove had gone mostly unnoticed and took up station in a far corner. We exchanged a strange look before he led my attention to the fact I still had my arms up, so I dropped them at his behest and continued on.

"If you're not in danger, I have reason to believe you're well on your way to it, so I want to separate you and speak with all of you as quick as possible. If we can get a fix on who's doing this, we have a better chance of shutting the connection down before anything bad can happen. If I can get the fellas outside first, then we can speak to the women, maybe make this go a little bit easier since people tend to share different stuff with different sexes."

I know, how progressive of me, but my main focus was on the men and I preferred to have everyone accuse me of being misogynistic than saddle myself with the trouble of trying to keep them calm while elaborating on the fact I thought this was an age-old case of misguided love. None of these men screamed "fighter"; in fact, two of them had to labor pretty mightily just to get out of their chairs. I couldn't take the time to read into every look exchanged, but the temperament of the room was impossible to miss: scared with a side of mistrusting.

The seer and I exchanged a look, and while I wasn't too keen to open myself up to someone who had the kind of sight that saw past a bad outfit and a sleep deprived disposition, I didn't shield myself from it. A lot passed between us, and she spoke up. "Go ahead gentleman, I can put a tea on and perhaps mister...?"

"Janzen." See, I could pick up on a hint.

"...Can better explain to us what is happening and has happened after he has spoken with everyone."

Gatekeeper, peacekeeper, and, if I had to guess, leader, I tried to impart as much respect as I could in a thankful nod at her intervention. I walked outside with Grove and two thick-bodied men, a stringy and almost strangely tall one, and a kid who is probably an inch shy of being considered a dwarf. I was not particularly sensitive, and generally you had to be a big fish for me to even grasp that you had any talent, but I was picking up nothing from any of them.

"Alright," I started. I cast a look at Grove, who, with the same proficient professionalism I had come to admire (and envy), stood vigil by the sidewalk. Scanning constantly. If I survived this, it would be nice to know I'd have my own Terminator.

"Spill. Who had the hots for Maria?"

As I'd spent the last five years being a sardonic recluse, my charming routine was rusty. Trying to get them to relax by way of camaraderie was my best bet, but when it worked I found out it wasn't all that helpful anyhow.

All of them raised their hands.

I took a breath to scold them, but I lost it with a shrug. She was beautiful, fierce and yet still delicate. It was a kind of contradictory thing, and, if I weren't busy being chased down by a death dealing hellion I would have probably spent a lot more time daydreaming after her.

"All right," I said, kneading the bridge of my nose. "Well, who here got rejected by her then?"

All the hands went up again.

"Son of a… Okay, which of you have a grudge about it, then, because look guys—this is the kind of thing that's easy to see when you take a s…" I trailed off. They were exchanging troubled looks, telltale shifting of weight from one foot to the other, and avoiding any kind of eye contact with me.

I'd eaten through what little patience I had. "I can switch this to the bones breaking part of the routine, if that's going to get me some answers." There was a rawness in me, the kind of ugliness that had a real attraction to violence. An old recess in my shamed soul that would admit to missing the thrill of snapping a head back with a thundering punch, or the feel of bone giving way. Menace wasn't a staple of who I was, but I knew, deep down inside, it was in me; it was in me and I wore it well.

"Frank!" Erupted the short one. Sharp and fox-faced, there was a cunning there that was still calculating despite being so scared.

"Who?" I snapped a look I know was dripping with malice and held each of them in it.

"He's upstairs—"

"—Still inside?!" None of them had pieced it together despite a pretty deliberate, heavy-handed approach on my part. I wanted to guess it was because good people usually couldn't make sense of bad stuff. They might acknowledge it, not be ignorant of it, but they are naive nonetheless. They didn't even piece together that as people who had made an advance on Maria, knew what she was, and had been rejected, that they would be the prime suspect in an investigation aimed to figure out who was trying to hurt her. If it wasn't so damned time consuming it would have been adorable.

Because this was destined to be a rough week, there was a scream inside as if on cue. I whirled to the door of the quaint little corner house, and without thought I was steamrolling inside. Adrenaline brought new life to my once-aching body and just as I was about to kick the door in, I turned around to instruct Grove, who has the sharpened instinct of a soldier and the fearlessness of an archaic warrior…

… Only to find that he was still scanning the street.

I took a grim kind of satisfaction that he wasn't perfect, but the smile on my face was wiped clean when another scream poured out. Without anything in the way of conscious thought, I grabbed a small potted plant and hurled it at his immaculately kept truck, no doubt a source of pride for the man. It cracked hard off the back panel and gave it a good dent. The look of utter betrayal on the face of my new friend was not to be understated, but thankfully he was able to piece together that shit had hit the fan by the fact that I was already facing the door and putting a size eleven boot to the unhinged side.

If the Stalker was inside, it wouldn't have been the worst thing to ever happen. I had a good night of sleep in me, my new accomplice fast approaching, and the small space actually gave me something of an advantage. Even if they were fast, when something that big was confined to a tight space it'd become cumbersome. With tempered hope, I breathed some of the fire out of me and bull rushed inside.

It was a massacre.

Two of the women were dead, one was screaming in the hallway leading to the back of the house, and the rest were lifting meager spells of shielding to try and keep a horde of horrendous beasts at bay. It wasn't a Stalker.

It was vampires.

CHAPTER 7

ROUND 3

If a Stalker—an Abyss-born monstrosity at the top of the food chain—was a great white shark, then vampires were something along the lines of a barracuda. One was dangerous, especially in the wrong setting. Two were deadly. Three were capable of chewing their way through this whole crew of low-level casters.

Like their cousins, they had something of an immunity to magic, they were faster than most men, and they had an array of natural weaponry. The sheer sight of them paralyzed most people. Luckily, I had already had the abrupt introduction to their kind a long time ago. These weren't going to seduce you with old school eloquence, they weren't richly dressed or impossibly handsome. Vampires were an abomination, a collage of every awful predator out there to make the perfect murderer. This amalgamation included rotten nails that they sharpened with their own teeth, even a small scratch can cause a massive infection. There were many accounts of people out on some kind of nature preserve being cut unexpectedly by something unseen, only to fall ghastly ill that very night. It was a clever way of making an easy meal.

Forget the lore, too. The sunlight was an annoyance, but didn't do more than just get them to scamper off or shield their face if they were hell-bent on killing you. Religion wasn't a deterrent unless you were a believer, a real, unflinching believer.

Your best bet was to take their head off or stake their black heart. Luckily, shattering their skull would do just fine.

"Don't make eye contact!" I screamed to everyone, doing a clumsy pirouette so I could move inside while simultaneously spinning to face Grove and scream that warning a second time for his benefit.

It was a reptilian kind of trait, but their stare was arresting if they managed to capture you with it. It didn't hold for very long—it was more like it had a way of suspending what you were doing at that moment—but as anyone who'd ever been in the thick of a fight could tell you, one pause was all it took to get you killed.

I squared up with the two that had corralled the women into the corner of the house, their attention reluctantly split between me and the small sampling of people they seemed intent to harvest. Something was exchanged between them in a guttural, old dialect; one vampire kept pressing the magic barrier constructed by the few women who could cast and the other decided it would deal with me.

It turned toward me, fluid and predatory. I kept my gaze steady on its jawline. Beyond the blackened nails and surplus of acrid-smelling drool, they could almost pass for men—starved and deranged men who had a real opposition to hygiene, but men nonetheless.

Its jaw *popped*, the sickening sound echoed uncomfortably, as if the audible release was meant to make a mark shudder. They could unhinge their jaw, as this one just did, and instead of a traditional set of teeth with just elongated canines, they had rows and rows of teeth. The first row was all serrated, better to render flesh like their Stalker brethren; the next series were wickedly curved so that once they seized you, it was all but impossible to dislodge yourself.

Of course, like every predator that had settled itself on the top of its respective food chain for too long, this thing had a kind of complacency about it.

The vampire displayed its ferocious maw with an ear-piercing shriek, one I was happy to cut short with a crisp right hook to its nasty face. It didn't expect me to be unaffected by the display; it certainly didn't expect me to react to that vulgar show of feral rage with a punch; and it most certainly didn't expect that punch to be reinforced by a metal gauntlet that seemed to just come to life over my arm.

I used my other arm to snap out and snatch it by the rags that served as some kind of makeshift shirt and, before the thing could make sense of what happened through the violent ringing in its head, I delivered another rough right hook. I aimed for the temple, making sure to twist my entire body into it, and delivered as if I were going six inches behind the head. I wasn't a killer, but something like this was easy to go all-out on. There was a part of me, after being thrown around by the Stalker and hunted down by a beast I couldn't even hurt, that was itching for a fair fight. Plus, why justify it? I just wanted to break something. It mewled on the ground, which had the second vampire turning from the cornered women to the scene of me dropping a third vicious blow. This one, rained down from above, caught it right in the face and my reinforced fist was able feel the give of the cranium without much in the way of worry about my hand or that my fist actually cracked the floorboards beneath the mess which was once its head.

Behind me I heard a gunshot, a scuffle, and then another shot. I had to trust Grove was making do, and while the infection from a scratch was serious, it was nothing a good cycle of antibiotics couldn't correct. It was the mouth I was worried about. I reminded myself the guy had enough sense to prioritize threats and was a warrior, one who had held his own against worse already.

The second vampire was considering me, the women, and its fallen comrade at my feet as if debating what would be the best course of action. It was only when it turned away that I sent a boot stomping down, driving the well-made sole into the base of the neck of its crumpled companion. Disrespect from prey was enough to spur him; he whipped around and lunged, unhinged mouth and claws leading the way.

I offered up my right arm and it latched on, gambling on the chance that although my fist was suddenly steel-plated, maybe my forearm wasn't. Biting into the jacket was tough enough; the magic worked into it reinforced the hide so that it gave the protection of a hundred leather layers rather than just the one. With my main offensive arm tangled up it was hard to push any action, which the vampire immediately took advantage of. The monster tightened every inch of itself and exploded across the room. The force of our collision was enough to drive the air out of my lungs—I didn't feel the glass table break beneath me, but I heard it. Tangled limbs and chomping teeth kept me distracted and tied up, a severe disadvantage and the absolute last place you'd want to be in this kind of situation.

It was smarter than I would have liked, and after a few swipes at my midsection and flank it had taken to just punching. The give of my leather jacket was great against ripping and clawing, but impact was impact, and with the vampire's strength every hit felt like it was rearranging all my innards. Its breath made me want to vomit. It wasn't anything to do with having a weak stomach, either; the actual smell gave me a kind of vertigo. I kept wrestling while trying to search for a way out. My bag of marbles was neatly tucked beneath my waistline which was covered by the jacket, my bracer was under the sleeve, and my metal arm was being gnawed on for all it was worth. To make matters worse, I looked up and Grove wasn't faring well. If my glimpse was enough to tell, he was bloodied up pretty well and trying to dance out of the reach of this damn thing. That was the way of a fight, though.

Military men coveted the element of surprise; one successful offensive could turn the tide of an entire war. Just as I was about to try something stupid, one of the women roared out and smashed the bastard in the back of the head. It wasn't enough to hurt it, but the thing in all that supreme arrogance just kept applying pressure on me by way of a single arm as if that was enough while casting an angry glare at her.

Three things happened. One, they locked eyes and she froze in horror. I'd long speculated on whether it was a magical trapping or just a byproduct of their natural gifts, but now wasn't the time to debate that. Two, the monster was still very much an animal and was deliberating between an easy meal and myself.

Three, I got my left arm free enough to punch it out and slide the bracer over my sleeve. I locked all of my focus into it, and suddenly the leather went from being the length of my entire wrist to just two thinner strappings; one at the top of my wrist and beginning of my hand, the other at the mid-level of my forearm. The rest slithered up and spun around, creating a small shield on my left arm about the size of a buckler. Normally the leather didn't hold up all that great, it was one of my first creations and I kept it for a mix of nostalgia and because, in terms of a last-ditch effort, it wasn't a bad idea to have a shield.

The only difference was the emblem Kaycee had presented to me, an emblem which didn't resist the incantation but instead bolstered it. Instead of just a crude leather shield, it was a crude leather shield emblazoned with the shining splendor of silver in the center. It wasn't my best work, but I gave the distracted vampire a good rabbit punch to the side of its head. My fist didn't connect; instead, the shield did, and while the leather just annoyed it, the feel of that silver sent it shrieking. It leapt off me with a stunted grace and flailed, crashing into the far wall. Dazed, covered in that putrid spittle of the vampire, and my right side half torn to shreds, I got to my feet and looked to Grove. I give a sign of reloading, the kind of reloading done on the old western rifles.

Like the one gifted to him this morning. I didn't have time to see if he figured it out; with a recklessness that was not exactly well thought-out, I charged at the vampire. I caught it before it had gotten upright, shielding against the wild clawing while driving him back with my steel-covered arm.

I knew how to fight, but being that I was quick and bulky when I didn't have a lot of space to work with, I couldn't help but throw all my body mass at something. The vampire and I crashed against one another with bone-breaking force, hurtling both of us out the far window. Outside was better for me because sunlight, while not deadly, was disturbing to them. My standing theory was that vampires saw less in the traditional way and more like a heat spectrum. I got my shield arm up, instinct guiding me more than skill, just in time to feel the force of an attempted overhand.

Another hiss wailed out, the silver burning the flesh that it caught, and I lifted my steel fist to fire off a spike. It found purchase with enough force to turn it around; I didn't get up, instead I sent a nice sharp punch with my shield arm into the thing's groin.

I heard a gunshot from inside, but this one was loud.

Monster or not, an uppercut to the groin was going to hurt, and when it doubled over I got beneath my shield and stood up into it. I caught the monster on the broad face of my shield, hoisting it high so I could twist and deposit it over the railing of the porch. I turned in time to see Grove, bloodied but not beaten, methodically stalking a fallen vampire. I slapped the bottom of my arm, a silent signal to my newfound friend that the blade on the bottom was silver. I caught a glimpse of him coming down with all his weight on the prone monster out of my peripheral because I was already turning my attention back to the vampire in the front yard.

The thing was badly burnt, horribly disfigured by the touch of the silver shield. It was blinded by the sun and crawling toward the hedge in a pitiful attempt to escape. My thundering heart was power-pumping adrenaline to every inch of me. I didn't get my start marveling at the wonder of magic and manipulate it to my whim. I cut my teeth breaking bones. I grew through asphalt. Out-connived the liars and triple-crossed double-crossers. Truth was, I wasn't some altruistic savior, nothing about redemption written in religion resonated with me. I surrounded the last piece of decency in me with unkempt violence so nothing awful could have at it again without a fight.

Standing over this vampire, there was no hesitation or remorse. Some less-primal part of me acknowledged another shot sounding off, that the women weren't screaming any longer. The frightened men we'd taken outside finally braved inside and all the while I just watched this thing try and scamper off, pulling itself forward with fistfuls of dirt and grass.

Vampires were used as fodder. They were usually at the beckon of someone else. Henchmen that took delight in the death. I grabbed it with my metal hand, let it catch my eye with its own. I didn't freeze. That answered one morbid curiosity.

It wasn't magic, just fear.

Its pupils narrowed to tight slits, a decidedly inhuman action that probably just gave good, God-fearing people pause. I stared at it. Its eyes didn't even give me an iota of hesitation. I saw, I *felt* the fear coming off of it. That wince-inducing *pop* of the unhinged jaw wasn't even enough to make me reconsider. I grabbed it by the throat, and when its maw split open as if to hiss I released it and swung my shield arm down, smashing that snapping vortex of teeth and dislodging half a dozen or so. Before it could thrash enough to whip its head from the silver, I sent a boot into its bottom jaw to stamp it shut.

Dropping all my weight behind the foot to take a knee on the things neck, I held my place on his esophagus until I felt rather than saw the last bit of life escape him. I turned toward the house, the disarray was hopefully quiet enough given this was an hour when most people worked. The proud tradition of nine-to-five which made slaves of us all. Taking a fistful of hair, I dragged the corpse to the hedge and tossed it into the thicket; the foliage wasn't going to conceal it from anyone inside, but if you just drove by and cast a cursory look over at the house it would be easy to miss the window and nothing would look to out of place.

Once back inside, I saw Grove; while there was nothing in the form of panic written across his face, I could tell he was still processing. Guy was taking a huge bite for the second time in as many days and was still with me. You had to admire that. Both of us were covered in the blood of our enemies—very Viking of us—though he had the looks to pull it off. Vampires bled, but it was a mucousy black blood, coagulated, and corrupted.

This wasn't a pretty life. The remaining members of the coven were checking on one another, and luckily a few of them were now of sound enough mind to start gathering some basic medical supplies. A few weren't coping nearly as well, but I didn't have time for them.

"Clean the glass up," I directed the heavy-set man I'd interrogated outside. I gave an up-nod with my chin at the window I'd thrown myself out. I locked eyes with the fox faced guy and implored him with a sneer. "And where is Frank?" The guy who fit my bill was conspicuously missing during this attack and now we had a full flock of frightened, traumatized people huddled around one another to go with a vampire attack in broad daylight. Vampires were taxing because there were always more than we realized, and they could hold a grudge. They skirted the edge of our everyday life and when you took down one, another three showed up with a vendetta. Cheap muscle usually loyal to a quick fix or payment and little else.

Of course, a big, life-threatening boss would be enough to inspire fidelity and the Stalker fit that motive to a tee.

"Hey, where's… *Shit*, what's-her-face?" It was around now I realized I had done little in the way of an introduction, and my streak of being one of the most abrasive people alive seemed to be holding strong. The bewildered looks I got from everyone who was busying themselves with bandaging, cleaning, or consoling is telling enough. Two of their friends were dead, and if I had to guess, the woman in the hallway who still hadn't moved had passed as well. In fact, the look I directed that way was picked up by Grove who'd had the decency to check, and with a grim shake of his head buried her beneath a jacket.

I really liked that guy.

I turned back to the living room. I knew this was a tragedy the likes of which they had never dealt with; I knew that shock was holding firm to their ability to make sense out of what I was saying. I also knew that time was limited; a second attack was probably being primed as we spoke and I had to get on the heels of whoever was doing this.

"Glasses!" The yell startled them, and the look of sheer terror that was transfixed on most their faces reminded me why I never got into the hero game. With a perpetually scowling face, patchwork tattooing, and a temper that rivaled any horror story you hear about a step-dad, I didn't fit the mold. Besides, it wasn't often I had been told that I inspired a sense of safety. Beggars couldn't be choosers, and maybe if I survived this I could turn boy wonder, Grove, into a mascot.

"Up… Upstairs… She… She tried to keep them from coming down." The woman who spoke up was wearing a hijab and had an accent that told me that she was a recent transplant. Looking around at the mayhem, the girl was the least distraught and I could see it in her face that that was becoming more and more apparent to her. Bias told me she'd maybe seen some bloody stuff in her life; though I didn't want to have any preconceived notions, it was hard to miss that a lot of the Middle East was a war zone. When you had witnessed massacres, you couldn't tell if the people who did it were men or monsters.

Sometimes they were one and the same.

"Look, we need you to move quickly, the police—" I started.

"They won't be coming," she said, cutting me off. I stayed quiet for once and she continued, "There's a sound insulating spell on the house, for privacy…" she trailed off. She needed to get out of here.

"Here," I said, taking out my keys and handing them over to her. I knelt so we could share in a quiet conversation. "Take everyone to my apartment. It's safe against this kind of stuff. My dog is friendly, but he's gonna look like a brute."

My pitbull had clipped ears—that was how I rescued him, I wasn't an asshole—but it did dissuade a lot of people from wanting to pet him. Whatever, I didn't mind having the whole sidewalk when we took our strolls.

"Some tummy rubs and he's all yours. You need to get everyone there, now; do you understand me? Here's the address." I filled it out on a notepad and handed it over to her. Pen and paper, people, still essential even in the digital age.

"Now," I said, trying to smile, though I could taste the copper in my mouth so I wisely decided to keep it tight lipped. A bloodied smile was not the placating gesture I was looking for. "Repeat that all back to me, including the address?"

That threw her, but I had her do it. Twice. Whenever dealing with a highly stressful situation, people tended to retain very little. Hell, in an everyday conversation people retained very little.

Repetition was a technique I used to make sure someone really understood something.

My mother did it to me, she knew I was a rambunctious knucklehead that had the attention span of a gnat on caffeine.

We stood up together.

"Everyone, you're going to follow—"

"—Alari."

"You're going to follow Alari. She's going to take you somewhere safe." I looked around, pulled a purse off the wall and with the grace of a gentleman dumped all the contents on the floor. Grove moved to join us in the living room, but I crisply shook my head no. I mouthed *watch the stairs* and Grove snapped back around, that gun-axe hybrid at the ready.

"Put anything you can be tracked with in here and leave it. Cellphone, nifty watch, any charm you know is locked in to your person that you've shared with the group—all of it, in here." Nobody moved, and while my knee-jerk reaction was to snap at them, I just exhaled through gritted teeth.

"We're out of time people and the first attack is usually just to soften everyone up, so *now* would be great." It wasn't dishonest, but it also wasn't a whole truth. I worked best in the grey. This world had a pretty severe divide. We had decadence, death, and duplicity on one side and the other was something warmer, inviting, and altogether innocent. I'd started off bad, took a pilgrimage to the good, and somehow a more organic evolution brought me here.

To the middle.

Existentialism wasn't my forte, and now wasn't the time to grow reflective on the progress of my path. When the bag was heavy with all their stuff I looked to Alari, a look I'd given many times in my life: it was a look that invited her to take over.

She did and, while we'd only had a short exchange, I was strangely proud of her. She ushered everyone out, escorting them into the cars outside, cars we would have to stow away in some out of the way parking garage or something later. It wasn't but a minute or two later they were off. I walked past the two dead bodies in the living room, did my best to appear reverent of the one in the hall, and joined Grove at the foot of the stairwell. The charlatan in me wasn't surprised, but it took until now for my heathen eyes to see he had a simple cross on a thin chain around his neck. Men of faith took this stuff especially hard because it shattered doctrine, but he seemed to be made of tougher stuff.

How I came across him was a minor miracle.

I took lead, calling forth my shield, and my metal gauntlet. Grove fell in one step behind me, on the right side, taking aim over my shoulder. We were working in perfect concert without ever having said a word about it. There was no vindication to be found in violence. I never got into this work for redemption.

Those women didn't deserve to die, and whenever I found the next fiend I was going to carve it up for the trespass it had visited on good people. That was the worst nightmare of bad guys, not that they'll come across a good guy. It's coming up against one of their own.

Give me righteous punishment over divine justice any day.

To my right there was a muted shout and I swiveled to face the room. Naturally, Grove had elevated out of his crouch to get a better line of sight and we both paused at the doorway. Shelving my inner monologue about faith, darkness, all that divisive insanity, I cracked the door open with a booming kick.

Following the explosion of splinters, I caught the charging vampire head on. Luckily, I was expecting it and absorbed most of the momentum with my bent knees, leaning into my shield arm. The first blast had me rocking back, but, with the reinforcement of Grove, I jockeyed to a stalemate with the savage vampire rampaging on the other side of my buckler. The sizzling flesh was a fitting soundtrack to my grim delight and with a roar of defiance I managed to shove my arm up and away, sending it stumbling backward. It hardly got enough time to stabilize as Grove opted for the big-ass revolver on his hip instead of the rifle. While it didn't have silver infused in the ammunition, I could tell the caliber was larger than anyone of sound mind should carry, and when the loud crack was done ruining what was left of my hearing I witnessed it twist the vampire around.

The second shot split its skull open like an axe wound. It was disgusting, stomach churning, and *awesome*.

It fell, dead before the body hit the floor, and I had no qualm with stepping on it as I walked over it. There, I saw the mousy seer, the unofficial leader of this quaint, peaceful group, cowering. She was untouched, which spoke to her ability. My guess was that she staved off at least two of them before they all managed to get downstairs and wreak havoc on her people.

We were not so far removed from our animal selves, and she was shaking like a leaf and blocking her face from the horror she was expecting to face. Abruptly it stopped when she realized she wasn't being torn apart by some bloodthirsty bastard. I tried to smile and she leapt up and into me.

I accepted the hug for as long as necessary. When we parted, I allowed her the classic indignant huff and dignifying straightening of her clothing. She was arranging her glasses, though they seemed to have stayed settled throughout the whole ordeal.

She was cute, probably my age, modestly dressed, and I would guess more than a little of her moxie was feigned. Didn't matter, I wasn't going to criticize a leader for bravado if it meant keeping the composure of her people in the face of danger.

"And your name?" I asked, coming around to manners I hadn't previously displayed.

"Jackie."

***

We spent an hour cleaning up the house. Grove and I dug a pit in the backyard near her compost pile to bury the vampires in a half-assed mass grave. Better than they deserved. Jackie had asked us not to bury the three coven members, and told us that they would look after their own. While we were digging, she knelt beside the bodies, muttering an incantation that was probably some sort of preservation spell. I relayed the happenings to Kaycee, and while she was still lending a supportive ear, I could sense that her time as an ally was coming to an end. There was a part of me that was angry at that, but I reminded myself she had gone way outside her wheelhouse as it stood.

I was mostly mad because of fatigue. Fatigue and the absence of an actual lead. I had a name, but after talking with Jackie, her skepticism told me that Frank wasn't all that accomplished of a practitioner. In fact, she was pretty candid in saying that only she and Maria had any real talent. I still needed to hunt this guy down.

Worn down to the bone, I had that sickening feeling of seeing children dancing on a grave I was soon destined for. The weariness was soul-sucking, siphoning out a lot of my fight which was all that kept me standing at this point. I waited until we'd gotten Jackie situated in her car, given explicit directions to my apartment, and made sure that the navigational system had the address.

Watching her drive off was exhausting. Not because I was just tired, or worn down in the physical sense. It was having chased down anything resembling a lead and ending up more confused and lost for it. Fading headlights were a fitting eulogy of my dying hope. I had an inability to do this job in the same fashion as those I'd so respected. The Polaroid images danced around in my pensive mind: good people and wild times, explosive adventures and at the end of the day the sun shone through the high-piling shit. Even when it ended ugly, we got through it. It was the promise of a new day that made whatever this one threw at us manageable.

The urge to haunt my local watering hole and forget any of this happened was strong. To forget myself in a biting blend of booze while a well-dressed harlot ten years past anything remotely resembling a prime latched onto my side for a bevy of free beer and to swap stories of yesteryear. I'd looked at the bottom of a lot of bottles though, and while I'd found a lot in the way of headaches, misery, and regrets, I'd yet to discover any kind of worthwhile answer.

It had probably been longer than I cared to admit when I come out of it. Grove was steadfast by my side and it was a cold comfort. There was a divinity in difference, and I had a feeling we were of a different make, he and I, but set upon the same path. We wore scars like badges, had buried better men than us, and couldn't quite shake the chorus of ghosts still calling our names. The neighborhood was going to start bustling to life sometime soon, and it was best we left. The outside of the house looked respectable but the interior was shredded, and the shrouded bodies were an ominous remainder.

"Bad juju, amigo." As a courtesy, I waited until Grove and I were standing face to face, each scanning our respective view of the opposite side of the road we were parked on. "And worse yet, the best we have to go on is a guy named Frank, who is in the wind and it's getting close to sundown." I watched his focus shift from my face to the sky.

"We can stow Maria away with Kaycee for another night, tops."

There was a questioning stare, an unspoken inquiry.

"The dollar trick can play for a day, a neutral with a leaning isn't going to stop the world, but it's when someone in the middle is outright playing favorite that it'll get complicated. That's throwing off the balance, and throwing off the balance is a death sentence in our world."

Our earned a smirk, and I resisted the urge to slug him in the arm solely on the grounds that he'd probably return the gesture and every inch of me was deadlocked in burning agony. I was currently held together by dollar-store duct tape and an unraveling thread, but I knew how important an appearance was.

"I have to talk to Kaycee about Maria, anyway." The lie she uttered the other night was curious before, but troublesome now. If this was less about some lovesick puppy going rabid and more about whatever it was Maria could do or was, then we were looking at a whole new set of challenges and worries.

"I need you to go to my apartment, check on the dog and get their cars somewhere, anywhere else; make sure those idiots we left aren't doing anything they shouldn't. Use your gut," I waved off that something out of the ordinary for him and something out of the ordinary for them might be worlds apart.

I've overstated how much I believe in instinct.

You know what? I haven't. Instinct is huge. Evolution has gotten us through the murk of uncivilized, catapulted us to the top of a once supremely competitive food chain and whether you realize it or not, has led you more often to good than bad. Instinct is important and even if it was wrong, the chance of it being right was so much larger that to me, it was the right call to follow. Even when wrong.

"I need you to find everything out about Frank, too. If they can't give you much I'm going to go out on a limb and guess you've got a source, or contact, or something that can maybe get us in the general vicinity of a clue?"

Grove nodded. If it wasn't for the fact that his gaze kept checking my mouth whenever I spoke, I'd have sworn the guy could hear. I resisted the urge to try and test if any other sense had become heightened. One, out of respect, but mostly because the only thing that came to mind was to test his sense of smell by farting, and even I had a limit on immaturity when my life was in danger.

With what I was guessing Grove did in the military, the expected professional track after his service was law enforcement or private security. While his limitation prevented him from exploring those avenues, I would guess he had any number of people who still respected and cared for him enough that they'd help him with a name. Given the sense of confidence he had about the task I couldn't imagine I was far off.

What was unexpected was the half-pat, half-punch to the shoulder I got whilst turning away.

There was a comeuppance well on its way to me for punching out of my weight class on this. I was downright meddling now, and even though I had some modicum of time before people started to piece together the wake of mayhem I'd left, we were now working against a clock.

"Look, man—"

A brisk wave cut me short. "Spare me the Hallmark moment."

I laughed. I couldn't help it. A nihilistic outlook with an optimistic heart made for enough of a headache, having someone to call me out on it was refreshing. "Do we hug or something?"

I got spun around by a sharp jab to the shoulder, and turned enough to make sure he had a good vantage point of my mouth.

"Check them out at my apartment and find Frank. I'll be in touch in two hours."

Grove didn't ask after where I was going, and while in the future that may be disconcerting if we made it past this whole clusterfuck and we ever again found ourselves staring down the proverbial barrel of a gun, right now it was a relief.

CHAPTER 8

NEUTRALITY

I watched the city pass by, this place I had laid down dead roots. Cheap men made expensive talk with overpriced women, the type that wore their scarlet letters as less a brand and more an award. Kaycee's shop was just on the cusp of the ghetto and downtown, that weird barrier that the middle class maintained. A thankless vanguard between the corrupt and the cowardly, though I found the terms fitting for thug and banker alike.

Hell, thug and banker were themselves interchangeable.

Fate in the form of a non-native Uber driver brought me by my second home. I couldn't tell if it was the bloodlust, fatigue, or withdrawal that had my hands so unsteady. We'd long arrived at the magic shop, but I ignored the driver for so long he was starting to fidget uncomfortably.

Just before he was about to ask me to leave for the fifth or sixth time, I got out. Measuring the entrance and the sidewalk laid out before it, I didn't need to tell myself I was stalling because not even I was that disillusioned.

When I walked in, two of her three kids were huddled beside her. Kaycee had the look of a career women balancing motherhood. Hair knotted high, a few rogue strands escaping the bun. Easy dress that was functional and durable.

The bell chimed with a pitch higher than before. Kaycee hadn't acknowledged me as of yet, and when my cursory inspection of the shop turned a bit more investigatorial and I saw no sign of Maria, my general stress turned to pointed concern.

"Kayc—"

"Wait."

It was homework, I realized, while one of her steady hands kept her youngest settled on the small stool beside her. Those rambunctious kids knew not to test her, and maybe I should have taken it as a sign.

Hindsight.

"Kay—"

"*Wait.*"

Power was a real thing, even if it couldn't be seen. It didn't rattle the rafters or walls, it was a kind of feeling. A sharp sensation that in no uncertain terms told you something without it being said. It was also different depending on which side of it you were on.

A Bengal tiger behind the security of double-panel glass or thick, caging bars was beautiful, graceful, and regal. In the wild, in shifting grass, soundlessly stalking toward you, I would wager that the description drastically changes.

I tried to disguise the scared stiffening as defiance and less a subconscious betrayal to the whiplash of her authority. Stupidly lingering at the door, I waited until she excused each child, carrying on the power play she'd established by making a show of checking each one over before sending them upstairs.

We held each other in a stare that conveyed a lot from our respective sides of the big showroom.

"I got three dead, Kaycee. Three. Dead."

She didn't blink.

"I need you to start filling in some blanks for me or there's more to come." Not ideal wording, but backpedaling now was going to kill momentum and the time for kid gloves was long gone.

"Somebody is after her, and the only way they get her is probably through me. Is that what you want? You willing to keep true to a long dead code if it's going to mean me dead?"

That one landed, though I'd have taken a softening of her glower rather than an almost predatory curl of her lip.

"You know what, you want to play all strong and silent? Keep to the code of conduct laid out in rune-stones and hieroglyphics fine, fuck it."

Rummaging into my coat set her to an unnatural stillness, confirming my suspicion that she was ready to attack and expecting as much from myself. I dropped a miniaturized chalk board at my feet, only as big as the span of my hand. I waited until she managed to tear her glare from my face to the floor.

"If I am going to die, you get to watch. You want to play in the middle, you can, and you can also live through what I did when I watched them all die."

Zachariah had been her friend. The men and women with him the same. Loyalties complicated friendship.

She winced with me when I cut my palm open. I extended it over the archaic symbol drawn in the heart of the chalkboard and closed my hand into a fist, blood dripping freely.

There's power in blood.

"Cura'sha."

Splattering blood was the only soundtrack to our Eastwoodian stare down.

"Cura'sha."

The second utterance, infused with blood, with the conviction of a madman ready to be martyred carried weight with it. It went from showdown to showtime.

"Cura—"

When I tried to explain to people that elves weren't us, it was a struggle to get them to understand the gravity of so simple a statement. Sure, they could witness the fact that they appreciated and viewed time differently. That their behavior was much more methodical or whimsical. All of that was fine. It wasn't until someone saw one *move* that they understood. Move, and move with *purpose*.

Kaycee crossed the entire room in a blink, ramming her fist so far into my sternum I doubled over and the only thing that kept me on my feet was the steely strength of her assaulting arm. Something snarky was on the tip of my tongue, and while I didn't have the oxygen to push it out, there was no need, because she was shifting to deliver a right hook that would have made any middleweight champion pale in envy.

I was a stout guy, so to take me off my feet was tough work for anyone, even the eight-foot-tall humanoid hellion chasing me down every nook and cranny of this city exerted some energy when molly-whopping me clear across the street. Kaycee didn't seem to break a sweat. While I couldn't tell you with any kind of reliable accuracy what she looked like after, laboring wasn't it. A little heavy, and short, but she managed to make it over to my prone body in what felt like an instant. Before this I never thought people actually picked anyone up by the lapel of their jacket, but here I was, hoisted above the squat woman I'd called *sister* for the better part of a decade and a half while being fixated by a stare that hurt worst than any haymaker.

"You think I don't hate this?!" she growled. My body vaguely felt the reverberating effect of being careened into the heavy bookshelves behind me.

"Tip-toeing an invisible line, speaking in riddles that'll send my friends, *my friends,* down a potentially dangerous path half ready for what they're about to face?!"

I was ashamed of the wetness touching the corner of her unblinking eyes. As usual, I hadn't taken the time to view the dilemma from her point of view. The fact that she was bound by a timeless station rigorously policed and that she had, in fact, already bent some serious rules on my behalf.

Still, I was committed. I hoped the tooth I spit out conveyed as much. Without resisting, I swallowed a mouthful of blood.

"If I fought it here, I'd have hurt it..."

She's piecing it together now.

"And if it's here, you are allowed to finish it..."

Usually I benefited from one of her spaced out think seshes. Right now, pinned between well-made oak (I'd have to thank her husband for crafting such unyielding wood) and a pissed off, pint-sized Amazon, wasn't such an occasion. I do my best to seem nonchalant, it's admittedly a hard look to pull off while your feet are dangling.

I was less put down and more shoved into the shelf and discarded. More pride than body was hurt, though both had taken a good beating.

"My children—"

"Have a mother who can tear the fabric of reality if she has a mind to, and I know who your husband is."

I wore a grim smirk that oozed with smugness when she acknowledged my accusation. In truth, I didn't know who her husband was, but I'd suspected. Another fact to consider when daring some stupid stunt against them. Still, busted lip and down a tooth, I couldn't help but smile. The ploy worked and she was now reluctantly fixing my jacket.

"She's a Wanderer," Kaycee said.

Pulling me by the hand, she set me at the kiddie table. My bad knee screamed in mute protest, but I knew better than to derail her. She vanished in the back, though her voice carried immaculately.

"A Wanderer is someone who can go through the In-Between."

I knew the lore. The In-Between separated the Abyss, the Veil, and our world; it was an almost living and organic energy. It was one of the longest-living mysteries in our world, too. It also coated most of the world we know. There were focal points that were thin and could be braved if one wanted to come here, but for the most part the In-Between was a no-go for anyone. Anyone save maybe like, a primordial or deity-level power. Those could maybe manage it.

The In-Between, from the little I knew, was said to be a kind of living energy. This sentient energy trapped anything in it, horribly mutating them and their innate gifts. There were rumored to be multi-headed vampires, mages gone rabid with an endless well of energy to draw from, even the *Cura'sha,* but even more fearsome if you can imagine. Anything with the misfortune of falling into this would either be absorbed, converted, or ripped to shreds. It seemed there was less a golden standard of what would happen and more a *dealer's choice* kind of thing.

Kaycee returned with the small med kit I'd known so well. Sitting on the edge of the table, she set to work on my face. The bite of the alcohol burn was doubled by the fact she was not doing it with any kind of tenderness. I pretended not to mind, and she gathered my face to make me hold her stare while she continued.

"A Wanderer is valuable, to either side, and rare."

"How rare?"

Sighing, she worked out something in her head. It had to be frustrating for a woman of the highest education to try and compound centuries of knowledge in short, simplified sentences. I needed to learn to be more appreciative of all she'd done.

Did.

Was doing.

"I'd say you find one maybe… One out of a million people have the talent? We discover maybe one out of a hundred of those? Every sentient species has a history of them, and it's fuzzy on what exactly they can do. What's most popular is espionage, an emissary or I know that there's something about using them to lock in a connection from one world to the next."

That last bit seemed to fit the bill.

"Wanderers have a natural proclivity for...?"

"Anything. Everything. They're attuned to all energies. It's why the last bit isn't that popular, usually by the time they're revealed they are a considerable power themselves and incredibly useful."

"So, if we're dealing with a real authority they're less inclined to kill her and more, what, interested in cultivating her gift? Recruit?"

Kaycee nodded, but the chewing lip was propelling me to keep thinking without actually prodding me on. Tip-toeing that line.

"Of course, sending something from the Abyss isn't exactly a welcoming party."

That earned me a slow nod, and a softer dab on my swollen lip.

"Where is she?"

Kaycee went very quiet, finishing her work in a fashion that told me any interruption would mean that this amicable peace would become very strained. The butterfly bandage tasted off and I clapped my dry mouth.

I was thirsty. The copper tinge didn't do much for my appetite even though I'd yet to eat today.

"I had to send her off."

I set my teeth and a rare show of maturity killed my snappish comeback in my throat. Kaycee was waiting, expectantly, yet softened when nothing sniped out.

"Those who keep the barrier of the In-Between can't allow a disturbance to the balance, and I was made aware that I was on the verge of it."

Another conspiratorial group that was too shadowy for my liking. The repercussion for upsetting the balance when you were a keeper was grave, though. Nobody had ever survived it. Even people who were close enough to witness it never seemed to want to tell the tale. In an equally rare showing of wisdom, I let the subject die.

"Where?"

Kaycee sat beside me, taking my rough hand in her smaller pair and depositing some aspirin in it. The side of her mouth tugged into a little smirk. "Do I have to do everything?"

Without resisting it, I laughed, a kind of rolling chuckle that ended in a very unbecoming chortle. A kind of burped, bark of laughter.

"She'd go somewhere safe," I said, stating the obvious. Kaycee bade me forward with a tempered, tolerating expression. "But she isn't stupid... Or selfish."

That meant she wouldn't go to her makeshift coven, neither would she risk her father. She didn't know where I lived.

"Stereotypes are ugly, but often..."

Hispanic. Catholic. I leapt out of my kiddie seat, catapulting it back in a series of tumbles.

"She went to church."

"'Atta boy."

I was almost out the door when I heard from behind me.

"You best put that chair back else you want another ass whooping."

She was gone before I even had the chance to even turn around, but I did as asked and with minimal muttering.

CHAPTER 9

FRANK

After narrowing down the choice of church to three, all in her neighborhood, I was about to start crossing them off the list when my phone vibrated. There was an address. Grove was nothing if not concise. I responded with some very expressive emoticons; the soldier just sent back one. A rude one. To be fair, it was the only sign I understand in sign language, so there was that.

An Uber later, I met him at the address he'd given. We were sharing silence shoulder-to-shoulder in what was quickly becoming our routine. In a refreshing break from tradition, it was he who broke it with a rough poke at my busted lip. As a paragon of maturity, I let out a grunt and kicked him. It was nice to know in the middle of all this mayhem two men could prove that no matter the circumstance or setting, guys would revert to schoolyard antics if given the opportunity.

I waved my defeat from a headlock and straightened out, and while he was usually Mr. Dour, I could tell he was preening a little.

"Kaycee and I had a disagreement about politics."

That seemed to sate my partner's curiosity, and we turned toward the apartment complex. While the Stalker was ever-present in my mind, especially now that it was dark out, we were in a shoddy part of town. Denizens of the criminal element were all about, and if someone was on the lookout for us, we had such a wide array of potential Judas' there was no way to mitigate the risk of us being seen getting reported without handing out every slip of silver I'd ever come across.

Battling the mythical beast of a shadow hell, the fantasy famous vampires, and whatever else might come our way had a way of corrupting your sense of mortality. A stray bullet could still do the trick. If the beneficiary of this scheme wanted to hedge bets, a nice fat purse to a fix-starved gangbanger would certainly make the odds of them winning out all the more favorable.

The shove I received from Grove to garner my attention worked, and I looked at the tablet.

"Maria is at a church," I answered.

An eyebrow encouraged me to elaborate.

"It's as good a protection as we can provide, amigo. If she's a believer, it'll hold for a spell. There's power in belief and, truthfully, we only lasted this long on a mix of surprise and luck. Lotta luck. The Stalker didn't think there was a protection sigil up the first time," I said, ticking a finger to accompany my storytelling. "The second time, I caught it because it didn't think I was anything but a dude, which isn't far from the truth. The vampire nest we rattled with a fine kicking was only survived because of you, which I don't think they counted on; you or the fact you don't scare. So what I mean, buddy, is we're kind of out of aces up our sleeves."

Grove wore a dark, dark smile and that bad part of me I kept stowed away in my own personal abysmal blackness loved it. "Not quite."

The soldier didn't finish, and I didn't push. We headed to the second story of the apartment complex, apartment 213. I managed to corral Grove just before he was set to kick the damn thing clear off the hinges. Luckily, the guy was of a mind to hear me out. Slap-shoving him to the side of the entrance, I jabbed at my eyes and pointed outward.

First, I tried the locked door, which didn't budge, much to his smug satisfaction. I flashed my own self-satisfied expression, kneeling down while tugging my necklace up out of my shirt. To most, it seemed just a very peculiar assortment of jingling metal. I set each end of the steel into the key slot, murmured an incantation and watched all the small slivers slide inside. They morphed and gelled, the individual layers congealing into a solid key that I grabbed and turned.

I knelt a jester and arose a conqueror, though to little fanfare. Unlocking the door cost me my necklace; the trick was useful, but it was a one-off and I'd have to go and remake the trinket.

Inside was in disarray and we weren't even in long enough for our eyes to adjust to the dimly lit hallway when I heard a cry for help cut short by a menacing growl.

***

I'd learned enough to know that instead of charging headlong I need to make some pretense of a plan. That, and Grove was only working off my rapidly-changing body language.

Company, I mouthed, adding a caveat with biting teeth. A gun and knife more appeared in his hand than were drawn, and while I knew I needed to outfit him a bit better, I couldn't help but be impressed. This guy was hard to shake, as stalwart and steady as the most venerable warrior of our little underworld. Bravado and bravery were two very different things, and his bravery wasn't some falsified disguise. I slipped under his guard and called my shield up. The last doorway was where the attacker was, and I hoped to creep up behind them and make short work of whatever was lurking behind door number one. That dream was shattered by the *crunch* beneath my feet as I clumsily stepped over the broken glass from the fallen lamp.

I didn't even have time to warn my partner before the thing, bounding on all fours, tore through the door, and came right at us. I managed to get my shield on it, though it wasn't as easy as our first go-around. Instead of headlong charging into it and challenging mine and Grove's combined strength and weight, it grasped the edge of my shield and used the fact that I was strapped to it against me. I stumbled and fell through the bedroom door, busting it open and falling right on the dying body of the very man we'd come to find.

Beneath me, ripped to bloody ribbons, was Frank.

Dying wasn't pretty. It wasn't dignified, either. We reflected the very way we were taken out of this world. If it was peaceful, under the haze of medication, we just slipped away with little fuss. If your innards were scattered across your bedroom floor, gouged out by the sharp, pestilent claws of some god-awful monster it was not peaceful.

When taken in violence, you left violently.

I tried to get loose of him, but he seized my arms, his vice-grip lassoing me close enough to smell that unmistakable scent of death. Hollywood dolled it up for you, but people dying grabbed, clawed, ripped, and screamed. They begged for help. Nobody caressed your face, nobody tried to impart some loving tidbit to their family on their dying breath. They smelled like shit, bled everywhere, and were generally panicked.

Behind me was the classic ruckus of a fight, the remaining furniture being crashed into and the roar of both beast and men locked in mortal combat. I had a penchant for the theatrical, but in a dark room and, given the element of surprise, it was likely Grove was not doing well. It was only one, but this thing wasn't as mindless as the rest of the horde we'd squared off with earlier.

"Frank," I screamed, my now-metal hand clamping over his mouth. "Frank! FRANK!" I hoisted his limp body up to make sure we're eye-to-eye. "Frank!" I jumped on the flash of recognition that passed his panicked stare.

"The more you move, the more you bleed; the more you bleed, the quicker you die. You have to stay still, my man," I said, ushering him down with gentleness I was hard fought to manage, I shuffled to a knee and grabbed a nearby curtain to cast over his exposed stomach.

The truth was, he was dead. Blackened blood, shallow breathing, even when calm his heart rate was through the roof. He was dead, but I needed him to not know that, I needed to talk to him.

"Grove!"

I cursed as soon as it came out my mouth, so I had to look away to try and make sense of all the chaos being conducted by the two warriors. Of course, after not seeing anything, it abruptly went quiet. One hand on the gutted schmuck beneath me, the other tentatively raised to ready myself for whatever came next.

I released a breath I hadn't realized I was holding when Grove came from around the corner, looking every bit the Nordic warrior I was starting to imagine him as. The gun was holstered, that once-pristine shirt now a mess of blood. Judging from the tearing, I guessed it was both his and the vampire's, but luckily it was a lot harder to catch a vampiric infection than you'd imagine.

Knife in one hand, it was the claw-hammer in the other that had my attention. Old, well-made, wooden handled and the rustic metal turned vibrant and ethereal about halfway up.

"Silver."

Resourceful bastard, and clever. The heavy-faced, many-ridged side complimented nicely by the sharpened spike side opposite it. I managed to wipe the cruel grin from my face before turning to the initial victim, who was blanched and growing more pale by the minute.

Grove situated himself out of eyesight but gave me a very crisp shake of his head. Apparently, the soldier with all his venerable experience on the battlefield came to the same conclusion as me.

This guy was dead meat.

I was not above dark humor and bad punnage; luckily, I had the decency to keep that thought to myself.

"Frank—Frank, hear my voice, man; help is coming, you gotta hold on."

The bill set by the other four men didn't fit here. Frank was probably late twenties, healthy, and actually not bad-looking. There was one of those competitive cycling bikes and a vast array of pictures scattered all over of him engaged in really sociable stuff. More than a few with Maria.

I wasn't above a touch of jealousy.

"Who is after her?" I jutted a finger at the wall and felt thankful that Grove didn't see fit to act reproachful about the command, and instead just got a picture of Maria to show Frank. "Maria is in danger Frank. A lot."

He gasped and one of his hands snagged the arm I was using to apply pressure.

"She was wa-wa-wa-"

He's stuck and running out of time.

"Maria was wanted, yeah? She's wanted?"

"By everyone... Needed..."

Color me confused, but before I could ask a death rattle wrapped its insidious, unrelenting fingers around him. Like I said, a violent death was exactly as it sounded. The poor guy seized, and I was torn between a morbid fascination—I saw myself in that instance, on the ground, writhing in agony while fighting for air—and the need for another answer.

***

Grove and I looked like the macabre aftermath of some low-budget slasher film. The claw hammer dipped in silver was a stroke of actual genius, and I entertained using it as an icebreaker, but instead I just kind of grumped. We made it to his truck and managed to wipe the excess gore off us and switched into another pair of shirts he had in a bag in his trunk.

Again, I had to hold my breath and more slither than slip into one of his shirts.

Not bothering with the radio, the monotone GPS was all we had in the way of noise. We checked the first two churches with little luck. One guy thought we'd made it all up in the search for some kind of penance, the other thought us a little unseemly to be searching out a woman in the dead of night who was in need of refuge. Looking back, I could see why that might have been a bit off-putting. At some point, I nodded off in the car, but as anyone who's ever been dog-tired could attest, there was a difference between passing out and sleeping.

Literally slapping the sleep off my face, we poured out of the car only to suddenly fall still. There was a dread seizing the ambient air, a kind of loathsome feeling that triggered our fight or flight response, and it managed to get ahold of both of us at once.

There was living darkness at the mouth of the alley on the farthest end of the street. I turned from it to the church and back to Grove.

"MARIA! GO!"

The problem with good men was just how righteous they tended to be. My fleet-footed friend had stuck by a code of ethics that had dictated the majority of his adult life, causing him to stand absolutely still at a time when I need him moving.

"I *might* die, she *will* die!"

My infamous dramatization driven home by the overemphasis, I finally got him to buckle and bee-line for the church. I glanced back to the road and there was nothing. That eerie, unnatural stillness. Our city was every bit as wild as anywhere in the world, and like anything else, in a sense it was alive. It was alive and being very, very quiet.

A kingpin predator was on the move, and despite my lack of faith I was moving toward the church while surveying as much of the street as possible.

Whether it was the fatigue, knowing I'd danced with the devil too often in too short a time, or just survival instinct kicking in, I made a mad dash for the cathedral. It was old and big and named Saint *Something*. My insolence all but guaranteed this wouldn't work out well for me, and as if the eye in the sky was listening,

I felt that big, bastard beast land on Grove's rundown pickup truck we'd taken over. Crumpling steel gave way to the massive monster, windows burst out glass all over the street and all the tires exploded from the pressure. An alarm attempted to sound off but seemed to choke on itself.

Still, I'd bought myself enough ground and, taking the stairs three stairs at a time, I couldn't help but ask for a little bit of love from the man upstairs. Maybe, despite my profound insolence in the past, he had a soft spot for the underdog trying to do what was right. My prayer was answered when I hit the beautifully carved, thick, reinforced door with a full head of steam.

I damn near bounced down the stairwell from the ricochet.

Now, half-conscious, the still-aware side of me was expecting to be eaten alive. To be devoured by that awful maw, and to have the scraps tossed to the beggar's nest of vampires this thing kept on retainer. Instead, I had three distinct memories.

A priest walking outside.

The monstrosity screeching to a stop before it braved the last step of the steps it'd been taking four at a time.

And the realization that the door was pull, not push.

CHAPTER 10

CHURCH

Being rendered unconscious with any kind of regularity was not ideal. I was fortunate this time because I hadn't completely lost consciousness; I was aware of the fact that a pair of strong hands had gotten a firm hold of me and managed to wrangle me inside. I was wrestled up roughly, mentally present enough to cooperate with Maria's arms slipping under me so I could find my footing before I ate the floor. Grove burst back outside, of course; the soldier wasn't about to leave the priest all alone out there.

I kept trying to turn back around, but between the sheer fatigue, Maria's insistence, and the fact that I couldn't hear any kind of pandemonium breaking loose, I didn't push it. Truthfully, I felt as safe as I had during this whole ordeal. The interior of the church was simple, the usual face of the faith cast at the head of the church and yet here it didn't come across as gaudy to me. I suspected Maria had been the one to take the time and light the candles still flickering with life. She had a lot to pray for, and the generosity of heart to do so sincerely.

She eased me down on the closest pew, kneeling down for a hasty inspection of my person. Usually a woman so beautiful taking the time to dote on me would have my attention undivided.

Instead, my bleary gaze was holding firm on Christ. The door closed behind us, the sound echoed from the heaviness of the door. It was tough, both the sound and my head could attest to the thickness of it. My surprise had to be apparent when Grove stepped to the foot of the altar, going over something to himself before kissing the feet of Christ. I was acknowledged by him long enough for him to sign that he was going to the roof to take a look around.

I couldn't think of a better thing for him to do, and right now, we could use the breather. Maria's probing hands reached my chest and I burst out with a fit of laughter. It tickled. I was only human.

"I'm okay," I managed through a delirious smile.

She swatted me. It was a gift. "You need to stop this right now!" I was hit a second, and third time, tears glistening in her kind, soulful eyes. "You can't die for me, that's it. This is it, I w—"

"Maria." The priest's voice cut through her ramping anxiety; simply speaking her name seemed to mandate that she calm down. There was a tenderness in the utterance complemented by an affectionate authority; it invoked a lot in her, and he conveyed it with a single word. You had to respect that kind of power, unless you were me.

I hated the church, a bunch of sycophants and liars and just a good face on a bad idea, if you asked me. Nobody did, thankfully. Maria used my shoulder to steady herself while standing, giving a brisk nod to the man with the white collar; she really had composed herself swiftly.

"Would you get us some tea? I think these two would like some as well."

I turned to give the priest my full attention. He was younger than expected, bald by choice. Since it was a Latino area, I expected to see the community reflected in one of their sacred leaders, but he was white. I saw a kind of smugness in him—but not from his status. It was the kind of thing I saw in really bright people. The brilliant type who couldn't help but come across as a little condescending, made worse by the fact that they were usually right. Perpetually wearing an almost self-satisfied smirk. In Maria's absence, we shared the solitude of silence, neither moving to break it.

He was taller than me. Thin, though not to the bone. He moved with the confidence of man who knew what was beneath his feet. Not a swagger or empty bravado. He stationed himself on the dais before the mantle of his lord, openly taking my inventory while I brazenly did the same.

The guy was the portrait of collected calm in the face of the calamity he'd just stared down outside. I, by unfavorable contrast, was a mess. Tattered leather jacket, some bruising on the right side of my face and mouth. Aviator glasses tucked into the pocket of my haggard jeans. Shoes I should have stopped wearing ten years ago.

I'd talk to a dog if it was making sufficient eye contact, so suffering to me was the stillness of silence.

"So, you handled the killer mutt pretty well. Not your first rodeo, Padre?" The sarcasm anchoring the Spanish version of his title wasn't lost on him, the glean in those very calm eyes told me as much.

"Maria told me a demon was after her," he said, shrugging.

"And you believed her?"

"Who am I to not?"

I felt my eyes narrow, and I knew my scowl was damn near ear-to-ear. "So, you just believe anyone whenever they tell you that?"

"You're angry and looking for a fight; if you'd like, we can see if that thing is still nearby?" he offered calmly. Not what I expected out of a holy man, especially one who just stood toe-to-toe with a damned hunter of the Abyss. I was acting like a juvenile, petulant ass and he'd called me on it. A lot of the fire in my chest deflated in a breath.

"Excuse me if it's hard to swallow that this kind of thing is new to you *and* you just came out the other end untouched, serene as a virgin mother and acting as if this is all part of your day job."

"The shepherd doth not just keep the flock, at times he's tasked with keeping the wolf at bay." There was a human moment in the pious servant, a kind of visible shake and laugh that was carrying him off into his own headspace. I loved a good back and forth, but as a perpetual daydreamer, I respected the need to slip into a pensive pause so I waited, dutifully. Plus, I knew he was jarring me a little, and I could appreciate that. People of faith tended to be very severe and dour; he was almost lackadaisical and serene.

"Was that a demon?" It was the earnestness of his question that took a lot of my gusto.

Chewing on an answer, the conflict was evident on my face. "I think... Not in the way you mean it. I'm afraid we don't see a lot in the way of your agency, but, yeah, I mean... Sort of. Demon does fit the bill."

We were back to the crux of a believer and an antagonistic nonbeliever.

"Not a big fan of the house of God?" he asked.

"You guys are a little too quiet in all of this for my liking."

"Seems we answered when called."

That was a point, and while I know he was aiming it as a jab in our verbal sparring, the fact that the church held something as wretched as the Stalker was new. I hadn't ever thought of trying holy ground, or something as radical as a religious weapon, but this seemed to hold a lot more weight than I was ever made aware of. One of the men Zachariah ran with a decade past came across as a kind of knight or paladin, but I thought that was more a byproduct of my nerd-dom than actually being based in any kind of truth. In all my time under his tutelage, nothing like this had ever been touched on; and even though my tenure was a few years long, in the grand scheme that was barely enough time to make a dent in all that was out there.

"Nah, not really what I was getting at, Father. I'm not any kind of authority on all of this, but my understanding is that it's not really governed or run by a Heaven or Hell kind of thing. Though..." I thought back to my first lesson, the craftsmanship and the power of belief, I remembered how vehement Zachariah was about the strength in conviction. "I have been told belief is kind of the basis of all power in—" I waved my hand in the air. My brain was a bit too bottomed out to make sense of this for him, "—all of this."

"So, by that logic and what you've seen, was God not just brought into this?"

"Saying you manifested God is a little arrogant, ain't it? Don't you guys got one of them seven truths about arrogance and pride."

"I wasn't saying I manifested God, and that's Buddhism."

"Same shit, different box."

"Can't win them all," he said, grunting to a stand. The priest was a little wobbly though I have the decency to refrain from asking after it. "And I guess this means you aren't going to want a pamphlet on the way out? I was sure I would get a donation out of you, the very least."

"Money is the root of all evil and yet the Church is always asking after it."

"You're confusing Disney values with Christian ones."

"One and the same."

"I wonder if the gates of the Magic Kingdom would have kept your monster out," he said dryly.

It was never fun for a smartass to be struck dumb, but the back and forth was won because the last quip cut to the heart of my cynicism. There was a lot about his establishment that I was against. This church was simple, modest, comfortable, spacious, and filled with love. The priest was brave and engaging, down-to-earth, approachable and, better still, able to take my unwarranted contempt in stride.

"Thanks," I said.

He gave an inquiring *hm* as if he hadn't heard me, but when I sourly went to repeat myself I caught the glimmer in his eyes again. I smiled, despite myself.

"I do not think it was my belief, so your appreciation is undeserved. A church is simply a building without belief, and I am just a man without faith; I still am, sure, but a vessel too." We shared a look to the far end of the church. Maria was busy in her own world, riddled by concern and distraught with guilt. Any decent human being would be in despair over what had happened in pursuit of their person, and since Maria seemed better than most, I couldn't even imagine the state she was in. I also couldn't conjure up the magnitude of strength it must have taken to stand upright.

"I never got your name," I said.

"You seemed more inclined to insult the bedrock of my belief and mission." Good natured and funny, not even a flinch in the face of all my barely checked disdain.

We shared a grin.

"Justin," he said.

"Father Justin?"

"Sure."

I struggled up to my feet; we met in the middle for a firm handshake.

"What's with the informality? Trying to be cool for all the kids, what with their wireless internet and rock-n-roll?"

That got me a chuckle. "My last name is Handy, plus I figured since you've all but called me a charlatan we shouldn't have to stand on ceremony."

"Father… Handy?" I winced, then grinned despite myself.

"I softballed that one to you, though I think it's time you saw to your charge."

The phrasing caught me, and when I'd followed his line of sight to Maria, again I was taking the time to dedicate all of her to memory. To say she was sexy would demean the truth of it; plus, in a church, while she was mourning, that was tactless even by my standards. She had none of the plastic motif that passed as pretty these days, her appeal was timeless.

Father Handy was gone by the time I turned around.

I hesitated before heading over to Maria; one of my marbles was right by where the priest had been standing. I leaned down to drop it in my bag. There was a joke about losing my marbles, but I was too exhausted to make it work, and besides, I wasn't sure Maria was in the mood for it. She was watching me in complete silence, her expression unreadable as I approached.

"You know, for all we've been through, the fact we've only had one or two conversations makes it feel like every time I want to talk to you I'm breaking the ice all over again." I motioned at the emptiness beside her on the pew. She accepted with a small turn of her hand, and I settled in.

"It couldn't be because you're awful at talking to women? Or men? Or even your friends?" she asked, a brow arched.

It was nice to laugh among all this madness. We shared a spirited one.

"You picked up on that?" I asked, struggling through a body-rumbling chuckle.

"I have eyes and ears. Grove is down one of the two and I bet even he's said something to the same effect." There was a glimmer in her eyes—dampness from laughing, maybe, but beyond that, it seemed like there was a desperate desire for her to be herself, to pretend things were normal, despite everything.

"Several times. Him and a lot of others."

I could feel her gaze on me; she was studious when not having her door kicked down or being chased across the city. "That doesn't really bother you, does it? I can kind of tell."

"Honestly? It doesn't. I haven't done a lot right in my life. Next to nothing, really. I got me right, though. I know who I am, and while I'll crack on myself a lot I don't *hate* hate myself, so in truth if I rub people wrong or someone isn't too keen on me, that's fine. They don't have to live with me, I do."

"Being okay with who you are is a pretty big deal, if anything I would say at your age that's not bad."

"How old do you think I am?" I asked.

Scrutinizing me, she was barely able to check her grin. "Not a day over forty."

I pulled a wounded face. "You're sitting on my bad side, to be fair."

"Your bad side?"

"Bad side," I said, gesturing to the side she was on, highlighting my busted lip. "Worse side." I turned my face and displayed the side with the blackening eye.

"If you learned to keep your foot out of your mouth, it might be more tolerable," she said. I had been chided worse, but never by better. Despite the lacking comfort of the pew, a cruel design I suspected from the church so nobody could enjoy a Sunday siesta, I was at ease for the first time since this mayhem started. Even when at the magic shop I knew it was under the pretense of barter, and that at any moment the luxury of a reprieve could be taken from us all.

"You're awful forgiving of me now, even though I tore half your house down."

"You also saved my life, and my father's. I'm not an idiot, Janzen, I know you came back into a life you'd left behind for me. To help me, though I can't for the life of me figure out why."

"You're hot."

She hit me in the back of my concussed head with enough force to set my teeth into each other. I rubbed at the ache, hoping to disperse the pain some.

She gestured at me, slender hands thrown up in mock disdain. "See? Just when I am trying to say something decent you go and turn it on its head."

I smiled, my heavy eyes fighting off a wave of fatigue that threatened to drown me.

"Why?" she asked with a sudden seriousness.

"Grove told me that all it's gonna take for bad to beat us out is for good men to do nothing. It's an old quote, it does hold truth, though. Anyway," I continued, but a yawn stole a lot of my thunder and I felt the sag in my body start to favor a side. I wanted to fight off Maria as she eased me down, but truthfully it was nice to feel her hands on mine.

"I didn't see any good men... Figured I'd do in a pinch. Beggars and choosers, you know."

A wry smile appeared on her face. "You lay the self-loathing thing on pretty thick, you know? It's especially hard to buy with all the good I've seen you do just in the past few days."

"They ran out of traditional armor at the anti-hero store, so I got stuck with a bad sense of humor and a worse view of self."

"Ah, I see. Could be a good niche market though, you know? Discounted hero work."

"Yeah, except you get what you pay for and last I checked this one was *pro bono* which is Latin for 'I'm an idiot'."

"No, it's not." She broke and humored my own attempts at it with a laugh. Soft fingers threaded through my hair, easing my aching head.

"Agree to disagree."

Most people, being social creatures, had an inherent and incessant need to fill any void with noise. Sharing silence comfortably showed a kind of kinship, a closeness that couldn't be faked. We both basked in it for a while, allowing the conversation to wax and wane naturally.

"Tell me about your people," she said. To ensure that I couldn't escape seriousness of the question with a clever side-step, she drove it home. "The ones who died."

What I admired most was the way she managed to balance both resolve and compassion. She knew this was a tough thing to talk about and yet she was unrelenting.

"Zachariah was my teacher and the leader. He was an artificer."

"Like you? I heard Kaycee mention that about you…"

I shook my head. "No, not like me, I never even got beyond being an apprentice."

"She made it sound like you were something of a prodigy." I looked at her, but there was no teasing in her voice or visage.

"Zachariah was very invested in me and had a tendency to get overly excited about stuff, I was okay though. No better or worse, I'd imagine."

We fell silent but she held on to hers longer, letting me know I wasn't going to get out of this so easily.

"They took me in, all of them, really, and helped bring me up. Zachariah owned an antique shop, right across the street from Kaycee's place, actually, and everyone operated out of there."

"How many were there?"

"Five, with a sixth who would drop in on occasion. Someone who knew someone kind of thing, depending on what they were working on."

"What happened?"

"I still don't really know. I know there was a fight. They all seemed fidgety, even Bhalore—he was a Paladin, big and brave, tough as hell and just the nicest guy ever. Scared, looking back on it."

I tried to sit up and she seized me, settling me back down with a wordless command. I'd like to say I grudgingly accepted, but that would have been an outright lie. I was stealing strength from her and finding comfort in it.

"They didn't take me or tell me where they had gone, it took me two days to get on a trail and hunt them down. I usually tagged along by then, I wasn't just riding the bench. I got to a sewer clearing, one that is kind of like a focal point from a lot of intersecting tunnels. What I found?"

I shuddered at the memory and I hate clichés, but it was tough not to walk back in the eye of your mind and see all your dead loved ones without having a visceral reaction.

"All of them dead, though they put up a hell of a fight. Hell of a fight. The place was in ruins, the walls barely standing, and the roof even took a good pounding. It ruined the street above them; it's how I found them. All of them dead there, except Zach. Zach chased down whatever took them all out and I found him a few hours later, down one of the sewer pipes. Heart ripped out, mouth and eyes wide open."

"I'm so sorry, Janzen."

I ignored the obligatory nicety, though she'd meant it in earnest. I finished the story, now more for my sake than hers. "I cleaned them all up, took them home, closed up shop... And never looked back. I just left."

"Just like that? You never tried to..." she trailed off, afraid of offending me.

"Whatever it was, I wasn't up to snuff, and half the reason it all went to hell was because I wasn't there. That fight was close, they had whatever it was beaten or close to. I could have been the difference. If they just had one more distraction, one more fighter, it could have turned the tide of all of it. Instead I sat on my ass, waiting up all night like some freeloading leech. Not only did it cost all of them everything, it cost this city. I got out. I wasn't made for this life."

"I don't know," she countered. She'd listened to my petulant whining about all that had unfairly befallen me and still kept rolling her fingers through my hair. "Get the look down and you could make a pretty good hero, I bet."

I muttered something about how next time, we could construct a six-foot-tall, hard bodied, handsome hero, but I doubt any of it came out legibly. I remembered her gifting me a kiss on my heavy head before I fell fast asleep.

***

It was still dark out when I woke up. Grove was sound asleep and Maria, too. They had a common area for homeless in the back, it was where I deposited the blanket someone had been nice enough to cast over me while I racked out on the rigid pew. Hard surface be damned, I couldn't deny it was some of the best sleep I'd ever gotten. Revitalized, the nagging aches and lingering stiffness seemed lifted. I sent a text message to Kaycee, and prepared one for Grove and Maria when they woke.

On my way out of the church I ran into another priest. We exchanged pleasantries and I made him promise to keep an eye on the two in the back. I was surprised that he was, in fact, surprised, someone was here.

I told him Father Handy let us in, mockingly describing the man.

He informed me nobody worked here by that name.

And nobody fit that description.

CHAPTER 11

MORE MUSCLE

I didn't have time to spend wrestling with the implications of the missing priest. While I didn't believe in coincidences anymore, I didn't have the luxury to sort through it. The sun was just now reaching for the sky, the fire of life starting to split the sea of darkness and gain a brilliant foothold on the horizon. I sucked down the sludge they were passing for coffee at a local diner across the street, along with some sugar-caked pastry.

I had an hour or so before the rough and tumble of the morning commute took off, so I got to work.

First, I took a look at the hammered-in truck, thankful that neither Grove nor I had been inside. From there I gauged the signature of the damage, where the Stalker must have launched itself from to impact the makeshift landing platform in that fashion. It was the very unsexy grunt-work that I spoke about before. It occurred to me that I wasn't really sure just what this thing was capable of. Hell, the most I knew was that it stank, it was damnably fast, and it had a dozen or so names.

I got to the top of a three-story residential building and in the far corner I got my first break. There was distinct clawing—not your usual wear-and-tear of corrosion— but deep, unmistakable imprints.

A high ground perch wasn't surprising. I took advantage of the still-rising sun to look over the whole scene from the night before. I hadn't been able to revisit any other of the attack sites, so I was hoping that this would give me a better insight to how it operated. I read the summary of the Art of War once, this seemed to kind of fit the bill.

High ground. Pretty common practice, but the issue was that it couldn't have been hunting us. It must have been here, lying in wait for Maria. We must have just made an easy target. I vaguely recalled the feeling of dread and how it bounced around the whole street before we'd been able to pinpoint it. Initially I thought it was because this thing was so agile that it was careening all around with such tremendous speed we hadn't been able to track it.

Now I wasn't so sure. An illusion could get you killed if you were committed, and while I wasn't about to bank that this thing could wield any serviceable magic, living in a world of the dark arts, it had probably picked up on a few things.

I walked the line to the other end of the rooftop, where an alley split it from another three-story structure. Another kudo given to my day job while I take out a military grade flashlight. Actually, I am not sure who determined the grade of the flashlight, it might just be clever marketing, but it's disturbingly bright. I searched the far wall of the adjacent building until I found what I was looking for.

Claw marks.

Trudging down the fire escape confirmed my suspicion of the concussion; I got vertigo just from the downward trip and had to sit down twice. The beatings I'd taken so far were supposed to be met with ice, pampering and bedrest. Despite what our silver screen action heroes have shown us, we weren't supposed to take this bad of a clobbering repeatedly in so short a time.

I rested twice on the very short trip. Once on the ground, I continued to Nancy Drew. I marked what I roughly guessed the distance between each claw was. How far it got with each jump. It was guesswork, but from what I could tell it took two jumps to get it to the roof. One to the opposite building and the other launching it sheer over the cowl of the roof. Made each leap roughly fifteen feet.

How this thing managed to maneuver the city without any fanfare was baffling. Now, being stumped is tough, but being vexed while fighting off a migraine on shitty coffee and a three-day-old piece of cardboard they passed off as a pastry was downright cruel. I tried to forget the fact that this thing was as nimble as an Olympic gymnast, strong as any ten men, with accelerated healing and possibly versed in some kind of magical craft, and instead forced myself to walk down my lead. No way it came from the street side. It was bright; the residential building is beside the diner I'd just left and a pretty well-known bar. The church across the street stayed fairly illuminated at night. Even skulking or with a glamour, that was a tough trick to pull off.

I took out the 80s-era aviators and rescanned all I'd gone over. While it was tough to make anything out in the already-darkened alley because of the lenses, the incantation I'd crafted into them allowed me to see magic. It was just basic stuff, sure, but the beauty of keeping stuff simple was that everything started off that way: simple. Surprisingly, the clawed-up wall had magic residue, kind of like a fingerprint, and it was then I found my trail.

No matter how fantastic, mythical, preposterous, or powerful, when something is in our world, they have to play by our rules. They may be able to bend a lot, break a few, but the big stuff was hard to get around. I was so absorbed and overwhelmed in the magnitude of taking this thing on, I had forgotten to take a step back and start applying some practical, problem solving application.

How it had moved around unseen was my first question, and I got the answer as I stumbled on a big sewer trench in the back of the alley. It was spindled and gaunt, though strong, it could slip into one of these. It was using the sewer. The sewer networked throughout the whole city. It also probably masked that pungent odor, unless that was what had been creating it.

I got my notebook out and started to write, texting Grove between jotting to invite him to the diner and soundboard off him what I'd learned, and formulated the beginning of something that might end up resembling a plan.

***

Maria, being on the frayed edges of the life, knew about the bar I was planning to go and visit and the proprietor I was about to speak with. She wore a conflicted face from the fusion of warring emotion, the amalgamation of concern, grief, exhaustion, and even anger, was just so adorable on her. Eventually she agreed, and we left the church before the early evening. The church as a sanctum had the distinct feeling of a one-night reprieve. My gut was telling me that we had to keep moving forward.

It wasn't yet dark when the taxi arrived. Gale had a place that was never full or bustling, neither was it ever empty or desolate. I'd been here on the heels of an all-nighter and it was still busy, same as the afternoon and right before closing. Truth is, after I lost touch with a lot of people, and just outright lost the rest, I wasn't in a good headspace. I wasn't sure I was now.

Without the burly doorman, there was only the short waif of a man who didn't blink. While that was unnerving, it wasn't nearly as intimidating as a guy who looked like he was half mastodon and half colossus.

"Ah, Mr. Robinson, very good," he said while not bothering to acknowledge me; he was instead busying himself with a tablet. That was rude, but it wasn't strange. What *was* strange was the podium he was behind was holding up a second tablet; somehow the man was occupying himself with the one tablet whilst still involved with the other.

"Friends? Hm." He continued his tapping. "Go ahead, Artificer."

"How di-"

"I thought 'apprentice' would be a bit demeaning in front of your company, and given that you look worse than you did just three days prior, and *that's* saying something given the state you'd been in at that time, I wasn't going to contribute to your continued misfortune."

"You're a real peach, Mr…?"

"Donovan. Donovan Dee."

"Doorman extraordinaire?" The sarcasm all but drooled out of my mouth.

"Tinkerer."

That gave me pause.

A Tinkerer was an entity associated with keeping the balance, an emissary of the In-Between. They were frequently gnomes. Innovative, brilliant and lethal. Partitioning their mind allowed them to compartmentalize somehow so they could take on several tedious tasks at once. Not just multitasking either; they could write poetry while figuring out some elaborate puzzle. On the surface, none of that sounded dangerous, but trust me, it was. They blended mechanics, machining and magic seamlessly. Not like an Artificer, either. We were basically a watered-down bastardization of them.

"Warrior. Strong."

Grove paused, considering him and then me. With a stout shake of my head I waved him forward, until the Tinkerer reached out to suspend his momentum.

"You won't go in unarmed and yet I cannot let you be armed." Sighing, the slight man just kept on reading a self-scrolling book on the tablet laid across the mantle of the podium while doodling some kind of theorem on the other one. "But you stink of honor. Will you only draw your weapon if threatened, and justly so?"

For the first time, seeing an elf, magic, fighting a demon, and being introduced to a world of what most would consider make-believe, he was stumped. I only offered a shrug when those pleading baby blues search me and at length, there was another nod.

"Say it."

"Yes," he answered. Grove wasn't self-conscious about anything save the tenor of his voice. It was a small discomfort to bear for entry, though.

When Maria stepped up, radiating beauty and kindness, was the first time we got the undivided attention of the toy-sized Tinkerer.

"My, oh my, she is going to want to meet you."

I cast a look at the skyline, the encroaching darkness eating away at the last sliver of sunlight; it was a doomsday clock flirting with an ugly end, the finality of night meant the lack of a haven. While I didn't think our enemy was right on us, it wasn't a chance I was willing to take.

"Donovan, I really have to insist we go inside."

I'd interrupted him, a fact embellished by the way his open mouth stayed so during my said interruption. It still did when turning to regard me with those big, unblinking eyes.

"I know well why you're here, and I am quite sure we're safe. I, at the least, am safe, and she, now, too, is safe."

He was like a backwater Yoda with the poetic punctuating at the end of every statement. I, for once, fell silent to get across that I wasn't playing a game.

"Fine," he said, abruptly snapping back to the two tablets. "Go inside. Take your warrior and Wanderer. I don't know why you're so anxious to get in when it's very likely she won't let you leave."

***

As usual the normal hustle and bustle of the bar was present. The reserved atmosphere was a little less animated. Instead of the tenor of some live artist, the electronic jukebox was churning out some top forty nonsense.

I mouthed to Grove: *out of nowhere and fast.*

My living shadow took up a sentry post by the stairwell we'd walked down, and managed to order himself a water while adopting his customary stance of everlasting vigilance. Maria was visibly torn between taking up residence beside our mutual guardian, or follow after me. Curiosity managed to get the best of her because not long after I sidled up to the bar, she joined me.

"Little dead in here," I said.

Gale's lips spread into a mirthless smile, a single chortle telling me I'd said something funny despite being unaware of the fact.

"Where's the kid?" I asked, casting a glance at the empty stage.

"Killed himself."

That's why. I muttered a curse that was also something like a prayer. My condolences to Gale would be wasted, but who would I be if I didn't try?

"Sorry to hear it. Guy was talented; really, really talented."

Something softened her reservation and she acquiesced with a nod. "Second one this year. The curse of the gifted, I suppose. Artists never do well."

Stalling would have been disingenuous, and still I found myself kind of fascinated. Gale never gave much in the way of herself, even a glimpse of what was beneath the cool exterior. Those who frequented the bar with any regularity still couldn't tell you anything concrete about the woman. Now it was my turn to take on the mantle of stony silence to encourage her to continue.

"They share their heartbreak, mourning the worst moments of their life. We hear about their sorrow and tragedy in such singsong melancholia and because they do it so beautifully, our thunderous applause, the one escape they can't help but chase, is our way of encouraging them to break their heart all over again for our morbid entertainment."

"When you say it like that it's almost cannibalistic."

"As it was in the beginning…"

She trailed off, leaving me to guess the rest which was reasonably easy.

"So, no live music tonight?" It was said with an unintentionally thick lament. Maybe it was fatigue but between the way she'd so eloquently described the nature of a performance when wrought with a stirring sincerity and hearing of another lost to something so insidious as suicide hit me more than expected.

"Unless you or the young lady will be providing your services, I am afraid not."

"Oh, she's great, actually, so that's kind of serendipitous." I straightened up excitedly. The beginning of a plan was taking shape in my head. Less a plan and more a ploy. It was a cheap way to buy us some time, but we were in need of precisely that. While it might infuriate Gale, should the truth of it come to light, it wasn't like I had a lot in the way of choices. Maria wore an expression that could only aptly be described as flabbergasted. It took a pair of kicks to get her to chime in, adopting my ruse with me and punctuating it with a sweet smile. I had a bad habit of concocting a scheme and forgetting to share it with the class, that and the fact that while I'd become a bit inoculated to the effect Gale could have, Maria had not. She was a little awe-stricken.

"You got the band, and it's not like you have anyone lined up to audition."

Gale, considering the empty stage, gave an almost imperceptible nod.

"Why not. You're hired. One night only though," she said, her feline gaze flitting over each of us. "And if you're terrible you don't get paid."

It was all I could do to keep from screaming. Maria, still in a perfectly perplexed stupor as to what just transpired, let me lead her to the stage. I placated Grove with a comically cheesy thumbs-up and deposited Maria with the stagehand. "Trust me," I cut her off, pleading for her to take this leap with me. She had to think I was crazy, but if we showed our hand too soon we'd be in it even worse than we already were.

I left a dumbfounded Maria at the stage, gifting an equally confused Grove a hearty pat on the shoulder as I ambled past and finally returned to my seat at the bar. Gale was both indifferent to the happenings while simultaneously aware of them. She epitomized how I imagined royalty, which, guessing by the reverence reserved for her, might not be that far off the mark.

"You going to tell me what that's about?" She uncapped a beer for me—some brand I'd never heard of, but I didn't complain. It had a zesty quality with a back-end bite that was satisfying.

"Just needed to buy some alone time," I said.

"So you bring two people into my bar?"

I hesitated, feeling a little sheepish. She had every right to be suspicious, but she lacked the interest to follow that line of inquiry. We were both waiting for Maria as she had a little huddle session with the band. The shrewd woman mixed a razor-sharp awareness with a lukewarm regard, a kind of living paradox existed in her stare. I shifted gears to press for more information.

"You know anything about Heaven?"

That grabbed the full of her attention. A perfectly shaped eyebrow asked what her voice would not bother to.

"I had a weird run-in at a church," I said, trying to keep my fidgeting to a minimum, but between her being dead-set on my person with those unnerving eyes and the fact that I was wrestling with taking on a whole new spectrum of power in this wildly unpredictable world I was living in, made me more than a little uneasy. "And just couldn't help but wonder. Kind of realized that I might not be seeing the whole picture."

Her eyebrow twitched, almost reading as a blasé dismissal, but she kept silent. The lighting dimmed; the stagehand started to scurry back and forth. I heard the pop of a bottle and a moment later saw that she was cradling the same beer she'd served me casually poised in an elegant hand. One I imagined belonging to a pianist.

"I don't really know." She settled her hip into the bar, watching the stage as Maria prepped. "This whole thing we're in is far more vast than you could ever hope to imagine," she said. I knew it wasn't aimed as a slight, yet before I could push past the sting of it she kept on. "And the same could be said of myself. It's like the ocean, the deeper you go the deeper it will get. I may seem a big fish to you because you're staying so close to the shore, but the depths I have braved? They have shown me that at the edge of the maps there are true monsters."

My struggle to grasp the magnitude of that statement must have been obvious, so she put it in line with my own metaphor.

"Imagine every time you take a step back, the picture you're trying to look at just kept getting bigger and bigger. I am telling you that, as far as I have gone, that is a truth that is still holding."

Gale was the undisputed power in the city and as far and wide as I had gone there was yet to be anyone whom I had come across that managed to shake me to my foundation the way she did. To hear her say that she was closer my end of the spectrum than the opposite side wasn't just sobering. It was downright horrifying.

"So there is...?"

"I said I don't know, and what I meant by that is: I don't know. There very well could be. Santa isn't real, but the Boogeyman is. Who is to say there isn't some variation of angel, or god, or messiah? Before men, the Good Book said that this was a world plagued by beasts and giants. It very well could have just meant us. Even in my world there is much unknown, the Queen herself could not hope to understand the sheer vastness of the Veil, so how you'd expect me to know everything about everywhere else is preposterous."

"Great, so you're telling me in ten years I've learned next to nothing."

"If we're really taking into account everything I know, and everything I think I do not know, I would say you've really learned closer to nothing than next to it."

Despite ourselves we shared a smile, the joke was well-aimed and even as it landed I couldn't feel too badly spurned by someone such as herself taking the time to educate me. Especially since I was on the verge of betraying our quasi-friendship in the name of safety. Betraying might have been a strong word, but there was definitely some mild manipulation going on.

Maria started to sing and my relief was so surreal I felt myself visibly relax. The sigh wouldn't have seemed to out of sort especially since I was drinking in the middle of what could accurately be called a rough week. Gale saw it for something more, the sagacity of the woman was a product of time, intuition, and perceptiveness. She was almost arrogantly apathetic but that didn't mean she wasn't paying attention. Lucky for me I didn't have to bear the brunt of her daunting scrutiny for too long.

Maria cut an octave above a simple hymn, her voice wafted through the place like a delectable aroma. Something about it soothed almost immediately, kneading the tension out of me and every downtrodden loser that haunted the bar. I couldn't understand what it was she was saying, but it didn't take long for me to pick up that she was singing in Spanish. Instead of taking away from the influence of the song, it seemed to enhance it. We could focus on the melody, it kept us present. As impressed as I was, I couldn't help but wonder if the stage had a magical property to it or if this amazing woman, thrown into the thick of all this madness, was just that magnificent.

"You got lucky," Gale said, her witticism in resplendence. I deflected the implication with a cheesy grin.

So much of my own personal baggage washed away on the waves of Maria's Spanish serenade. It was a gift that the soulful, young witch was blissfully unaware she'd given. Four songs and two beers later it was all going on without incident. But I should have guessed that this wasn't the week for any kind of miracle, even a minor one.

The upstairs entrance door crashed open, the rancorous bang was followed by the stairwell wood groaning in protest as it barely shouldered the weight of the descending Stalker.

CHAPTER 12

CHALLENGE

The music screeched to a stop, which before this I'd figured to be some Hollywood fabrication, but it actually does cut off in an almost broken belch when someone is shocked. Most of the people took refuge in the far corners of the room. The first clue that something was amiss came in the form of a troubled expression sweeping over Grove. His retreat from the base of the stairwell was surprising, since I hadn't seen the kid back down once.

Then I saw why.

It was me.

Well, a mutilated bastardization of me.

Gaunt and skinny, with gangly arms and a sunken face. Shirtless and filthy. Tattered rags served as something resembling trousers while big, gnarled feet scoffed sluggishly over the floor. It was me, but it wasn't; it was what a nightmare reflection of me would look like. This thing was wearing my face in an attempt to scare and demoralize me and my camp. It was working.

It moved in a halting, unnatural manner; it struggled to turn its head, which then suddenly snapped in the direction it fought to look. Its milky white eyes were unblinking, the yellow iris at the heart blazed in the dim club. My grotesque impostor fixated on Grove and gave a foul hiss, though when it sought me, those dead eyes lingered for a lot longer. It wasn't until it caught the scent of Maria that the creature seemed to come alive, pivoting sharply to square itself with the direction of the stage.

"AH! Wait. You sure you want to do that?" I asked in a smug tone. I watched the thing deliberate while calculating the distance between it, its intended target, and myself. "She's working here, you know."

Behind me there was a mirthless snort. "You little bastard."

The back of my neck prickled and I looked back at Gale somewhat apologetically. See, the rule was, this was unofficial neutral ground. The common understanding hadn't been reached by some kind of formal agreement or accord. The forces that jockeyed for ground in this part of the world knew not to trespass because Gale wouldn't tolerate any kind of contentious challenge to her station or a threat being laid upon one of her people.

She'd fought hard to make that line both clear and beyond reproach. Her people weren't trifled with, not that she didn't keep considerably powerful people in her company, but even those who weren't were deemed untouchable.

Tonight, she'd agreed to let Maria be one of her people.

I would worry about the woman who could reduce me to ash with little more than a thought *after* I got done staring down my disgustingly warped doppelgänger. The beast looked from me to Gale and something akin to acknowledgement flashed in those bright, burning eyes.

The creature regarded Gale, then Maria, who was struck still by fear. There was a slow, willful shake of the head by the keeper and whatever passed between the Stalker and the Matron did so in complete silence. Gale was going to be furious with me. I could try and spin this but there was no getting around just how underhanded what I had just done was. Duplicitous behavior against a woman who may well have invented vindictiveness was an idiotic move.

I was out of options. The church wasn't going to hold, we weren't anywhere close to honing in on who actually conjured this thing up and pulled it from the other side, and the fact that the intermittent attacks were becoming more and more frequent put me dead smack in the middle of desperation.

I found that perfect cocktail of bravery and bravado and actually slid out of my stool to cross the distance between us. The only impediment I was working with was a sturdy table and, while normally that would be enough space to make me somewhat comfortable, I'd witnessed firsthand what this thing could do. How it moved, hunted, what it could endure, and that it kept coming despite having thrown everything I've got at it made me a little kamikaze crazy.

It was wearing my face, poorly, and shifting that unblinking gawk between me and Maria. When it spoke, the mouth moved, just not in sync with what was being uttered. It was like a deranged ventriloquist that wouldn't time the cadence of the bloodless blue lips with what was being said. Plus, when it moved that mouth it was stilted, the bone popping grotesquely as if all that mass was having trouble contouring into this deceptive metamorphosis.

"If you are her champ-i-on we fight. Fight." The echoed word was harsh and guttural. "No more game. Game! Fight. *Fight.*"

Now, I was scared. Maria was downright terror-stricken. Grove? Grove was attentive despite being rattled, which I admired and was a little thankful for. It helped me to know I wasn't the only one horrified by what was transpiring.

"Why doesn't the one tugging your leash come out and try to actually talk with us?"

"Talk. No. No! Champ-i-on, fight. Fight."

Its snarling maw protruded a bit, apparently fighting the urge to shape-shift back into its true form and come after me. I had a feeling that Gale was the only thing that was keeping me upright, even if by now I was sure she was entertaining the idea of green-lighting this thing to take my head off of my shoulders.

"You're not very smart, are you?" I asked.

"Talk. Time. All waste. Human waste enough of Turashan time." A meaty hand smacked hard against its bony chest. While I was aware it was some kind of twisted, deformed reflection of myself, I actually got a little bit worried that the thing might hurt itself—me—with the strike. Compartmentalizing was going to be a big priority for me, should I see the light of another day.

The way it phrased the last bit hadn't escaped me, though this wasn't the time.

"You want a high noon thing, then?"

That blank stare devoid of any emotion seemed to be its default expression, so it took me longer than I care to admit to realize that the thing was confused about my reference.

I cleared it up for him. "Tomorrow, eight. Warehouse district. You'll find me. We'll finish this."

Crooked and toothy, the countenance of the mirror-me spasmed and twitched until it contoured a sickly smile. As if I would benefit from that image being seared into my rattled brain.

"Die well."

When it cackled, it did so with a slack-jawed disposition, meaning the throaty and phlegmy sound was coming out of an unmoving mouth, creepy and daunting. Despite our terse back-and-forth, a part of me thought that if I could manage to avoid this death trap, there might be a chance of dodging the one I'd square off against when Gale got my undivided attention.

"*Cura'sha nasci*," a deep voice growled in a slow drawl.

Two things happened when I heard the insult come from across the room. One, I knew it was going to be an issue because it was notoriously tough to dissuade Xander from locking horns with anyone short-sighted enough to make him mad. Two, the malice dripping from that single curse was so tangible I couldn't help but start to think if this might present an opening for finishing this before it started.

I fought hard to temper the influx of hope that if Xander and the Stalker went blow for blow, I could pick a prime spot to sneak in and keep the tide in favor of the brawny doorman or end it if said opening was too tempting. Plus, my curiosity had been chomping at the bit for over a decade to learn what it was the hulk of a security guard was. All I knew was that the primal stuff that I had crossed, the kind of beasts that were faster than any two men and strong as any four, didn't want any part of him. I got a very *king of the jungle* vibe from the man affectionately known as the Regulator.

Back in real time, the nasty nightmare spun on the newly-entered Xander and let loose a shriek that died off in a hiss. It called him something in a tongue I couldn't quite make out, but even if I didn't speak the language, recognition was universal. Pawning a fight off on someone else was a shitty and cowardly way of operating, but if this worked out I'd live to fight another day and I could add that to the laundry list of stuff that I'd have to repent for. Dead men didn't redeem themselves, so I was ready to take this.

Grove was too, and we both waited for that one signal. The calm before the storm was about to snap, we just needed an eye-blink, insult, shift in wind, anything. Whatever it was that cued them, I missed it, and as they each took a second step they started to shift into their true forms: a Stalker, and what looked like a similar kind of creature, though less gaunt and abysmal.

"ENOUGH!"

I'd heard every kind of yell there was to be heard. Screams enhanced by a magical touch, a death metal band live in concert, an angry mom, a despairing rage; there wasn't one I hadn't come across in my twenty-five years, so I thought. Until I heard Gale call us all to attention.

The power of her command actually coursed through my body. Lights flickered. Electronics either erupted, cut off, or got taken to task by a surge of pure energy. The Regulator and Stalker stopped their evolution into what it is they each are and judging by their astonished faces, I'd have to guess it wasn't voluntary.

"This is *my* establishment, and I will not tolerate this type of disrespect. *Ever.*"

Gale was alive with an intensity I couldn't even properly convey. The green of her gaze was vibrant, bright with fury, and the ferocious feel coming off of her was enough to make me take an involuntary step back.

She was livid, and as a result the puissance laying long dormant inside of her was extending itself outward. I could see crackles of energy reverberating off the walls, coiling around metallic piping, shaking everyone in attendance to our rotten cores; invisible, yet visible in their interference in the air. Gale was rasping, struggling to find some kind of center in her roughed breathing.

"Not under my roof." There was such a sincere threat in the way she spoke that I found myself letting go of a breath I didn't know I'd held when the pair of beasts slowly backed off one another.

"*Cura'sha.*" Xander spat the name with such open contempt that I realized to him, the mere mentioning of it was considered a curse. I couldn't say I didn't agree, but this thing had chased me all across Cleveland, leading me down a violent rabbit hole that was aimed straight at Hell.

The Stalker was looking at Gale with a practiced wariness, ignoring the jab by the doorman. Perspective was seeing something I'd bamboozled into getting hit by a two-ton truck and then simply shrugging it off regress instinctively from a woman I wouldn't guess weighed much more than a hundred pounds. I noticed she no longer wore a tolerant expression either, this one was wrought with antipathy.

"You. Will. Sit," she dictated to Xander, though two stunned denizens and I were quicker to comply than he was. It would have been funny if I hadn't managed to raise the ire of an actual demigod.

"Nobody will be exercising their vendettas out in my establishment," she continued. When her fixed gaze narrowed, Xander actually seemed to shrink. "Especially if you're *my* charge. And you," she said turning her head toward the Stalker. Her bared teeth sparkled with an ivory ostentatiousness, it made her somehow more menacing. "Coming in here with the intent to harm, or kill, in *my* home? That is a rudeness I am going to forgive only once." There was no need to anchor the threat with an example; the magnitude of her presence was actually suffocating.

Gale exhaled fumes of tar-black smoke, then sucked in a calming breath. She deliberated for what seemed an eternity but couldn't have been more than a moment or two. "Figure this out. Now."

Pushing my luck would have been incredibly stupid, and truthfully, I wasn't sure I had managed to clear myself of repercussions as it was. Instead of dawdling, I regarded the spurned Stalker, staring into its putrid face with a hard-fought levelness. "Tomorrow night, you and I will end this."

I drop a crumpled piece of paper on the table that still sat between us. On it was an address.

"If you can't read, I'm sure you'll figure it out."

That sunken, gaunt face twitched and convulsed, which in and of itself wasn't unsettling; what was was how the dark eyes devoid of any life stayed fixated on me all the while. It snatched up the paper and walked out, a silent sneer trying to bait Xander but falling short. Once it vanished from sight I felt all the tension that was knotted up inside of me release.

I should have known it wouldn't last.

***

"You two!" Gale shouted, her fervor renewed ten-fold, and though I didn't see her move I was thrown clear across the room by an invisible force. Through the haze of pain I actually recalled hearing the wooden wall that caught me give a little, the protesting timber starting to snap under the amount of pressure it took to keep me upright. Grove managed to dodge a wild swing by Xander, who erupted into motion in unison with whatever Gale had just cast at me.

Despite dodging the initial blow, the hand that shot forward afterward expanded in size three times over and snatched him by the throat and chest, hoisting him up and pinning him to the wall so that he shared in my unfavorable position. Xander's hand started to change with the expansion, black-clawed and golden-furred. I couldn't discern much, what with choking on the blood filling my mouth and the waves of nausea, but I did my best to file it away inside of my mind, making a mental inventory could come in handy if I ever ended up on the wrong side of this bunch.

Well, more so than I was right now.

"No, don—" Maria began, but Gale snapped her fingers and Maria involuntarily snapped her mouth shut. Confusion swept over her face and the panicked expression looked from me to the woman who was no longer behind the bar but was instead standing in front of me. How she'd made the move in the blink of an eye I couldn't be sure, but if she could manipulate time the way she could command us with magic, then I may not have been far off when I called her a demigod.

The Stalker hadn't been keen on crossing her and those things usually put the fear of God into anyone they came across. She'd told it to shut the fuck up and sit down, and it did.

Grove suddenly acted, reaching for something quickly but not quickly enough. The move earned him a broken arm judging by the way Xander intercepted it and painfully cocked it back. Still, as the soldier howled in pain, he used the distraction to reach with his good arm to draw out a hand-cannon. With a barbaric viciousness, Grove actually muzzle-punched the Regulator right in the maw, breaking teeth to get the barrel inside of his now grinning and bloodied mouth. Their standoff was much more visceral than any I had ever witnessed before.

Even more alarming was that if Gale had even noticed, which I actually doubted, she did an immaculate job of maintaining utter indifference to it. The weight of her attention was settled squarely on me.

"You think you can just use my lenience, my compassion, as a bargaining chip to try and snake your way out of a mess you made?" she asked.

I probably could have managed to speak, though it would have been terse and throaty, but I opted instead to just exaggerate a gasp and cough. She waved off whatever incantation she'd listlessly thrown at me and suddenly I was no longer suspended upright.

Now I was spewing spittle and gasping for air while kneeling in front of her heeled boots.

"Tell me why I don't pike your head to my front door as a reminder why it is not in the best interest of anyone to try and take advantage of my niceties?"

I was begging my mind to get creative and conjure something up that was equal parts sense and wit, something that might make whatever shred of compassion she'd still had in her, at least entertain reconsidering the killing of me.

Nada. Bupkis. Nothing. All I could do was envision me managing to jump out of a gigantic frying pan and into a fire. My coughing was a little more dignified by the time I swayed myself upright, still kneeling. It was half from just sheer exhaustion and half because I hoped the showing of subjugation might earn me some goodwill.

"Ain't her fault she is what she is," I fought to my feet. "And it ain't her fault the people who could have actually helped her are long gone now." If I was going to meet my maker, I am going to stare the one doing the delivering eye-to-eye. I met the fury of her green gaze with my own hard-eyed stare.

"I guess I was just hoping that even if I went about it in a way that was shitty, you weren't so cold hearted of a bitch that you'd let me get by. I couldn't afford you saying no. She couldn't." I looked to Maria, caught in the middle of all of this madness. Sure, she was dabbling in the art, but what she knew wouldn't even qualify as rudimentary. What I saw wasn't just her, though. What I saw was my reason for helping her. I was helping her because once, long ago, I knew some good people I'd loved and admired who would have taken this kind of thing on. They would have charged headlong into danger in the name of shielding an innocent. They wouldn't ask for recompense, monetary compensation or fame. When I was helping those people help others, I felt good. I didn't stare at myself in the mirror with revulsion. I was helping Maria so I could maybe start to live with the man I was and forget the one I had become these last five dark years.

Gathering conviction and strength I turned to give Gale a last defiant answer, but she was already walking back to her bar. Xander put Grove down, looking once more fully human, and the soldier was kind enough to retract the hammer from the pistol he'd firmly shoved inside of Xander's mouth and pull it out. In a demented way, Xander's respect for my partner had just amplified considerably—those meaty fingers fixing Grove's shirt some before trudging upstairs to take a position at the entrance was a pretty big indicator of that.

Calling me confused would be short-selling it. The proprietor was making another mixed drink and adopting her stony silence once again, withdrawn and kind of lackadaisical like she was more enduring the day than enjoying it. Maria was about to step down but the barkeep interrupted.

"I've got you today and tomorrow and you still owe me songs."

Having her out of the way was helpful, having her out of the way and knowing she'd be safeguarded was no small miracle. Maria was searching my face for something, but all I could muster was a half-smile. Sadly, I didn't have time to hold her hand and work her through all that was happening. I very rarely walked into a bad situation and came out on top.

Everyone inside was either gawking or still. Stillness was a natural reaction. The fight or flight response had all the empirical data and scientific know-how in the world behind it, but I would always argue that there was a third option: freezing. It was the worst thing you can do when in an awful situation, though I was guilty of having done it. As if moving would somehow draw attention to you. I don't know if it was completely unwarranted, but there was an irrevocable humor to having Gale yell out, "Well?" and seeing the entire bar come back to life. At the behest of the piano player Maria fell into another song, one that I couldn't place, but it was lovely.

I sauntered over to Grove, riding the euphoric high of it all having worked out. I was knocked off the high horse when my mute friend right-hooked me across the jaw. It garnered the attention of the bar keep, but when Grove signed a *sorry* to her, she half-shrugged and gave a full and sincere smile. Apparently, there was some flexibility to the house rules if you'd been an ass, and while my jaw was already swelling I couldn't say it was completely unwarranted.

Grove helped me up and we both walked out, never to bring the issue up again.

***

I was barely inside of Grove's apartment before he handed me an ice pack. During the drive we didn't broach the subject, though I may have exaggerated the tenderness of it when moving my jaw absently. I had a penchant for theatrics. Maria was safe for the rest of this day and at least until the next one. It gave us time, just not as much as I would have liked.

"So, we're seriously going to just fight this thing?" he asked. Dutiful and diligent, Grove was emphatic on seeing this fight through. With the epiphany I'd been wrestling with back at the nightclub, I had started to come to terms with my own reasons for finishing this fight. Him I couldn't quite get, though I wouldn't be surprised if some of his reasons were in the same vein as my own.

"Only thing to do, except this time we're not going to just react or go in cold. I've got a plan."

An unflattering skepticism held firm on his handsome face.

"I have an idea, at least." I leaned down over the island table in the center of his modest kitchen and started to write out everything I was going to need. To his credit, the unflattering skepticism was still holding strong. "What? I do!"

A noncommittal grunt was the best I was going to get, so I rose above it by throwing the paper with my instructions on it at his face. "Fuck you."

We both laughed, but his tapered off by the time he gave a once-over to the list of what I wanted. He lifted the roughed-up paper as if that was somehow going to sway my mind, but I doubled down with a nod. "Burn it after."

"This'll take me a little while," he said.

"We need to get everything here tonight. Seal this place shut and get to work. Get some sleep, food, and if we're lucky we might be able to catch this thing on a bad enough day that we come out the other end of this victorious."

I fished out my tattered wallet and handed it over. "Max the blue one out, then the black. If we need to use the red, though, I can't promise how much is on it."

"What're you going to do?"

"I've got some more tools to work on."

"That carving stuff?" he asked, sounding unimpressed with my contribution to the plan.

I laughed and nodded.

"Yeah, kind of, the carving is only half of it. You have to exert a lot of will and focus into it, too. It's exhausting and tedious. It's why I want to do as much as I can now, so that when I sleep I have as little as possible left tomorrow so I'm not dragging ass for our showdown."

"If we live, and don't get arrested, you're going to be broke."

"My lease is almost up anyway," I shrugged.

"No." He saw where that was going.

I smiled ear to ear, a twinkle of mischief in my still-swollen eye. "I already got my stuff moved into the guest bedroom."

Remember earlier when I said the other side of this business was the long, tedious process of investigation or preparation? We were in the thick of that now. We managed to break bread in the form of an overcooked pizza. I learned that Grove was originally from Minnesota, a lumberjack outdoorsman who had a proud family history of military service.

By two in the morning, he was poring over some city ordinance map for our still-evolving plan and I was busy carving into the two bats I'd retrieved from Kaycee's. Five years ago, they had been a brainchild of mine, a simple series of incantations that could deliver some real hurt even if there wasn't much in the way of finesse to them. A lot of my own backstory had been shared, though one thing still perplexed me about Grove.

"You seriously don't want to know *anything* else? I mean, you just kind of jumped right into the deep end and started swimming with sharks."

Grove deliberated before spinning his finger over itself in a circle, a sign I'd learned that meant to repeat myself so he could catch whatever he'd missed. After I echoed my statement the guy just shrugged.

I felt like we were destined for some more shared silence when I caught his eyes lingering on the bat I'd been working on.

"Why don't you just finish a bunch of these and hand them out? That doesn't seem that hard, no offense."

None was taken, and I understood the origin of the question. It was one I had asked ten years ago.

"Each sigil is different," I said, placing a finger just above the grip of the bat's base. That's where it started. "And the next one above it will be unique to it, because I am trying to get it to work in concert. There's no set order or blueprint. This wood was alive, it's communicating with the magic, the magic is being translated through it so it's unique. Plus, it's exhausting."

His dubiousness wasn't disrespectful, though I could tell he was having a hard time believing that carving could be that taxing.

"Every time I create a sigil I am pouring focus, a piece of myself into it, to bring it to life. This sigil," I said, moving my finger from the first one to the second, "is unique. I had to feel what it needed to connect with the first, that feeling is an effort. It's honestly like jogging, or swimming, just the navigating and when you actually pour power into it while carving that's like a full sprint. It's a mental discipline, and focus, will, magic, whatever you want to call it, is born from a mix of... well, the soul, your own emotional investment and concentration."

Self-deprecation was my go-to defense mechanism and I wrestled with making fun of my own craft, but I decided against it. This wasn't the time to install doubt or damage whatever confidence he'd started to harbor in me. It wasn't the time to doubt myself, either. If I was going to win, I couldn't go in half-cocked. I had enough enemies in front of me, I didn't need to make one of myself.

"Sounds tough."

"Most people who train never make a single thing, the bridging of the sigils is something that can't be taught. Like, it can, to an extent, there's some universal stuff out there, but something that's going to work reliably is anchored to the person it's owned by."

"You must be pretty good." There was a searching sincerity in his voice, understanding now that he saw the multiple bridges I had carved.

"I..." There was a breath I was holding, and in it was an answer that might very well dictate my mindset going into this. Your mindset could be the deciding factor in something so dangerous and it would be surprising if it wasn't. For years, I had let the self-loathing leash me, dragging me through incessant misery that became so habitual I had forgotten what it felt like to simply feel good. Grove was done with his own assembly of preparation, satisfied with the duffel bags of supplies at his feet and the last checklist he'd gone through while having a back and forth with me.

"I was," I said.

Grove smirked, that fastidious focus allowed an air of approval to flash over it.

"I am."

Though I worked well into the morning and slept as hard as I had in recollection, I finished both of the bats.

CHAPTER 13

SETTING THE STAGE

Since I'd found sleep so serenely, I expected to wake up with a sense of dread, a cloud of impending doom suffocating any semblance of sanity I had left.

Instead, I felt good. Very good.

Grove kicked me out of bed before it could be considered afternoon. We got a meal and set to putting into motion the plan we'd concocted.

I took a long look at myself in the mirror. I was a week behind the need to shave and, with my heritage, it had become the beginning of an unkempt beard. My face was shaped by hardship, fists, and a pair of recklessly-lived decades; if I cleaned up, slept, and maybe smiled, I wouldn't be so bad looking. Could be I would do those very things if I got out of this alive. Might be nice to take a sober girl out instead of some drunk one home.

We got out at about noon. There was a cooling breeze coming off the lake and it was a nice drive. As with every great storm, there was a calm we were determined to bask in before it hit. I wasn't complaining. It allowed me to reflect. I wasn't thinking through the plan; I was pretty sure Grove was obsessing over that. Meddling with my own plan wasn't going to help my anxiety, and at this point there was nowhere to go but forward. We'd done all we could and to spend all my energy fixated on it would just wrap me up in a bundle of smothering anxiety, which would turn to fear, then into doubt, and would ultimately lead to me making a mistake or thinking this whole thing was one.

I was committed, I had conviction in that commitment and it felt good. Even liberating. The fight wasn't finished, far from it; hell, I didn't even have anything in the way of a resolution since I knew quite literally nothing about why it was here or who had put together the scheme to bring it over.

But I had a course.

We had been torn between riding in a rickety pick-up truck with expired tags and an outdated registration that Kaycee kept out back of her store or borrowing Maria's car. Reliability and subtlety were the essential crux of this plan working out, so we'd squeezed into her Smart Car. We packed a few dozen explosives in the back, duffle bags with every gun imaginable, and I was covered head to toe in all my trinkets.

Kaycee opened her personal door located in the alley beside her shop and squirreled away behind a concrete partition that protruded out. Sunday afternoon had a kind of optimism to it, it seemed to be when most of us had decompressed from the chaos of our weekly obligations that the best part of who we are and could be found its way to the surface. It was sunny with a cooling breeze, the perfect day; I knew because I'd spent the last two hours at the park with my pooch.

Max was more than a dog. Maybe that wasn't exactly right; Max was precisely a dog, a big and warm ball of love and affection, free from any judgment and capable of loving somebody more than himself. As often as I pulled stuff from out of his stubborn mouth he kept just as much out of my own; namely the barrel of a gun or a handful of pills. The truth is I wouldn't have made it through my worst times without being able to clutch that burly furball. If this didn't work out, I needed to have him with somebody I not only trusted, but more importantly somebody I loved. Somebody who would love him as much as I did, because while to everyone else he may have just been another happy-go-lucky mutt, to me he was my best friend, confidant and savior.

Kaycee seemed a bit confused at the sight of me holding a leash in one hand and a box full of food and toys in the other. Curiosity lent itself to something else, something more serious and all at once sincere; I didn't have to say a thing before she took the box from me and gave a single, solemn nod.

I knelt down and, even though he was at no risk of overhearing, Grove had the decency to turn around and pretend to scan our surroundings.

"Alright amigo," I said. Max stirred to a stand, half-anxious to go inside and run amok with her children but also picking up that something was amiss with me. "Gonna need you to hold up here and keep everyone safe and sound while I take care of some stuff."

The anxiety washed out of me as he gave an almost too-perfect tilt of his head. For a second I smiled, I smiled and thought of nothing else; I smiled and did nothing else, just lived in this single moment. Just a boy and his dog.

"Paw?"

Max sat.

I put my hand out and tapped it, repeating my command.

Max barked, before laying down.

"Atta boy." Laughing in defeat, it was a humbling reminder of my place in all of this. I gave my chest a good pat and he leapt up, giving me a makeshift hug and a series of slobbering kisses.

"You'll work on it when you're back." Kaycee said sharply, a stern reminder that she wasn't at all thrilled with the happenings.

"I'll be back for him."

"Damn right you will, this dog has worse manners than you."

Acquiescing with a smile, I creaked, cracked and popped to a stand just as Grove turned around. I was aware of how ugly the reality was of what was going on; I was also keenly aware that Kaycee didn't want to visit that reality more than she had to. There was a plea in my eyes as I geared up to say what I had to, but she cut me off in a kind fashion.

"I've got him, I promise."

I'd be lying if I said I wasn't choked up; any words I could have said would have stumbled out of my mouth, so I just nodded. She kept the door open just long enough for me to see her lower a hand and him obediently deposit a paw in it, before taking off down the hall in a clumsy sprint after the laughing children who were calling him on.

***

Our limited timeframe made it impossible to stop by the remnants of Maria's coven, plus if they could get through this by burying their collective heads in the sand, it would be for the best. They'd already lost a quarter of their people and, while this was not only too real for them, it was also an eventuality that showing up would be a reminder that they had stock in this fight but no say on how it would go down. That was tough, and being reminded of that wasn't helpful.

Our last stop was the surprising one. Grove and I crammed ourselves into the car and headed to the bar we'd managed to stash Maria in. Luckily Gale was a green-eyed hurricane and while she'd be dead-set on us in the aftermath of all this, I was content for now knowing that Maria was safe. Plus, my confidence about there being an "after" this showdown was pretty shaky and it was hard to worry myself with what was behind the big, bad, demonic wolf monster that was hellbent on killing me.

Grove waited in the car.

"You're a special kind of stupid." Donovan seemed more terse and abrasive than I recalled, fixing me with an angry eye. Xander was steady sleeping beside him, balancing all that mass on the slip of a stool.

"I didn't come to try and check on the proceedings below," I said. I moved deliberately in my approach so as not to startle either of the gentleman. A tinkerer was lethal because they had a plan for every plan, a contingency for every failure and a failsafe should none of those work out. Xander, while not as methodical and meticulous, could probably cross the distance between us in a second and rip me limb from limb in half the time it took him to reach me. "I came to talk to you."

I produced each bat I'd been working on. Stalemated, Donovan and I endured a stare-off while I held them out to him. Taking some artistic license, I had crafted a holster for each of them so that the wooden bat hung off my hip, the aluminum across my back. A modernized swordsman was the look I was going for even if it was my subconscious that directed me down that path. Mock all you want, no matter how enlightened you are or severe a situation, there was an innate need to try and look your best. If I was going to die, I wanted to try and pull off *cool*.

What seemed a year was no more than half a minute. Thirty seconds to stand there stupidly is an eternity. Gnomes were another long-lived race, so they had a different perspective on patience, an irritable consistency in this life that I had conveniently forgotten just how annoying it was.

"Bring it over here," he said. I did as directed, shifting to circle the podium he was at while the short stack swiveled to square off with me. "Hold on to it, too."

Waving away the aluminum, I twirled it once before slapping it across my back and feeling the self-collapsing latch I'd designed secure it. It felt cool up until I heard the mocking chortle of the doorman who'd been feigning sleep.

"Eat me."

"Don't tempt me," he drawled.

That straightened me up, given that I was starting to get a grasp on the fact that Xander was much more monster than man.

"This is a lot of absorption," Donovan mused.

"I figured I would be swinging a lot, and hard. If I could reuse that energy it would probably help if the fight lasted more than the first exchange."

"It's a good flow," Donovan said, smoothing a smaller hand over the glyphs and sigils I'd spiraled all around the base. "They're all speaking to each other, too."

That was a relief. Normally a tool was made with a lot of trial and error, but I didn't have that kind of time. Somebody as talented as Donovan could circumvent that process at a cost. Usually a steep one.

"It's for kinetic and magical energies?" His question felt rhetorical, but the look aimed my way bade an answer.

"I don't know everything this thing can do, I figured best to not hedge a bet."

After another episode of studious surveying, there seemed to be something in the spirit of approval. "Crude and simple," he said with a smirk that cut like his quips. "But clever. It'll be effective, too. Clever," he murmured the end to himself. "Very clever. Let's see the other one."

I secured the wooden bat to my hip and peeled the aluminum one off; I attempted to hand it all the way over to him but caught a reprimand in the form of a reproachful look.

"I need to see how the magic is communicating with you. That's part of it, you know."

The base of the bat narrowed, padded with the rubber mold to help sink your hand in, and that was where I held. Donovan reached for the business end and began his examination. "Elemental? Doesn't seem your area of expertise, if you could even be said to have one."

Counting to ten while I vividly imagined myself cracking him upside the head with the very bat he was holding, I reminded myself over and over, like a mantra, that this was for Maria and it was the only way we'd a chance in hell to see our way out of this alive.

"It isn't. Problem is I don't know what can damage this thing with any certainty outside of a big ol' hit."

"Light." Xander's unexpected interjection turned both of us toward him. Unmoved, and not looking as if that would change, I settled in the silence as if it would coax him to elaborate. It didn't. "This isn't as good as the other one in terms of work. It's recklessly done, too. Still, could be useful. Could be it'll be like a dynamite stick and kill you along with whatever you hit though." His shrug matched his tone, like he really wouldn't mind either way.

"Oh. Good."

"Have you charged them all?"

"Some, I didn't have a lot of time."

"You use Latin or Coptic?"

"Um, well, both... I uh..."

"How much of this is from your studies and how much from your intuition?" Donovan was a very monotone person by nature, with a boring and neutral constitution. *That* question didn't ring with the same timbre as the rest of them. Had I been making a mistake? At this juncture, it was too far gone to go back but it would behoove me to figure out if I had been fucking up or not.

"I'd say fifty-fifty," I answered.

Our continued free-falling into these spells of shared silence wasn't helping my already limping confidence, and this one was our longest yet.

"Interesting." Donovan disappeared into the podium, emerging with a glue stick and blank scrabble pieces. That was a new one, even for me, and I was the king of scavenging and corner-cutting in our shared field.

In a matter of a minute he'd scribbled and carved four insignia into the blank pieces, then carefully glued them just above the rubber grip of the bat.

"They'll come off first hit," he said. Unblinking eyes skimmed over my own craft as it collaborated with what he'd contributed. "Hopefully by then you'll have a full charge."

"And it doesn't blow up me too."

"Hard to tell," he answered matter-of-factly.

"Between jowls or evisceration, I'll take the latter over the teeth every time."

I strapped and checked each bat before taking on the discussion of payment. "I have money, it's just not a lot. If I get out of this I can make good on whatever it is you think you're owed."

"Whatever it is I think I am owed? You're an awful negotiator." That grating little bastard was wearing my every nerve, even if he'd saved me a week of time in the span of an hour.

"You take your tutelage with me from here out. One year."

You could have coughed and blown me off my feet at that moment. Donovan was a Tinkerer; the guy was so good at artificery he actually had the talent to cultivate something and breathe life into it. He belonged to the Beyond, a rumored world that existed somewhere within the In-Between itself; the Gnome Tinkerers were among the most respected of the denizens there. This wasn't a price paid, it was an honor. An outright honor. People would vie for this. People would kill for this. While I stood there flabbergasted and dumbstruck, the little guy crept off the stool to vanish below into the bar, but not before imparting one final thought to me.

"You're not the only one who respected and liked Zachariah. If you're finally going to show him the love you claimed to have for him by continuing his mission, then you can count me an ally."

I couldn't find my voice, and by the time I would have he'd been long gone. Smiling foolishly, I twisted my head over to Xander. I wasn't assuming anything at the time, though the fact that Zachariah had clout I could still call on was an unexpected bonus.

"I'd kill you for a candy bar."

"Buzzkill."

"Wuss."

"If that thing comes for her…"

"It'll have to see me dead first."

I offered my hand to Xander, who after a mostly mocking period of consideration, took it.

Using the hold, the behemoth roped me into him, wrapping me up in a one-armed hug. It was all for show, because that harsh voice was whispering in my ear while we embraced. "Light, kid. They got a shadow magic about them that's making the hide so tough, that's healing them up even if you get a good lick in."

When we parted, he was laughing loudly, compensating so whatever gimmick he was trying to sell might stick. I couldn't imagine Gale would take issue with them helping me, especially since Donovan had done so openly. Then again, Donovan and I had struck an accord. The woman coveted balance and saw herself as an enforcer of it. Donovan helping me could have been out of gain, warranted by our mutual craft or just the natural order.

Xander was invested, with an established and long-standing vendetta.

Or could just be that Xander just wanted to hug me and was a big boisterous bastard.

I didn't give it another thought. It was late in the afternoon and I wanted to have us well on our way before the sunlight was even starting to wane.

***

The warehouse district was in an ugly part of town. Worse than a ghetto, this was one of those neighborhoods that better resembled a war zone than anything that should have been on a city street in America. I was a mutt who grew up a slum dog, so I considered a haunt like this familiar stomping grounds. It was out of the way, the kind of hellhole the police wouldn't think twice about and anyone of the local populace probably steered clear of it after dark. It wasn't ideal, but it was as close to as I was going to get.

Grove and I had spent the last three hours assembling the stage we planned the night before. Having been on the losing side of every encounter was equal parts humiliating and humbling and still here we were, on our feet, ready to go another round. One advantage we had was arrogance. This thing was well aware of the fact there was a disparity in strength between us; it even went so far as to toy with me in battle when it was sure it had me dead-to-rights. Sadly, I couldn't rely on outright luck to see me out of every encounter.

Finality brought a kind of peace with it. One way or another, this was the last time I would be crossing paths with this thing.

"You think this is going to work?"

Pointing out that Grove was speaking more this last day was a surefire way to shut him up so I tactfully didn't. Whether it was because we'd become kindred in this suicide pact or the inevitable cold shunt of fear that snuck in when preparing for a fight, it was hard to say.

"I do," I said, meeting his eyes.

I never could begin to understand what it was that made men who served together so close, the constancy of the warfighter was starting to give me some kind of inkling of an understanding. Grove was ready to stand fast by my side against an unstoppable force, and should that enemy come with the support of an insurmountable number of sycophant vampires, I doubt it would make him flinch. Even if I was only going to be able to enjoy this kind of loyalty once, I was still thankful to have experienced it.

I silenced whatever he was about to say with a raised finger. It wasn't that we were in the thick of silence, it was the type of silence we'd been surrounded by. The law of the jungle still was a mandate in the world of man.

"It's time."

CHAPTER 14

SHOWDOWN

The warehouse we were in was flanked by two much larger ones. It was three stories with a spacious first floor, a condemned second from a bad fire and the third was much like the first. Except instead of a wide-open floor plan, there were intermittently placed steel pillars jutting out of the decrepit floor like battered tombstones. It was a project damned before it was even finished and they never bothered to restart. There wasn't even a real roof since the third story was just the skeleton of the structure.

When I saw the first vampire, I couldn't say I was all that surprised. Night had barely fallen and we were far from the zenith of darkness which this monster preferred. We'd won enough respect to merit consideration. It wasn't rocket science; the Stalker wanted to soften us up with the horde of vampires it kept on rotation before coming in for the kill. It wanted to snuff the light out of us itself, though. Last time I locked onto those treacherous eyes I knew as much.

The first vampire was a scout; I could sense a magic about it even though they didn't have any of their own. Judging from the glossed over look, I'd guess the Alpha had hijacked its body -- using the eyes of the vampire as its' own, turning the vampire into a vessel, a vehicle for it to spy with. Before it caught notice of us, I turned Grove and mouthed: *Get out.*

I fought off his hesitance with a reinforced grip and a pleading stare.

You can't carry me and you. Trust me.

The palpable anxiety finally subsided when he rapped his fist hard off my own and vanished out the back.

The vampire was an apex predator. It boasted a conglomeration of traits collected from all the top-tier predators, an aberrant abomination of pure lethality. Its forked tongue was tasting the air, trying to wrangle my scent from out of the atmosphere so it could fixate on me. Its fluid movement was a bit stilted, its sluggishness a result of the Stalker piggybacking its already stunted consciousness. That didn't make it any less dangerous, though.

Nearing my scent, that scaly disgrace of the natural order shuddered in excitement. It was just about to pounce and rip me apart, rend open my flesh and feast on my innards when a loud wail of music cut through the makeshift PA system we'd installed inside the warehouse. To its credit, the thing still stayed focus on my smell and tore through the cardboard box impeding it from where I must have been. My only regret was not being able to see the shock smeared across its ugly face when it realized I wasn't on the other side.

Its skull caved in with one well-aimed swing, the meaty spire of the bat wrung hard off the ugly bastard's now-disfigured head. Ambient energy resonated in the reverberating wooden shaft before being assimilated by the sigils carved into it. I took a grim gratification in stomping the confused look off its gruesome face as it lay there dying without ever knowing how I managed to throw my scent or befuddle its superior senses. How it, a predator of all mankind, could have been so thoroughly duped by a mere mortal. My glance cut to the dangling piece of dirty fabric nailed to the pillar in the center of the room just above the very box the vampire suspected I was in, a remnant of the shirt I shredded for this very reason. Suddenly the skin-searing, scalding hot shower and odor-eating lotion I had slathered myself in seemed worth it.

The communication device circling my ear gave a single chime sound, a predetermined, simplified kind of Morse code to tell me what was happening outside. Visitors. I didn't try to retreat upstairs; instead, I moved deeper into the spacious room with hand-picked and strategic clutter strewn about. All of it was designed. Emotionally removed from the fear of the fight, I looked at the prospect with a level head and started to try and discern what had worked for us in each of our crazed meetings and what hadn't.

I got another chime in my ear. Then another. It stopped at four. Four of them, and me. I dropped my free hand to the specialized radio on my hip and clicked a response, vibrating on his end to avoid the obstacle of his hearing impairment. My heart was beating in my eardrum, and, even with the steadying breaths I was trying to pace, it was hard to keep some of the panic out of me. It was like a war drum, my own blood providing the ominous soundtrack by beatboxing inside my head. Didn't matter now.

We had a plan. I was already in the fight.

I stared at the blackish gore splattered across my bat to remind myself that these weren't the monsters of lore. That these were worthless scavengers, things that feasted on fear and flesh and used the myth behind them to keep people afraid. I reminded myself it was okay to be afraid, too, but it wasn't okay to be a coward.

One by one they began to hesitantly pour into the shadowy warehouse.

I heard scuffling to the right of me and then, a gunshot.

Outside, Grove had just retired whatever backup they had been counting on. Legendary killer or not, when a round released a ballistic the size of a fist and it traveled at the speed of sound, no amount of fairytale fear mongering was going to keep you upright. Seizing the sudden element of surprise, I erupted out of my crouch, spinning to the right where a stunned looking vampire was regarding the way they had come in as if trying to make sense out of what was transpiring.

It managed to swing back on me in time to get a face-full of flashlight. Not just any flashlight, either. It was some gaudy, overpriced, tactical-looking flashlight that burned so bright there was a warning to use it responsibly in fear that it would blind someone. They moved best in darkness, and, if what I had been told was true, a lot of their toughness came from an innate magic harvested from the dark.

Ignoring a cringe-inducing hiss, I swung my bat overhead, connecting squarely at the top of its cranium. Not only with the force of the swing, or the toughness of the finely condensed wood, but also releasing the force of my first strike from the first victim. That kinetic energy lashed out, amplifying the concussion twice over. It was enough to actually split the bashed head, the fracture running so deep it cleaved the now dead, would-be assailant's skull in half.

With a thought, I allowed the bat to usurp the vibration of force still dancing through it, re-charging the sigil of power I had just released and starting to fill a second one.

Crude, but clever.

"All right motherfuckers," I challenged. I heard the deranged grin in my snarky voice. That cadence of heartbeats a new battle drumming inside of me, one that felt less like fear and more like adrenaline. The thrill of the fight. "Let's dance."

With a narrowing of focus, the shield-bracer on my flashlight arm awoke, spiraling around to keep my weak arm safe. The broken wristwatch expanded, a thin plating of durable steel coating my right arm.

The three remaining vampires seemed taken aback; the sheer brutality of my attack betrayed their understandings of my perceived limitations and I was sure that my newfound gumption to throw down with them was a bit off-putting.

One accepted my challenge, athletically bounding over the barrier of junk we'd constructed at the main entrance of the spacious room. I roared defiantly, charging headlong to meet him in a brutal exchange of physicality…

… And when the thing took another step forward, it hit the cluster of trash that concealed a pitfall that sent him careening down into the unforgiving concrete floor below. I heard bones snapping and one of those nightmare-invoking screams echo out of the opening, but I didn't have time to enjoy the success of my trap. The one on my right sprang into action in unison with the one in the middle, and the fierce fall fated to its comrade didn't even stall the thing, let alone slow him down. In order to bait the trap, I had to charge pretty hard at the opening myself, and by the time I had stuck my foot down hard enough to stop myself I wasn't exactly balanced.

That's when the thing hit me like a tidal wave of scaly flesh and claws. We ended up head over heels a few times, tumbling in a joined mess of flailing limbs. Whenever you were driven into the ground it was hard to maintain your wits, but when you were completely dislodged from the ground before being driven into it with another body crashing into you, it was impossible. Instinct more than any kind of know-how prompted me to lift my shield arm and I did so just in time to intercept the second vampire. I hadn't even gathered myself to a knee when the second one threw himself at me and I was thankful for the second time in as many days that the video-game inspired, arm-length armor I had made myself was holding firm. Razor teeth clamped down on the metal, tightening it to my own very vulnerable skin; the thing had thrown itself at me mouth first, leading the charge with an unhinged jaw that was ushering out rows upon rows of grisly teeth.

Time wasn't on my side against one of these things, and a pair was a formidable enemy. I didn't have the luxury of time to consider what I was doing, I had to just commit. Violent action would keep me forging ahead and that was my only chance. Standing, I lifted my left arm and brought the vampire up with me. I used to my advantage that the now-warped metal of my armor was tangled and capturing its cruelly serrated teeth and I wrenched it not only up but to the tip of its toes, stealing the stability that comes from being flat footed. That made it easier to drive it back and smash hard into the punishing concrete of the wall in the back of the room. The first vampire was fast approaching after recovering from its tumble, and in trying to stick with the theme of playing off their own viciousness and baiting them into mistakes with my own inaction, I waited, throwing a rabbit jab into the exposed midsection of the vampire still gnawing on my metallic arm. It wasn't until the other one was right on me that I ripped my arm back, swinging it in a wide arc and sending the silver-emblemed shield slamming into its stupid, exposed, mouth-leading face. Once you got past the fear of it, their preferred attacking method did have a glaring weakness: head first was no way to enter into a fight. Shoving off the one I had pinned between my arm and the wall, twisting with all I could sacrifice while not losing hold on the vampire caged between me and the wall so that I could reinforce the swing with some of my weight.

The searing sound of silver rubbing raw off their exposed flesh mixed with a howl of agony was another source of dark pride. During the whole encounter, I'd lost my wooden bat, the one which still had the lion's share of my confidence that would work, but this wasn't a time to be choosy. The shield on my arm collapsed with a thought so I could better reach the bat secured to my back. Cringing as the metal started to give on my arm, knowing the paralytic and infectious toxins in this things saliva would be enough to end this fight, I pushed past that fear.

It was the feel of the grip that seemed to double-down against my waning confidence. It silenced my mounting concern. It wasn't a legendary sword pulled from stone, it wasn't a long-lost artifact returned to a rightful wielder, yet when I got my sore fingers to wrap around it I suddenly felt invincible.

I wasn't some destined savior, heralded in prophecy, returned from the unknown to save the day.

I was just a punk kid a good man saw some promise in.

And when the bat connected hard into the midsection of the bastard-born beast I was fighting, I knew I was where I belonged.

A surge of electricity ran up and through the metal, pouring out at the point of impact and tangling the flesh of the undead into tight, agonizing knots. The convulsing jaw clamped down with renewed force on my arm before involuntarily letting it go. With a still somewhat-lucid presence of mind, I ripped my arm clean, doubled down on my grip, and, by the time the vampire stopped reeling from the shock—I know, I couldn't help myself—I was already cutting through the air with another full head of steam swing.

As the vampire was doubled over in pain, I connected clean with the lowered head, lifting it off bare feet and sending it sailing clear across the room. That impact crackled with an unseen power, ice pouring out of the bat and freezing the top half of the would-be killer solid. When the wall suddenly ended the momentum of his flight, half of him shattered into a dozen pieces, scattering about in a gruesome rain of frozen body parts.

The legs slid down and actually stood upright for a second before unceremoniously slumping over.

Outside was another gunshot. This one seemed to have a bit more clarity to it. It wasn't because the fight inside had settled, it wasn't even that it was over. My heart was no longer running rampant, beating wildly with a steroidal surge of fear and adrenaline.

It was steady, rhythmic, and strong.

***

The last shot signaled the end of the fourth vampire I had been tangled up with. Apparently watching one of its own get turned into an icicle and catapulted clear across a room was enough to dissuade it from pushing the issue any further. Unfortunately, Grove wasn't as forgiving as I was.

My radio chimed another few times, it wasn't quite panicked but it wasn't in the same restrained cadence we had rehearsed either. I didn't bother to inspect the twisted metal covering my arm, or the swelling side that was probably settling a lot deeper inside of me than I would have cared to admit. Quickly retracing my steps and throws, and fall downs, and well, the fight, I find my wooden bat and latch it to my hip. Time for phase two.

I ducked into the back of the room where the stairwell lead me up to the second story but not before dropping off a time-released box that had a mechanism inside of it. Between Grove and me, we found out we had a lot of workable knowledge. I was a capable carpenter and it seemed he was one of those hyper-dangerous, super well-trained secret agent types at one point.

"Don't you dare stray from the plan damnit..."

It was one thing to not judge someone for a disability, it was another not to admit that while I had found several advantages to his handicap that it still was a handicap at times. Grove was a soldier so I expected him to stick to the plan.

Grove was a soldier so I also expected him to put himself between anyone he cared about and harm.

There was a loud clatter of noise downstairs, and by putting together the fact that Grove seemed concerned and my sixth sense was outright screaming at me, I guessed that the whole vampire scourge thing was going to be a two-wave event instead of just a few lowly henchmen. Made sense. Even if I was riding a high right now, we didn't have a lot in the way of crafty trappings and my stamina was severely limited by the fact that at the end of the day I was just another everyman.

Before I started trampling across the second story floor, I reached down to my phone and switched the media player on. My playlist was the kind that made people with eclectic taste think I was crazy, but for now I stuck with the greatest of the 80s. Vampires had incredibly amplified sense, they could triangulate your position by any one alone. That was why I'd scattered dirty clothing of mine all around the downstairs, which confused the first vampire scout whose head I'd rearranged. It was also why we rigged little speakers all throughout the warehouse. It gave me enough cover to try and tight-rope walk my way across the floor without clueing them into where I was. If I could get to the third floor I would be ready for the big showdown; unfortunately, we hadn't come prepared for two different waves of the underlings. I thought the Stalker was going to be careful, not downright prudent. Especially since as of yet I hadn't really hurt it yet.

The mechanism I set up below triggered. It was an oversized, self-activating Zippo lighter. The debris we'd scattered below was all highly flammable, though we couldn't douse it in gasoline because of the hypersensitive nose of the predators we're trying to turn into prey. Smoke was billowing, the windows we had reinforced or outright boarded up would do their job of trapping the smoke inside. I hoped with enough inhalation and burn, the problem would take care of itself.

Initially my plan was to just dart to the top of the building, trying to bait the Stalker into a rooftop showdown. I heard the loud crack of the gun—apparently one of them had thought to try and escape from the way they'd come.

Two. Another gunshot barked out.

I hated these things. They were vermin. Lecherous, lowlife scavengers that fattened themselves on innocence. Logic left me since the day I delivered the package to a house I knew, on some level, was a target of some kind.

This was my city.

I turned to the stairwell. Two of them were ambling up and there was a third, badly burned, literally trying to crawl from the fast-growing inferno that was gaining momentum. The licking flames were a purification to their disease. It took them a moment to recognize that I was holding fast instead of turning tail. For some misguided reason, I wasn't pushing an offensive, either. It was important to me to show them that I wasn't afraid. That I wouldn't pale in the face of their gnarled skin, that abyss of columned, serrated, viciously curved teeth. I locked eyes with the one at the helm of their scorched trio, I let him leer and try and captivate me with those awful, slitted eyes.

When the confusion started to run rampant across his deformed face I smiled. A sadistic, smug smile.

With my two bats, it took me less than a minute to dispatch all three as I fell into a pattern of ruthless swings learned from a paladin knight a decade prior. The bat and swordplay weren't so far off, despite popular belief. Broadswords tended to have dull edges and only the point was sharp enough to pierce, so the way they fought in the time before this one lent itself to my weaponry quite well.

I gave no quarter. I froze one, the elemental bat helped me eviscerate the burnt one the rest of the way and the gathered kinetic energy allowed me to homerun the last one clear through a wall, crumbling to the dirty alley floor below.

When I started upstairs it was with a patient purpose, the stride determined but not hurried. Another classic tune clicked on my playlist and despite the moment, the gravity of this fight, the wisp of flame pluming out from the building and the significance of me squaring up with one of the most reviled and feared monsters in all the Abyss, I couldn't help but think...

...It was so cool to have a soundtrack to what was likely my final fight.

There was the bark of an engine, the squeal of tires and a crash so loud it rumbled the failing structure of the warehouse I was in. Grove and I had set a trap in the sewer system the Stalker was using to move unseen. We clogged up one exit, booby-trapped another and the third we put his badly beaten up SUV in front of.

At the first sign of the monster Grove had left his sniper perch, bricked the gas pedal and thrown the car into drive. It was a hit. The distractions of a burning building and the last of its henchmen being dealt with so succinctly had torn enough focus away from the Stalker that it hadn't paid attention to the road. It was the second time that tactic worked.

If it ain't broke...

Howling with a maddened laughter, I shouted a stream of obscenities at the thing below. The third floor was wide open, the skeletal steel pillars revealed there was once a plan to add a fourth floor that never saw the light of day and, because of our heroic (and criminal) actions, never would.

That didn't matter. The enraged Stalker hurled the car with such ferocity that it tumbled end over end back into the spot we'd concealed it. That didn't matter though, that rank odor was an acrid reminder that this thing bled. It bled, I'd bloodied it, and now?

I was going to kill it.

"Come on, you son of a bitch."

My challenging sneer followed it as it bounded off one wall before hurling itself to the metal stairwell of this building, which unhinged from the loosening screws and compromised pieces (us, naturally) that now kept it barely afloat. An undignified yelp sent scurrying limbs flailing while it freefell back into the alley, followed by a hand of my tricked-out marbles I'd fished out.

This wasn't a killing blow, but I know the impact would be enough to steal some air from its body and the one-two punch of that and marbles would keep it engaged with me.

I needed the time to hurry to the middle of the rooftop, the fire was starting to become an outright blaze and even though this desolate part of town was a proverbial no-man's land it wouldn't be long before some kind of authority came. Introducing something like this to the light of the general public was dangerous; there were entire organizations out there dedicated to making sure this very thing didn't happen, but what were they going to do?

Kill me?

I wanted to know that if I couldn't kill this thing a few dozen heavily armed police officers could maybe finish the fight. I used my time to wave frantically at the position we'd discussed Grove would move to next. I'd lost my flashlight and the radio worked for me, not so well for him, though the little light indicator was still an option. One of the contingencies we'd considered.

Tightening my grip on the bats, I saw a small flash of light from across the street that bolstered my confidence.

Confidence ripped clean out of me when I heard a crushing sound not twenty feet behind me. The Stalker had nixed the routine of scurrying up the building and just wholly cleared all three stories of the building to land square across from me.

It unwound all that impressive mass, stretching those long, powerful arms in a languid fashion. An explosion of foul breath washed across the expanse between us, molesting my exposed flesh and assaulting my every sense. Its flank and left leg looked mired, the black blood might have had a reddish hue to it, but in this light it was all but impossible to discern. That smattering of patchwork hair was freckled all over. Its body was thickly plated by the dense hide, an off-brown color. Its canine snout and reptilian eyes were crowned by a mohawk head of onyx hair. I realized nobody had ever really gotten the depiction of this thing right because it was so lethal and very few people engaged this thing up close and lived to tell.

Four minutes. The arch predator moved at a blur, and before I could get the wooden bat to cut across the air right in front of my face a blindingly fast swipe had sent those midnight nails into the shaft, just about six inches from my grip, cleaving it clear in half. I dropped it; the deflection was so damned powerful that it sent a painful vibration lancing through the weapon and into my unprepared arm.

Speaking of my unprepared arm, the Stalker's other hand clamped down on my metal arm. I heard and felt the steel give way. It warranted a scream, which I gave. I was suspended by my steel arm, stretched out to be cut clean in half like my bat. Another shot rang out—it cut hard into the assaulting shoulder of the Stalker and seemed to throw the aim of the swipe. It widened it the swing and bought me enough time to call out my shield. Altering the brunt of the impact, I less challenged the blow and more sought to deflect it.

Meanwhile, I focused on my arm to disengage the steel plating. My gauntlet expanded before folding into itself. Using the momentum gained by being hit by this thing, it actually gave me enough speed to get my arm out of the steel contraption before the thing wised up to what I was doing and crushed it completely. Naturally, the hit freed me but not gracefully. Luckily, I had managed to hurt this thing often enough that it didn't seem to be underestimating me anymore.

Small victories.

I was tumbling across the heated floor, the fire I was guessing having made its way to the second story, and the Stalker was in pursuit. Another shot rang out. Another. Four or five, I couldn't tell you, and though they didn't pierce that impenetrable skin, they did rattle it. Desperation inspired me to launch myself headlong to the right, tucking my head and actually doing not a half bad job of getting to my feet. The Stalker was swatting at the gunshots and so when I leapt, the swing it aimed at me was clumsy.

Though those claws did cut clean through a big steel pillar, so that's a cold comfort. If it hit me, at least I'd die quick. Sprinting, I got to the far end of the roof with it still in chase. Grove was starting to miss as the forest of steel sprouting from the floor was making a clear shot an impossibility even for his skill set. It didn't matter; I got to the button I was looking for and hit it as if I was mad at it.

That old-school, playground sound of spotlights coming to life chimed all around us. Light was born from every angle, pouring down all around us so bright it made me squint even in the dead of night. That, or the smoke, at this point I was too exhausted and delirious to tell.

Skidding to a stop, the thing veiled its face and hissed. Normally I would try to play it smart, take my old benefactor's advice to heart about analyzing the battlefield and gauging my opponent. Fuck that, this was his mission but my fight.

I screamed in defiance. I screamed at the ludicrousness of this. I cried havoc and let loose the dogs of war. In that scream I spit in the face of the doubters, I declared to my city and all the darkness harboring ill will that their misdeeds will no longer be met with complacent indifference. The hit I landed across the

Stalker's covered face was so hard it shot an adrenaline-stifling pain throughout my body, I released a sigil of power and let the ice burn its body. I stepped into the first swing but pivoted wide after, whipping my body into a spin to land a blow on the opposite side of its midsection. Another sigil of power released, this one a torrent of air which sent it sailing head over feet into a cluster of sprouted steel. My entire body was sapped, I could barely hear the screeching of AC/DC on the speakers we'd set up. The time for hiding was over, throwing off any scent or sense wasn't going to work.

It stood, and the roar it was going to use to signal its charge was cut short by another gunshot, except this one didn't just turn it or annoy it.

This one?

It punched into the arm, cutting through the hide, twisting sinew, fracturing bone, breaking out the other side of the shoulder before sailing into the bricking of the warehouse behind this one. There was a moment of utter silence.

Not literal silence.

The fire was cackling, the harrowing cry of sirens mingled with the actual soundtrack playing over the makeshift PA system we set up, except none of that existed in this instant. Just me and the bloodied nightmare. The singe marks of the ice burn on one arm, the swelling of its side and now?

A bloodied shoulder.

It gave off an irritated huff, its troubled snout clamping up and down, the disconcerting chewing a kind of contemplating sign, or so I thought. The arm it had deprived of the steel casing was hurting and I realized it was becoming difficult to extend it all the way. I had a broken rib or two but I didn't know for sure. I was sizing it up when it was just there, in front of me, sending its indomitable forehead into my face. There was an explosion of pain, the white-noise static that came with having your bell rung filled my ears and I didn't remember what happened to my bat though I knew I was without it. A hard hit sent me back into the air, which at a very stout two hundred pounds wasn't supposed to be as easy as this thing made it seem.

I couldn't hear it, and the franticness of the gunshots filled me with enough dread to get through the burning pain white-washing my broken face. I knew it was on me, and without thinking I untied the satchel on my hip where all my marbles where. They scattered all across the floor, but the thing had either seen them coming or wasn't fucking around with me anymore. With its speed it not only nimbly avoided every marble, but had me up and off my feet before all of them could be loosed from the bag.

It was quaking, though I suspected it wasn't just from rage. Even a magic entity had a physiognomy in our world, it had to have an anchored vessel to let it roam free and those could be damaged no matter how powerful the thing was in its world. I took a kind of grim satisfaction in knowing I had hurt it. Cleverly, it angled my body toward where Grove was, though judging from the chaos now dominating everything around me and how bad our plan had gone to shit, I would say he was on the move. The police had to be a minute out, the foundation of the warehouse was so compromised I could only hope we wouldn't be standing much longer and I had lost.

There was a studiousness in the visage of the Stalker, though with one eye now swollen shut I couldn't make much of it out.

"You fought better than your predecessor."

It was talking with a strange clarity it didn't have before. This thing wasn't really the loquacious type, so I wasn't that thrown when it wasn't all that eloquent. Now? Something was different.

"You alone did what none of them could, the whole troupe you respected and praised so well. Pious men are always the most broken when you break their heroes."

It dawned on me, one of those slow burning epiphanies that went from a whisper to a shout. That studious look wasn't studious at all, it was spellbound. Someone was using the Stalker as a conduit, much like it had with the first vampire earlier. I mistook the stilted movement as injury.

"Should have killed you then," I said. Laughing was hard to do when suffocating, plus a mouthful of my own blood made it more of a kind of gurgling.

"What's so funny?"

The demand was scathing and so I just doubled down on my effort to laugh, though it was a shit job because one, my heart wasn't in it, two my body was just a broken slab of meat and three I was being held up my damned neck.

"Yo—You're…Actually…"

I got my fist around a marble, the one without any identifying mark I'd found in the church and stowed away in the smaller pocket of my satchel.

"Monologuing... The hell did you pick this up from? Being a Bad Guy 101? Se— Seriously, have you not seen any movie ever?"

The look it gave me moved from annoyed to quizzical, though, just like my epiphany, it seemed that what I was insinuating was starting to gain some traction and it reared back to take my head clean off my shoulders.

I lifted my still working arm and crushed the marble right in front of its face. Ice. Fire. Whatever. Face to face would kill me for sure, but in the light if I could blind this thing the Cleveland police force or the soldier could surely finish the job. It was a good death.

Then, everything went still.

And a light so blinding it seemed to turn the heart of night into the peak of day erupted out of my hand. It was radiant, too. An exquisite brilliance that flowed out in every direction. The Stalker was broken from the connection to whatever was using it as a mouthpiece, and I hit the ground. I didn't double down or just crumple.

No, in fact, I felt good.

No.

I felt *great*.

The Stalker reeled, covering its coveted eyesight as if trying to keep it from being done any more damage. My sight was impeccable, my arm felt strong as ever and the reverberating aftereffect of the light that had been born from the crushed marble seemed to be the source of it all. I called up my shield and sent the silver-faced thick of it into the midsection of the beast, stepping out to the left so I could undercut it when the thing doubled over with an uppercut. Nearby, I saw my sheared bat and on a strange impulse I dove to collect it, and compose myself. I couldn't see the aluminum bat and I was a little light on offensive options.

A shot rang, except this time it wasn't from the building across the street but the one right beside us. Grove was on some kind of rundown window cleaner device and managed to score a hit with a handgun from a good distance. This hurt it, and it also turned the attention of the thing away from me as it blindly and clumsily swung around while shielding itself from the sting of the fast-fading secondary light. The man-made one opened it up to pain, this one seemed to cripple it.

When I barreled back after the beast like a one man stampede I noticed something, though it didn't register immediately—as the light faded, so did my renewed health. My sight was blurring and I was badly favoring my left side. With my shield arm, I dropped my weight and arm down on the reversed jointed knee of the Stalker, instead of following it up I moved right past it, hoping it would involuntarily whirl to that side and throw another sloppy haymaker.

It did, and Grove fired again, turning it around once more. The pain was mounting fast and while I didn't quite understand it, I swung with all my might with the half-cleaved bat. When it hit the back of the monster it opened up a brutal wound, something that didn't make any sense to me at all but I didn't question it. I rolled through it and let another shot take it in the chest. The light was dying out and so was my offensive.

I was bone-tired and when I ran through the last attack I stumbled, then kind of just fumbled and eventually collapsed on my knees. I caught myself with my left arm and before my right turned useless I clasped the broken bat to my hip.

Behind me the Stalker was bloodied, gasping and just as bad off as me.

"Ten seconds!"

Holy. Shit. I looked at the minefield of marbles, back at the Stalker now blinking away the last of its blindness and the little lift-platform Grove had lowered.

There was nothing in me at all except some weird obstinate streak to not die on my knees. The exertion it took to get to my feet was more damnably difficult than anything I had ever done. I knew this was serious because the visceral snap of the Stalker maw told me that this thing was done placating me. We erupted into motion at the same time, except with the kind of anger it was operating with—only I could get people this angry—it wasn't using all its facilities.

It slipped on one marble that didn't give, and when it tilted to see what had thrown off its trajectory it came down with all its weight on a second. An expanse of ice blossomed beneath it, long talons unable to find any purchase which sent it skittering wide before eating a face full of scalding roof.

Me? I was running. Well, a limping bastardization of sprinting, but I didn't dare look behind me. It roared again and then broke a marble of air, I could tell by the sound that swam out in every direction and the gust that swam all over me. Grove was letting off shots in rapid succession, sacrificing aim for volume.

Remember in the beginning of this sordid tale when I was taking all my stuff? I told you about the watch, the necklace, the marbles, the post-stylish bracer and finally, my boots? When I was first in this I had this bright idea that kinetic energy, my favorite kind of sigil release, was gathered by impact. Whether hard or constant, it kept growing. So my stroke of genius was storing a sigil in the sole of my boot so it would collect the ambient energy of me walking around and release it. Only problem? My work at the time was shit. It was rudimentary now, but back then it was awful. It was one giant release. When I tried kicking something it launched me across the room. If I used it for leaping it hurled me off target and with no way to coordinate myself mid-flight it was always a catastrophe. They were virtually useless.

I kept them as a reminder of my failure, that sometimes the best idea and intent cannot come together. Brilliance was often found in simplicity, and while this was a monumental waste of time I never forgot how proud Zachariah was. Lauding me for my unorthodox approach, my tenacity. He'd been proud of me. The guy begged me not to discard them, said they should be a memento at the very least. This was an accomplishment, because while I despised them this was proof that I could bring the craft to life.

Zachariah was sure one day I would use them.

And as the last second ticked off from the ten second warning, as the *whoosh* of air came all around me, as the bombs we'd set on the fire weakened foundation of the warehouse sounded off, I closed my eyes and sent the last of my function focus to my feet.

I released the sigil in my boot and just catapulted myself clear across the roof, to the slip of a platform where Grove was dual-wielding pistols to try and hold off the fast-approaching Stalker.

It was a weird sensation but I felt the ground give beneath me. We rigged it so it would collapse in on itself, sucking the middle of the structure into itself. That's where the Stalker was, where it clawed and fought for a good grasp to try and throw itself out of the condemned building.

Somehow, I hit the railing of the lift but, with nothing left in me and the last of the air (and fight) punched out of me by the brutal midair collision, I couldn't even muster the strength to try and hold on. Luckily, the soldier didn't just have a superhero physique but the strength that came with it. Grabbing my ass and headlocking me kept me stable, and with a mighty heave we both poured into the treacherous lift. One I suspected was decommissioned for being a perfectly shitty machine. I was beaten to the core of my being. I felt my spirit as broken as the body encasing it. Grove threw himself over me, the collapsing building spouting off debris and the fire at the heart of it very conveniently smothered for the most part by the collapse.

I didn't remember much after that; I watched the mountain of brick, steel and dirt long enough to make sure nothing would stir from it. I tried not to think of my numb, motionless arm, my laboring breath, the taste of copper in my mouth or the repercussions of being at the scene of a crime that could be called terrorist in nature. The darkness was calling me, even as Grove violently shook me and bade me to stay awake. I had nothing left, and so I slipped into the cold embrace of that nothingness.

CHAPTER 15

SETTLED DUST

My head had a particular soreness to it from being hurt for so long. Far as I could tell, it was dark and I was thankful for that. I wondered, not for the first time this week, just how many times somebody could be rendered unconscious without suffering long term consequences.

When I realized I wasn't in a hospital bed and that I wasn't handcuffed to the railing, I knew I had to be with someone we trusted. Since the bed wasn't crisp to the touch and tucked halfway under the mattress to the point of uselessness, I could surmise this wasn't Grove's place. Toys and decor led me to the conclusion that the single bed my busted body was in belonged to an adolescent. A boy, if the stereotype of robot fights and blue held true.

I was at Kaycee's. I had no way of telling how much time had passed, but the tenderness in my side made me believe it couldn't have been too long. Luckily, I didn't have to go Sherlock Holmes on the timeline and my whereabouts for long because, as if on cue, Kaycee was looking in on me.

"Hey-o," I said through a grimace. "What's the hap?"

"Really?" she answered. Only I could make someone blow past pity and settle on annoyance so swiftly. "You're lucky to be alive."

"You and I do not share the same definition of luck."

The end of the sentence was a struggle and I buckled down to fight off a wave of nausea produced by the insurmountable pain just ping-ponging around inside of me. She had the decency to wait in understanding silence while I dragged myself to the bathroom and attempted to put myself back together again.

My ribcage was so badly rocked that I wasn't surprised when I pissed blood. My left eye was almost comically blackened; I looked like a raccoon. With my already-sunken face from the sheer exhaustion I looked like I had skipped my entire thirties and landed squarely in the middle of my forties.

I was down a tooth in the back, the one right behind the molars I still needed to get removed. Just my luck, punched in the mouth by a freak of the netherworlds and it didn't even have the common courtesy to knock a tooth out that would have saved me a trip to the dentist. I forewent a shirt as I limped out of the bathroom, my one arm still virtually useless and my organs feeling as if they'd been rearranged by a sledgehammer.

"Is it dead?" I asked.

"Yes."

There was something new in her stare that I couldn't quite make out, but at the moment I didn't have the mental facilities to try and take too much on.

"Grove?"

"Jail."

I didn't need to give voice to the question as it was written all over my badly maimed face.

"Far as I could tell, after everything he got you into a car and managed to text me your location. I know he wanted to make sure the thing was dead and maybe he thought he could hold off any pursuit of you while we got you back here."

"How bad is it?"

"I don't know, the news called it a fire though there is some whisper that it was some kind of militant protest thing. Nothing about Grove."

I exhaled through gritted teeth; my composure and consciousness were coming at a cost. "Me?"

"Broken ribs, I think. I'm worried that shiner on your eye is an orbital fracture and you dislocated your arm. Grove managed to set it but I had to do it again when you got here. Stitches on the midsection and your eyebrow, too. You took a beating."

"Should see the other guy." Normally, that was a line reserved for when trying to save face. This time I could feel the edge in my voice when I said it, I could see the way she straightened up in response.

"You sure it's dead?"

After some hesitation, there was another nod.

"What?"

"Well," she said, rounding on me so that we could sit face-to-face. Me looking so haggard yet battle-hardened on a racecar bed, her trying to manage her balance on a tyke-sized seat. "Two things. There's a lot of rumblings about someone having killed a Stalker."

The accolades part could be a double-edged sword but now wasn't the time to make a pro-and-con list of what the after-effect of killing that thing would be.

"You're actually going to make me say it, aren't you?"

The tick of a smile died before it could truly come to life, her heavy eyes weighed down by a sympathetic sadness. "Maria is missing."

Just like that, my spirit was as defeated as my mutilated body. Maria was gone.

"Stop, Janz—STOP."

I had firsthand experience with just how strong Kaycee was. There was something about elvish anatomy—denser muscle or bone, I don't know—that amplified their strength considerably when compared to humans. She spun me around with little resistance. We were downstairs after a rather painful period of watching me struggle into tattered clothing. I was missing my steel-plated watch, the aluminum bat and all my marbles.

"I have to go."

"You'll die. Hell, you might still die, I have no way of knowing if you're bleeding internally and judging from the bruises that may very well be happening."

"If it's internal it doesn't really fit the description of bleeding."

"This isn't a time to be funny, damn you." The snap was so gut-wrenchingly instinctive that I actually flinched from it.

"You don't even have any gear left. What're you going to do, collapse in front of whoever took her as some kind of misguided symbol of stubbornness?"

Looking down at the bracer with the silver coin she'd gifted me in it, I knew she wasn't wrong. I had the shield and, well, half a bat on my hip.

The bat on my hip.

"Look at this."

I took it off and the urgency with which I carefully handed it over seemed to defuse some of our bickering. Her half-open mouth shut; the curious look at the bat was suspended to aim a suspicious one at me.

"I'm serious. The Stalker cut my absorption bat in half, and when it was all going to shit and I had nothing left, I hit him with the half I still had."

She ran her fingers over the handle, turning it over to examine my shoddy rush-job, and gave me a look that told me to get to the point.

"It opened his whole back up, Kay. I mean, bad. Gruesome. I have no idea how, but I don't want to touch the end of it at all."

"Interesting." Normally I'd take the noncommittal answer as some kind of sarcasm but she said it with a distracted edge that indicated that she was actually deep in thought.

"Yeah, at the time I didn't want to question it, but what the hell?"

A smile crept over her cherubic face before she rotated the bat to show me what she'd found. "One of your sigils wasn't desecrated when it was cut into the bat," she said, a free finger tapping the symbol she'd indicated. If you carved a sigil incorrectly—if it was altered or broken—there was usually not only a consequence, but the power inherent to the glyph was then destroyed.

"Okay, but how—"

"The Stalker isn't an Earthly monster. It's an abomination from the Abyss. The presence of it alone is kind of magical, plus they are said to have claws that can cut through anything."

"Far as I can tell, they can."

"Right. Well, if I was to guess, this sigil absorbed whatever it is about those claws that make them so hellishly sharp." The sigil, still resonating with power, was given another tap. "This might be one you think of enclosing..."

I took the bat back, eyeballing it warily. "This would be the funniest-looking knife in the world."

"They wouldn't see it coming."

That merited consideration. When a sigil was encircled, it trapped whatever power was inside it so that it continued to replicate that power. Very few glyphs are worth that. If you trapped, say, a fire sigil, then you would have to exert a lot of Focus to activate it; the amount of power in the fire sigil would be determined by how much of yourself was in it. That was why it was best to release them and recharge them unless you were an artificer and a practitioner. I wasn't.

This, though, wouldn't demand a big sacrifice of focus or will. Not in the least. Plus, encasing them was fairly easy; you just scribed a circle around the still holding sigil. It had to be a perfect circle with a very special kind of chalk-laden chisel.

I looked up at the clock. I'd slept most of the day away, plus the night before. "I need as much aspirin as I can take without shutting down my liver or kidneys, a chisel, and whatever you have left of Zachariah's."

Kaycee didn't like it, and as much was evident all across her face.

"I'm going to do this, so either get out of my way or get behind me on it Kaycee. I can't see this to the end and not finish it. Grove is in jail, we actually some-fucking-how killed the Stalker, and Maria is still in trouble."

"Fine," she said. There was a flash of pride, I think, in the narrowed glare I got. "But I don't know how well his stuff is going to work for you."

"Better than nothing."

"Painkillers?"

"No, I need to focus, moreso if it's not going to be my gear."

"I'll see what Jay can spare, too." Jay was her husband, though that wasn't his real name.

"You mean 'he who shall not be named'," I said, theatrically quoting with my fingers. Kaycee's husband was a complicated sort, and saying his true name was incredibly dangerous. "Nah, his stuff isn't really in line with what I know and do."

She hit me with a loose LEGO piece nearby for mocking her husband, though it wasn't with any real malice. "Well, sit down. I'll get it, order us some food, and we'll get to work."

"We?" If I sounded surprised, it was because I was expecting her to stay out of it for nominal neutrality.

"You're not going to be able to fix up what you've got, find out where Maria is and situate travel all on your own and in time. We got a few hours before it's dark, tops. If traditional storytelling has told me anything, that's what they're going to wait for."

I laughed. Hard. She wasn't sure if I was mocking her, so I explained. "Whoever is controlling the Stalker actually started monologuing to me."

"They spoke to you through it?" She was more shoving than settling me into the chair at the big work table.

"Well, yeah...?"

I got a slap to the back, one I couldn't say for sure was warranted but luck had been on my side enough this past week that I let it slide.

"When I get back, you're going to tell me everything it said. Everything. Talking through a Stalker isn't some paltry party trick;

that's breaking the will of a beast as old as the Shadow itself and manipulating it to your will. It makes a lot more sense. Summoning a Stalker is something any idiot could do if they stumbled across the know-how. Getting it to lock in on a particular target was a lot tougher, but doable, if you were strong enough or had something it wanted badly enough to be compliant. These aren't agreeable creatures, it's why people don't use them for this kind of work. Binding one to your will, though? That's heavy, heavy stuff but it would explain why this thing stayed so focused and fixated the whole time."

"So, bad? Basically? Bad news?"

"I can't do it. I don't know if Gale could, or could and still be able to go about her day-to-day life."

"Could have just said bad."

CHAPTER 16

FURTHER DOWN THE RABBIT HOLE

After my pow-wow with Kaycee, it was almost dark. I planned to follow the breadcrumbs to piece together what happened after I had passed out. I was on a steady diet of over-the-counter aspirin that didn't have enough punch to dull the steady throb of pain but was enough to keep my feet from falling out beneath me. I had to keep a sharp mind if I was going to make sense of all that had happened this long, so very long, week.

Just before I was about to leave, someone in a suit a size too big stopped me. She was cute, fit, and about my height which was tall for a woman but not abnormally so.

"Are you Janzen Robinson?" she asked.

"...Yeah?" I answered with some hesitation. My reluctance to answer was well-founded, because she tore back and sent a blistering slap across the front of my face. What she couldn't know was that the hand she shoved into my chest to hand over a letter was all that kept me upright in the aftermath.

Holding my face, looking dumber than usual, I looked at Kaycee as she stepped outside. Despite having witnessed the exchange, she didn't look surprised at all. In fact, she was digging around that oversized bag of hers trying to fish out keys.

"Who was that?" she said, sounding a little too smug.

"Another satisfied customer?"

Kaycee snorted. I opened the letter and distractedly situated myself in the passenger side of her minivan.

"For a guy who whines incessantly about being kept in the dark, you sure do take your sweet time to share with the class," she said.

"I don't whine," I whined.

She offered a flat look while I stuffed the letter into the glove box.

"It's Grove. He's in jail right now for some kind of obstruction of justice. He's claiming it was a militant activist group that he's been tracking on his own, that way they'll hopefully buy it without digging too deep. I guess he's telling me to steer clear, that I'll just muddy the whole thing up even more."

The good side of me hated having put my newest, and quite frankly only, friend in such a compromising situation, one that could ruin his entire life. The bad side of me hated not having the backup of such a competent fighter who hadn't once flinched in the face of real evil. Kneading the bridge of my nose, I lost myself in a debate as to whether or not it was broken. I shifted the top of it back and forth, wondering if it ever did that before.

Kaycee didn't bother to repeat herself. Well, first she hit me to lure me out of my daydream, and then she repeated herself. "Where we going?"

"Gale's."

That struck a nerve and commanded an unfavorable silence. Gale and Kaycee didn't exactly get on very well. I wasn't too keen on the specifics, though I knew as a half-elf Kaycee could serve as something akin to an ambassador from the Veil. Gale, who I had no real clue as to what she was, didn't enjoy anyone from that side of the world—the Veil—in her bar. For that matter, it seemed kind of funny that she disliked almost anyone unnatural in her establishment when it had become something of a mecca for unique individuals in the city.

"You think he's going to be all right?"

"I don't know... Kid is a war hero, he might not say as much but I gathered as much from what was going on at his apartment. If I was going to take this very thin limb I am on and run further down it, I would guess he's probably gotten reprimanded a few times for stepping over the duties specified for citizen watch. Probably a lot of times. So, this might not be wholly out of character. I guess I'm just worried about the bodies."

Kaycee gave a wry smirk that punctuated a chortle.

"I keep forgetting you're new to this, the field part. Stuff like that doesn't stick around. They get dusted pretty quickly. The vampires they'll find, but that will only help your case."

It was my turn to flip the expectant silence over to her.

"They still retain stuff like fingerprints and DNA. They've probably killed a few people or been close enough to a murder that their stuff will be on record. All the other stuff that's happened to them reverts back to what they had been originally, so they won't find an unhinged jaw or a buzz saw in their mouth."

Well, it seemed something finally broke our way. If a few of them came back with some dirt on their record, who was to say whatever line Grove was feeding them wasn't factual? The card stapled to the letter was that of a lawyer. Nice embossing, rich stuff, she wasn't cheap. Judging by her middle name, the same as his last, she was also his sister.

The slap made a lot more sense now.

We pulled up to the bar, which seemed to be having one of its better nights. The crowd was a blend of the make-believe, as I called it—those who were in the know about that world—and a smattering of people who just came because it was close.

"Have fun at school with your friends," she said dryly as I stepped out of the van.

"No lunch money?" I asked, hunching over to look at her through the window.

She sped off.

"Dad always gave me money," I lamented before moving to the entrance with a pronounced limp I was trying to fight through.

"Take the belt off, Mr. Robinson." The Tinkerer was as dry and indifferent as ever. It was strangely wounding. My old mentor would have been euphoric at my victory, but this one, the man I had come to terms with to learn under, couldn't even be bothered enough to look up at me.

"Bracer too."

I dropped it, after a rather embarrassing battle to free myself from it, on top of the belt with my effects. Donovan finally turned those intense, dark eyes on me to give me a cursory sweep.

"I won," I said.

"I came to work tonight."

The comeback wasn't just off-putting, but kind of threw me.

"We did what is expected of us, do not look for praise every time you do something right else your tenure with me will be a long and arduous one instead of an educational one. You did exactly as I knew you could," he said, then left me with a stinger. "And five years late."

Well, that was both disheartening and sobering. If this was going to be my new life, taking on the mantle of those who came before me, it suddenly got a lot more real. Real and dark. It was a thankless thing I was doing right now; if I continued, nothing about that would change. I shuffled through the door, looking over my shoulder once, but Donovan was already turned back toward the street. With the swiftness of a sleep deprived slug, I came to the conclusion that Donovan, whom I had just recently met, knew too much about me for it to fall under hearsay or coincidence.

My realization was interrupted by a mastodon of a man who abruptly wrapped me up in a ground-stealing hug. My feet drifted a clean foot or so from the floor they once seemed so content on. All I could smell was the musk of well-aged leather and some kind of bourbon. When I was finally set down, I aimed my best smile up.

Xander was either enjoying a night off, or the responsibilities he was seeing to could be done while cross-eyed drunk. I wasn't one to judge, what with my rich history of trying to accomplish complex tasks while absolutely shithoused.

"Like a darned wombat. Or Wolverine."

I got a nice shot to the arm. I knew it was supposed to be a masculine sign of affection, but since that shoulder had been dislocated less than a day ago, I couldn't really enjoy the significance of our bonding moment. It just hurt.

"Yeah, you know me...Honey badger all the way."

"Ha! Yes! Honey badger. Good." He laughed. Gale was giving me a look somewhere between bemused and plaintive. "You are named friend by me, Janzen... uh? Wizard? No. Don't tell me. Practitioner? The, uhm, what is it, smart men... Think much, all those measuring glasses and stuff—"

"Alchemist."

"Yes! Alchemist? What is it, then? You must tell me this and then the story of how you felled the *Cura'sha*."

That name had a way of slithering throughout the whole establishment, changing the ambiance with it. People became cautious, tossed a glance our way, huddled closer to one another. There was power in the name of a thing, there was power in the reputation of it, and there was power in the fear it seemed to inspire. I hated these facts, and I hated the Stalker for being able to do all of that just by the mere mention of its name.

"I dropped a building on it." My hands crumbled together and then expanded while I made the noise a building down when falling in on itself. In hindsight, I could have been a little more dark and mysterious about it. More comic book antihero and less after-school special. "And it's just Janzen."

I gave his big arm a good pat as I passed him to go and take refuge at a seat across from Gale. She had a new act—one that was decidedly not Maria, whom I had hoped would still be here though it was a day past our agreement. He was good; there was a little more bite to his soulfulness, and the way he was working that guitar, and at his age, I could tell he was a kind of prodigy. The precocious type who was the result of passion and talent coming together. I knew better than to speak while he was still playing, though I had more of Gale's attention than I would have expected.

She eyeballed me sidelong while throwing together a two-finger drink, neat. She never did something so simple and classy for the likes of me, and even though I wasn't a fan of the stuff, I could tell it was the good kind. It had that pretentious odor of wealth.

It stank of opulence and, what was that, oak?

It tasted like hot ass going down my gullet. I shotgunned it down. I wasn't sure if it was just my way of being petulant, showing that I hadn't changed that much or that I wouldn't, or if it was just that I was so dumb that the fact that she'd extended me an olive branch to the big kids table had flown right over my head.

I was angry about Maria, and that was a lot more difficult to swallow than the overpriced scotch I'd just chugged.

"Maybe I should put it in a sippy cup for you next time."

"Where is she." I could hear the tone I was taking with her, and didn't care.

"Not here."

It was the dismissiveness of her answer that had me on edge. That or the headache was doing the tango with my swollen stomach to make me perfectly mad.

"That one seemed kind of obvious."

"So did sipping a hundred-year-old glass of scotch instead of shooting it like a frat boy, but you have shown me never to underestimate the severity of your stupidity."

Even at full speed with every weapon I'd ever held at my disposal, I wasn't sure I could make a dent in this woman, and furthermore, it was unwise to even think about it. Xander, who I felt getting a lot closer, was a lot less jovial than during our interaction a minute before.

"Gale. Can you tell me anything about where Maria might have ended up?"

"She left. Something about her group being in trouble again."

Of course that would have been a weak spot for her. That little hodgepodge of people seemed to serve as some kind of surrogate family for her, and that was something I could relate to. The only odd thing was that it wasn't what I would have done if she was the priority; who would even think or know to go after them?

"Gale, can a group bring something over from the Abyss and control it?"

"Sure. Matter of fact, given the limitations of most people, that would probably be the smartest way to go."

"Fuck." It hit me like a ton of bricks. I was out of my stool, hammering an already sore fist down on top of the bar. "Fuck. I didn't—fuck..."

"It's your command of the English language that I find so appealing," she quipped flatly, watching the stage.

"Where is she, Gale? I need to know, now. She's in trouble, they aren't, it's a damn trap. Fuck."

My inability to string together anything even quasi-coherent was wearing thin, and so I tried to stall the full-blown anxiety attack I was in danger of falling victim to and tried to explain.

"Her old little coven, they played at innocent, but they have to be the people who called the Stalker over. They're the only people I've come across who knew, before all of this, that she's a Wanderer. I need to know where she went, Gale."

"I really didn't care to know; my obligation was over at that point, and if she wanted to leave..." She trailed off with that feline shrug, the haughty one of practiced indifference.

"Damnit, Gale, come on!"

The music screeched to a stop. I didn't actually think that kind of thing was possible, but silly me. I didn't get another word in before a massive paw pretending to be a human hand grabbed my agonized arm and whipped me around. Sadly, today wasn't a day I was going to play victim.

"Fuck off me, Lurch." I shoved him, though it was an exercise in futility. Luckily, Gale had calmed him with an upraised hand.

"Janzen—" she started, her tone verging on conciliatory.

"No." It seemed my reinforced ire surprised her. "No, Gale. I don't have time for your middle of the road bullshit. I am barely standing, my only friend lied to me about even knowing what a Wanderer is, my partner is in jail, and that thing knew about Zachariah. You want to live with your head in the sand, lofty and perfect in your throne of superiority where care and the innocent are beneath you? Fine. This is my city, though, and if you want to stay here you're going to play ball. Whatever is coming is big enough that they would drag a heavy hitter over to back off all the people playing by the rules from stepping over whatever line has you all so god damned scared. I don't have time to play connect-the-dots and I'm not some fucking Nancy Drew, so I need you to be straight with me and now. I don't have time for this."

Nausea was threatening me again. I gritted my teeth, not to stave off the burning anger rising inside of me but so I could steel myself against the waves of sickness.

"Tell me where she is."

Gale looked like she was deciding whether or not she was going to have Xander rip my arms from off my body and beat me to death with them. She was so frighteningly at ease on the proverbial throne I just accused her of being on that after my bout of illness and the rage started to subside, I started to remember just who it was I had been talking to.

"...She's a good person, and good people can get hu—"

"The lake. There's an address she scribbled down," she said, giving an up-nod which delegated to Xander the task of retrieving it. I felt more than heard the huff of indignant air as it crept down my spine. "There's thirteen of them hiding out at some small resort out there, she said. Not a good number."

"When is it ever?"

She eyed me with a tempered expression, one she'd probably had a lot of practice forging over those long-lived centuries. Again, that was just a guess. Gale might just be an incredibly able con artist for all I knew, but I doubted it.

"You're not going to make it out alive. You probably won't even be able to save her."

I was draped over the stool I'd been sitting on before my outburst, using it to keep me upright.

"Well, then maybe this will be just like those dime store noir novelettes."

"Why you?"

"Who else?" I tried to hold tight to my last shred of pride while straightening myself so I could take the address out of Xander's hand. "You ain't gonna do shit," I said. This had a lot less tone, I figured now wasn't a time to be biting. "And he's not going to." I cocked a hitched thumb at the big man. "Good people are at stake, real people. I know what it's like to have your whole life ripped from you." I memorized what was written down before stuffing it into my pocket. "If Maria is going to die, it's not going to be alone."

I was almost to the stairwell. The eerie silence that had fallen over the normally rowdy bar was unsettling, but luckily, I couldn't fixate on it since I was more concerned with putting one foot in front of the other.

"It's going to be on the water," Gale said, her clear voice cutting the tension and suspending my awkward trek up the stairs. "And if they need water, it's being used as some kind of conduit lubrication, so... It's going to be big."

That was both bleak and helpful. I smirked at her. "Thanks."

Just as I got to the door, Xander in tow to make sure I was properly escorted out, I tossed one last pleasantry at my burly buddy. "She wants me."

We both laughed, exchanged a firm grip, and I left.

CHAPTER 17

THE HUNT

It wasn't any colder, but it felt that way. It was probably blood loss and, of course, the fact that I was so utterly alone in all of this probably wasn't helping. Donovan didn't even acknowledge me as we stood beside one another. I was gawking and uncomfortable, he was just involved in whatever he was reading.

It started adding up without me even having to try and put the pieces together. The vampire attack against her ilk might have made sense if the Stalker was tracking me in the misguided hope of finding out where it was we'd stashed Maria away.

The mini-van pulled up and before I climbed in I chirped to Donovan, "Nice talking."

"Smartass."

"Better than being a dumbass."

And with the last word I slammed the door shut. Small victories were important on a day like this.

Kaycee gave me an overly concerned eye that I was dutifully, and childishly, ignoring. I pulled a folded piece of paper out of my pocket and pushed it at her. "Take me to this address, then you can be done."

"Where is this?" She ignored my glib attitude and scathing tone.

"Grove's. Need to pick some stuff up. I can't even be sure I'll be able to use Zachariah's stuff, or if it'll let me."

"I think it will," she said. And she smiled with such a motherly tenderness even I couldn't keep my sour face so sternly planted. Softening wasn't on the agenda, though. I was pissed. I was at it alone. Bad stuff was happening, and all these people who prattled on about balance and the precarious nature of this big unknown that governed said balance seemed to be ignoring the fact that if these people hurt Maria, if they did whatever they seemed hell-bent on doing, that it would in effect throw off the balance. "Where you headed after that?"

"Lake Erie. I got it. Grove has another car."

"I can take you."

"It's fine."

Snapping back and forth wasn't a healthy form of communication, but it's not like I was in an ideal headspace.

"Put your seatbelt on."

"Huh?"

She slammed on the brakes. The stop was jarring enough to send my badly battered body into the dashboard.

"Oh, are you fucking kidding me? Really?! Real mature." To emphasize, a horn blasted behind me.

"If you're going to act like a child, I'll treat you like one. Put. Your. Seatbelt. On."

"Okay, I don't know how many dramatic outbursts I have to deal with today, but this is fucking ridiculous." My attempt to get out was interrupted by her gunning the minivan (which, off-topic, had surprisingly good acceleration) and pinning me to my seat.

"You think you have the market cornered on misery, you snide prick?"

That threw me, and for once I didn't have a counter.

"You think I like the fact that I have to choose between my family and my friends every time you guys run off to fight? You think I want to watch you die, really?"

Thankfully she wasn't putting that inhuman strength into the stinging slaps she was drumming off my chest. It still hurt, but at this point everything hurt. Breathing hurt.

"You think I let you steal, accidentally left blankets out on cold nights, fought for an apprenticeship for you, because I don't care you, you nincompoop?"

"...Nincompoop."

"I have kids, fuck you!" She was laughing while crying, and I was glad the dagger of levity hit the right chord because she had me dead-to-rights. I was being a selfish, pity-party-for-one asshole.

"Kay," I started.

"Shut up. Just shut up." Her hands clenched the steering wheel, blanching her knuckles. "You don't get to leave me too, Janzen, not you. I won't let it. We are going to finish this fight, you and me."

"Kaycee, you can't—"

"Don't you tell me what I can and can't do, Janzen Eliot Robinson, I am the closest thing you've got to a mother and so long as I am here, I am done letting you go at it alone."

She was all teeth, fire and brimstone and when I made even a motion to speak she set on me with eyes burning so bright I couldn't help but reflexively lift both arms as if being arrested.

I seriously needed to stop doing that.

"You got it, mamabear."

A victorious nod seemed to calm her frayed nerves.

"All right, then."

"I don't know exactly where her people are, but when we get there, we'll scope out as much of the lake as we can until we figure it out. Grove's first."

***

There was little to no traffic, the evening was well on its way. I spent a lot of time reflecting on life and my city. Cleveland didn't fit the narrative of the sexy city. There was nobody poring over it poetically. Still, I couldn't help but love it. It was a city built by callused hands, driven by hard work, with a gritty attitude that shamelessly defined it. We loved our teams even when they were losing, we didn't get distracted by the glitz and glam. It was a bastion of truth to me, a lot of hard reality lived in every nook and cranny. While that was uncomfortable for some people, I couldn't help but like my truth to punch me in the face.

I loved my city for what it was.

There was a storm brewing over the lake—not an uncommon thing this time of the year, but the storyteller in me couldn't help but find it fitting. Kaycee and I shared the kind of silence only people who knew one another entirely could. When we talked, the conversation wasn't strained; we seemed to be just as at ease talking as we were in this cone of nothingness. There are two type of people before a fight. One is those who have to crawl inside of themselves to find whatever it is they're looking for—a reason to fight, the courage to see it through, or just reflection. The other is riddled by nerves and tends to power talk. I could go either way, so whenever someone picked one antic over the other I wasn't bothered by it.

The sun was taking its curtain call behind me; the backdrop of my city's humble skyline silhouetted against the ensuing storm was calming. My internal monologue mourned not being a more elegant wordsmith; I had a penchant for cursing too much and coming off as crude. Plus, I had to interject humor as a way to break the monotony of too much intensity.

I stared at a blank piece of paper for the whole drive, unable to think of a single person to write or what I would even want to say to them.

We pulled up to the first place, where I did a cursory inspection. It was the wrong address and I knew it, though when I got to the shore I could see a few places that fit the bill for isolated and private. I could eyeball about where we needed to go. Still, the routine remained the same for the next three places. When we got to the penned address, I did the same hasty once-over.

"We need to split up. You have to check up the road; I'll walk this line, and if nothing we meet up in an hour. This isn't going to be fast enough."

Kaycee didn't suspect anything; her reluctance was born from concern for my well-being. Good people who loved unremittingly didn't expect to be lied to. I was a good liar, I always had been. It was a horrible trait, but a useful talent. After a while she agreed, and with a hard slap to the side of the van door I sent her off, likely the last time I would see her.

I couldn't allow her to jeopardize her family. Unlike Gale, she was an actual emissary for one of the worlds and it would be hard to justify her involvement in all of this. I believed she would have seen this through with me, but I couldn't allow that. I understood the decision risked the life of Maria as well, but it was mine to make and enough good people had been hurt already.

Speaking of hurt, I turned to move to the shoreline and investigate when another crippling signal of pain paralyzed me. It arrested my momentum and doubled me over. I'd been surviving on aspirin and anti-inflammatories, but that was like using shoddy duct tape on an airplane. Sooner or later it was going to unravel, and I was flirting with sooner, having long ago blown past later.

I was on the verge of ending it before it began. I was so badly disoriented that it took me a good minute to grasp the grass and to realize that during this whole internal strife, it had started to rain. The waning fringe of my consciousness throbbed with encroaching darkness until I heard a voice.

"I don't mind that you're so beat up, or filthy, but I wish you'd make at least some kind of effort to dress your age."

I knew that voice, though it was impossible that he was here. It was sophisticated in the way only an English accent could be, full of an amicable understanding of my plight, and it was wetting my sunken eyes just to hear it.

Zachariah.

CHAPTER 18

ZACHARIAH

"... You're dead."

A disinterested shrug dismissed the question while also at least acknowledging it. It was a contradictory kind of aloofness mastered by the British.

"No. That's it, I know it. You're dead. That's the end, man."

"Many smarter than us hypothesize that death, is in fact, the beginning."

Great. I was puking blood, and the delusion I was suffering from was more interested in lecturing me than leaving me alone.

"Zachariah. No, I—I mean..."

"Think it through, rattle off what you know to be true. If it is not the likely, or the unlikely, then we can start to entertain the impossible, no?"

And as if to circumvent that entire process recited, he reached an arm down, which I took as a matter of muscle memory and was then, consequently, hoisted up by.

This week had been a long one. Monumentally so. The world beneath was complicated, so much so that the ageless creatures who studied it the whole of their extended lives still felt as if they hadn't even begun to scratch the surface. What I had jumped into was so far out of my depth I couldn't think of an apt enough metaphor to parallel it to.

But this?

"So what is it? Did I just drop dead?" I actually looked around at my feet to see if I was securing one Hollywood cliché by drifting above my own dead body. "Internal bleeding, the concussion?"

Zachariah was smiling the tolerant smile he wore so well. Class personified. The magnanimous man blended aristocratic pedigree with principled humility. I couldn't say for certain why I was seeing him, but I would be lying if my broken heart didn't sing a little at the sight.

"Fuck it." Apparition or not, the spectre was solid enough to steal a hug. I could tell it was caught unaware and yet when it returned the embrace I would swear there was a heartfelt tenderness in the shared touch.

"I see your ability to articulate yourself with such eloquence hasn't diminished in my absence," he said.

"I'm the Hemingway of the spoken word."

With reluctance, I extricated myself from the mirage of my old mentor, my eyes searching the shoreline I'd been eyeballing before nearly being subdued by the startling jolt of crippling pain running rampant throughout my broken body.

"You sent Kaycee off," he observed.

Maybe it was the life I'd lived, maybe the week I'd endured, or it could just be from blood loss, but I seemed to process this whole ghost mentor thing fairly well. I wasn't sure if it was because I missed him, or that on the list of crazy stuff that happened recently it barely ranked. "Not her fight. I've got no idea what I am stepping into, and even if she did make it out of this, that would only be messing up her life after, anyway."

"What are you up against?"

"A coven of what I thought was pretty novice practitioners. Maybe ten or so? They've got the girl."

"Ah," he remarked knowingly. "A girl, eh? Tell me, is the young miss pretty?"

"That's not what it's about."

Only the English could taint silence with so much smugness.

"She's not *not* pretty," I relented with a bark of unenthused laughter.

The placidness of the lake was pretty common given the hour. It wouldn't be long before the crawling rain crept up on us. It was cool out, though not so chilly as to have a bite. Clouds blocked out a lot of the starlight. The stretch of land I was at had a scattering of foliage with a thicket of trees blanketing the coast. There was one boat out in the water, which helped narrow down the suspects, so I had that going for me. I saw a gimmicky restaurant with a hokey lighthouse on the dock that doubled as an outside bar. They were just closing down but hadn't yet, which meant I wasn't too late. There was an unspoken accord that we don't operate in plain view, and no matter how far up the totem pole you perched, that was a pretty unbreakable rule.

"Ten on one isn't favorable," he warned.

"It's been that kind of week."

I would swear there's a flash of pride in the smirk we shared.

"Why this girl?"

"She's a Wanderer."

"Ah, I see."

Seeing something that wasn't there was usually a sign of some pretty gnarly psychosis. Engaging with it was no longer flirting with insanity, but outright going steady with it. Still, I didn't have a lot in the way of options. Maybe this was my subconscious mind manifesting itself? Maybe this was the ghost of my old friend.

"What do you see? I am still really fuzzy on all of that. I mean, what do you think they're going to do?"

When Zachariah contoured his face in the way I knew so well I understood that he'd fallen into deep thought. "It's a bit perplexing, how to condense what a Wanderer is in just one discussion let alone a dozen."

"I need the cliff notes, Z-man."

The quaint little bar was cleared out and it seemed the last of the staff was about to shuffle out for the night, which would mean not long after this little spot in the middle of nowhere would be absent any prying eye.

"Inside every Wanderer is a piece of the Beyond, the barrier that is keeping the Abyss, the Veil, and everywhere else from overlapping. The Beyond itself is a sentient force, a conscious power that can't be manipulated. Inside the Wanderer, though, is a fraction of it that can be cultivated, or used, by someone outside of the Beyond."

"Smaller words, simpler point."

Like old times the man seemed perturbed enough to lose that classic calm but with a steadying breath continued on.

"You can use a Wanderer to get from one world to the next, open bridges between them. The Beyond won't let everyone cross, that's why the emissaries of each world are far from the scariest things that are there. A Wanderer isn't so bound, and the power in them can be harvested. They're very valuable. This is only one use of that power, too. That's just what people do to a Wanderer, a Wanderer who is aware of their gift and taught tend to be very, very powerful."

"They all said Maria was unusually talented for how long she'd been involved in the lifestyle."

"She'd have a natural affinity so that does make sense."

The sky started to weep, the last car sputtered out of the parking lot and the lighting on the boat started to yawn awake. Torches. Very ritualistic.

"They're playing my song." The tension in my head was no longer doubling my vision, just blurring, so this half-cocked scheme of mine went from outright impossible to snowball's chance in hell.

"What are you working out in terms of plan?"

"...Uhm," I said, sheepishly shrugging. I tried to sell a smile that hadn't worked for a decade and probably wasn't as schoolboy-charming as I thought then.

"Truthfully man, most of my stuff is broken beyond repair. I've got some of your old gear with me, but I can't even say it'll work even if I figured out how to use it. We don't have allies; the city has been kind of bleak since we lost all of you. I didn't piece this travesty together until a few hours ago, so even if I was in good health, locked and loaded with pristine equipment this would still be a crapshoot."

"Janzen," he started. Just to hear the old man chide my name was beautiful. There was an age-old adage about not knowing what you've got until it's gone, and even if it's a hackneyed saying that's been beaten to death, the reason it's so resilient because of how true it is. "You're better than this."

"I'm really no—"

"Do you know why I took you on as a student?"

Zachariah used to berate me on the merit of interrupting, so to have him interject stopped me cold.

"Kaycee was soft on me and you owed her one?"

"No."

"Prickly charm?"

"No," he said, laughing. "Your natural proclivities weren't in your favor."

"In the interest of brevity, what with having to try and save a girl from a crazed cult of lunatics, why don't we skip to the part where you bring me into the know?"

"Shrewdness and a good moral compass."

I'll admit, that didn't have the montage-inspiring moment I was hoping for but it also felt real.

"There are smarter people, no doubt, but if there is someone who can think on their feet the way you can, I haven't seen them. I watched you before I took you in. Never stealing from someone who couldn't afford it, never playing a hustle out so far that you'd bankrupt them. You stayed charitable, too. Sharing a score with those as downtrodden as you, so much so that you weren't ever going to elevate your station because of your need to see those you cared about kept safe. We all lived such a black and white life, but that isn't the way the world really is. People deal in such absolutes in this life and those who are in the middle tend to be duplicitous and self-serving. That wasn't the case with you. With you, I wasn't looking for someone to carry out my legacy, I was trying to find someone who was destined to forge their own. To make their own legacy. A better one than mine."

A soft breeze could have toppled me over, and not because I was badly bruised on every inch of my body. We never did the sharing-is-caring talk and while the old man wasn't cruel, neither was he outwardly affectionate. I was aware that there was a love between us, but to hear that it walked hand-in-hand with a respect broke the floodgates. I was too tired to outright sob, and that same exhaustion made it impossible to try and stave off the tears that were flowing freely down my face.

I was aware that this all might not even be real. I was also aware it didn't matter. It was a balm for the soul, the dark recess in which I kept all this locked up was finally able to let it go. The chasm just gave way and when I breathed, it felt like for the first time.

"You can do better."

I looked at the bar, where a soon-to-be-embarrassed custodian was belting karaoke into a broomstick while spinning it around. From the shanty lighthouse, to the big boat still stirring to life and finally the backpack full of gear I'd lugged along.

"... I have an idea."

"You should bring my gloves." Zachariah allowed that statesmanlike disposition to light up with a touch of mischief at the mention of them. They were his trademark. They were both his Sistine Chapel and swan song.

"What? No. Those looked ridiculous."

"Nice leather bracelet."

"Fuck you."

My heart wasn't in the ribbing, despite my unstoppable smile; my mind sluggishly started to turn some wheels and develop something starting to resemble an idea.

"Bring them," he said. There was an insistence that drew me out of my contemplative strategizing. I exchanged a look where he punctuated the sentiment with a smiling nod. By now, the crazy plan I'd constructed could use something with that much firepower. They were well-stitched and black as the night that surrounded us. My mentor had embroidered his initials on the top, and the palm had a complex formula of alchemy and artificery that was simply astounding. It wasn't just the complexity of it that made them remarkable, but the calligraphy, the way the science, craft and art all blended so spectacularly.

"I wouldn't even know how to use them."

"Bollocks." The curse accentuated the statement because the man was a saint when it came to vulgarity. Within the murky darkness, given the coming fight and the overall feel of dread trying to suffocate any semblance of sanity I had left, it felt good to laugh.

"They might not even work for me, they were yours. This was your best work. It's probably attuned to you."

"Then I guess it's a good thing I'm always with you."

As quick as he'd come, he was gone. I wasn't sure if that was real, but I didn't have time to run through a checklist about it. Maria was in trouble, the singing custodian was almost done with his one-man act, and I had a rendezvous with destiny. I pocketed the gloves, adjusted the leather bracer and double-checked my half-bat. I retrieved the backpack and quietly moved to the restaurant, keeping the ship in my line of sight the entire time.

It was time to show that the faith others had in me wasn't misplaced.

CHAPTER 19

BLOOD AND WATER

I left the gimmicky restaurant out another hundred bucks with only a crummy to-go bag to show for it. At the shoreline, I stashed all my more sensitive stuff inside the plastic bag and knotted it as best I could. The water was cold as hell, but it was a good distraction from my unreasonable fear of being in water when I can't see anything beneath it. Give me a mutated apex predator from another dimension any day over swimming at night.

I got to the boat and just drifted at the ass end of it for a minute, trying to listen to the soundtrack of the happenings on board and seeing if I could gather anything useful. It was a big boat, the kind a newlywed couple might host a party on or be actually married on. It reminded me of something you took out on a school field trip. My best guess was there were only a dozen or so of them left, and following that line of guesswork, I also had to imagine they weren't expecting anything in the way of an interruption. That was a pair of things I had going for me. The boat was big enough to get lost on if only a dozen or so people were mulling around, and given that it seemed to be getting more animated, I would think they had their attention elsewhere. Plus, the city was without anything resembling a protector, and the only fool who came forward—that would be me—was in their minds most likely having his bones picked clean by a rabid Stalker.

Wrestling my body weight up wasn't as easy as it used to be at full strength, which meant when I heaved my ass on board it was in a very undignified, wheezing, grimacing fashion. It was a poignant reminder that I was on my last leg. That didn't change anything. There wasn't anyone left, and there was no way I would sit on the sideline while some girl was martyred on a slab of stone for some misguided belief system or dark, undeserving godling.

I ducked into the engine room. The loud purring of the engine lugging idly along concealed the reassembling of my effects. I was still soaked, so now I had a good shiver to accompany the dull ache that was steadily growing. I wedged my bracer down my left arm and strapped those old, gnarled boots on. I clasped the half-bat to my hip, and on the other side I hung my old mentor's signature gloves. Finally, I slid on the leather biker jacket and readjusted the pistol I'd taken from Grove's place.

At this point I was willing to cut corners and break rules.

This rendezvous point wasn't exactly subtle, and yet I knew they shouldn't expect any kind of trouble. It wasn't like they fit the motif of evildoers. Most of them had just a generic, suburban, harmless next door neighbor thing going on. Plus, I would bet this was either legally rented or one of them worked for the company that subleased out this damn boat.

It wasn't the first time tonight I had come to miss Grove. I had forgotten what a comfort it was to be staring down a hardship with someone reliable by your side. Slipping out of the engine room, I scaled the wall to the second story. This thing had an outlier where people could work around, a two-story construct in the middle of it, and in the front was a spacious area where I imagined the majority of them would congregate. I paused my progress, falling still to see if there was any kind of alarm raised. It was around then that I started to hear someone out at the front of the boat. A speaker, female, though I couldn't discern what she'd been saying. I surveyed the second story to find it mostly desolate, though I could make out a pair of silhouettes at the way front through a glass panel. As I crept forward, I passed by what looked like a lumpy sheet of canvas, which didn't make sense until I peeled back a corner and saw the three dead bodies from Jackie's house. All signs pointed to them making an attempt at resurrection, which was considered very dark magic for good reason. There was an inherent wrongness in bringing people back, it was only ever a facsimile of life. The spark was gone forever.

Subterfuge wasn't really my thing, but I knew enough to walk lightly and stick to the shadows. The speaker was at it again, and with more fervor—there was a charge to the atmosphere, which told me in no uncertain terms that whatever was at work here wasn't good.

When I got to the front of the boat, or bow since we're all nautical, all I could see inside were the dumpy guy and the fox-faced one. Earlier I'd felt guilty about not taking the time to even ask after their names, but now? Fuck 'em. Their attention, rapt and undivided, was fixed on whatever was happening in front of them. It took the fox-faced kid a full second to register that his buddy had been pistol whipped so hard that he was unconscious before he hit the floor. It was a calculated risk since I couldn't see what it was that had them so spellbound below. Luckily, no alarm was set off, and by the time the kid thought to jump to the call of action, I had him by the scruff of his weird robe and a gun firmly planted against the flat of his forehead.

Soaked, shivering, pale from blood loss and sunken-eyed from sleep deprivation, I had to imagine that I cut a pretty menacing portrait. Gauging from the reaction of the slick-talking youngster I had pinned between the wall and myself, I wasn't wrong. It was important to get one of them alone, and as much as I wanted to split my attention between the guy I was about to interrogate and whatever ceremony had just commenced below it was important to get through this quickly if I was going to have any kind of real chance at understanding what it was they were up to and how best to disrupt it. It was also vital to single one out because they struck me as the zealous type.

Zealots, like bullies, were at their most dangerous when the numbers favored them. You take a gang away from a loudmouthed ruffian and suddenly he's got to stand and deliver on all the shit he's talked by way of his own merit, which they aren't big on. It was easier to get one of these fanatics to break if they didn't have another believer beside them.

This was all guesswork, I hadn't actually broken one yet.

I was about to.

"You're a pretty clever kid," I started. Steel resolve is all that kept my teeth from chattering. "So, I don't think I have to spell out what I'm going to ask you."

We exchanged a look that, when coupled with the application of pressure from the gun barrel to his cranium, seemed to convey what it is I wanted: silence.

"What is going on out there?"

"It's a cere—"

The hand I had on his mouth curled into a fist and turned in, sending the thick-plated bone of my elbow into the side of his head. I doubled him over with an air-stealing knee to the solar plexus. Everything in the diminutive guy wanted to collapse, but I reeled him back upright with a fist full of his hair. I re-stamped his head with the muzzle.

"Try again."

"It's a spell."

"More."

"Jackie... She... She is in communion with the Mistress. The Mistress told her how to open a bridge between us and her using Maria."

"Who is the Mistress?"

"Man... I—I don't... I don't kno—"

He broke off into a sob because, in order to punctuate my willingness to escalate this conversation, I had racked the hammer of the pistol back. I wasn't even sure what that did, though my guess would be it's a kind of cocking? Honestly, I knew next to nothing about the weapon, but enough television told me that this was a great way to drive home a point for a final time. Regardless of my limited understanding on how to operate the gun, I knew enough to be dangerous, and everything written on my face said that I was willing to put him in a body bag.

"She's from the Abyss, that's all I know, I swear—I *swear*, man. We got into this because it was like, real magic, it was *big*. Not the piddling stuff we've been doing. It got out of hand, though. Jackie reached into this darkness and it started to rub off on her. Before we know it, she's plotting on Maria, turning people against her. When people disagreed she either bullied them, outright threatened them, or ghosted them like she did Frank."

"Frank didn't want to go along with it?" Time was limited, because on a raised dais above the amassed assembly of the rest of the coven was Jackie—presiding over all of them, with Maria bound to something beside her. There was a circlet of some kind that seemed to keep her suspended.

"Nah man, not at all, and Frank was the only one who could actually do more than a stupid scry spell and tarot card stuff. It's why she had him killed."

"The Stalker?"

Tears in his eyes, he's frantically nodding.

"It was a gift from the Mistress. Frank wasn't like, great, you know? But he was good and nobody wanted to try him one-on-one, not even two-on-one. The Mistress gifted the Stalker to Jackie as a reward for her fidelity and Jackie used it to keep us in line. She said it was to show us the rewards that could be gained by staying faithful but... She let it hurt us, all of us, and torment us and...worse."

"It feeds off fear," I offered, though I wasn't sure what kind of comfort it would provide at this point.

"Maria sensed something was after her, she kept trying to come to us for help and we kept telling her she was imagining it. That's when Frank knew something was about to actually go down, it's why he sent her home and showed her how to protect herself."

Fractured trust didn't allow my heart to go soft and start bleeding for him, though I stopped trying to break him in half. With my hand still on the scruff of his robe I leaned toward the window they'd been peering through to see what was happening.

Jackie was vivacious, an absolutely possessed grin taking her ear-to-ear. It was a stark deviation from the scarred girl I'd met earlier.

"How's she contact this Mistress?"

"Through the Stalker... Which," he paused as it started to dawn on him. This meek, manipulated kid stiffened and stood a bit more upright. "Where is it?"

My dark smile said enough that I didn't have to.

"No... you?" There was an exuberant smile that was a vivid reminder of why I once used to love doing what my old entourage and I used to do.

"What's next then, are you going to go down there? I can help, please, I don't want to see Maria hurt..." he said.

"When you wake up, you just make sure you get out of here, okay?"

The flash of confusion was an unasked question I answered in the form of a harsh tug, drawing him into a chokehold. I wasn't taller than a lot of people, but he was the rare exception. I lifted him off his feet, collapsed his windpipe and felt that lithe frame go limp. Instead of casting him off, I actually escorted the pipsqueak all the way down. I knew what it was like to be in quicksand, when one bad choice had gotten you so deep that any action in any direction was going to lead to an even more damning one. The fat one I zip-tied to the railing. It took everything in me not to put a bullet in him, though before I could answer to my anger I imagined how many of them felt trapped because they just fell in with a charismatic demagogue who didn't stop staring into the abyss even after the Abyss started staring back.

I steadied myself on the steering column while I waited for a wave of drowsiness to wash over me. This was it—a rescue against a devout cult trying to call on some mysterious darkling from the Abyss while I was at half speed and barely able to see straight. When I could finally count to ten without grimacing or running out of air, I started to try and get a line of coherent thought in gear. First, I would retract the anchor. Pressing the button was another blind leap of faith since I knew nothing about a boat, let alone this one big, and wasn't sure what that would entail.

Luckily, no alarm sounded, and it seemed however the anchor was being retracted wasn't a very loud one. The rabble-rouser outside was feeding her followers some diatribe about ascension and their own vigorous response was doing a bang-up job of muting any noise I might have been making. Coaxing the engine to life, I put it in motion at the slowest possible speed.

Now that the boat was moving and I had two down, it was time for some good old-fashioned reconnaissance. Grove was the card-carrying badass at this kind of stuff; he'd have probably come back with an entire situational report about who was what-handed, their height, weight, favorite color and best point of entry and best chance at a successful extraction.

Me? I counted eight, not including Jackie at the raised dais with a petrified Maria beside her. Eight might not have been a tall order in my prime with all my own equipment but it would still be an uphill climb. Given where I was now, I just couldn't see how this would workout in my favor. Maybe if I could run the boat ashore without anyone really taking note beforehand, I would have a chance to split the group—and if I worked fast enough, I could put them down and get to Maria.

The problem was I knew just how hurt I was, and even without that, taking all these people on successfully was me being very optimistic.

I'd been lost in thought when I heard a culminating shriek capped off by booming applause from the handful below. Jackie grabbed the spherical contraption they'd suspended Maria in before reaching over and ripping her top clean off.

My blood boiled, my already pale knuckles whitened even worse and I felt the metallic railing I was holding onto start to give way as I let out a series of slurred curses.

She'd carved a sigil into Maria's stomach, bloodying her skin and scarring it for life. The sadistically carved rune was being fed by her still-living blood, amplifying whatever it was meant to do with the dark craft. Blood magic was bad enough; it was a whole new level of fiendish when harvested from a living source.

I was so drunk on rage that I couldn't even feel the exhaustion that had hampered me this whole time. The fire raging inside of me whitewashed the once-debilitating aches that made every movement a sluggish one. I barely remembered kicking the door open; I couldn't tell you what I screamed at Jackie when I stood across from her on the raised platform with the mass of her followers separating us below, and I didn't know when I had slipped on the gloves entrusted to me by Zachariah.

I just remembered the explosion, and the heat.

***

The gloves were an heirloom. Their craftsmanship was unique, the knowhow a well-kept secret, that had been bestowed down the very long and prestigious line of Zachariah's family. Runework was a subject that could be studied for a lifetime and one could still not come even remotely close to unlocking all the complex intricacies of the craft. The left glove could bring fire to life, and force-fed it a steady stream of pure oxygen. It was an onyx glove, and the multiplex stitching was blood red. It was a virtual flamethrower, though the problem was that the flame wasn't concentrated and dispersed widely the minute it left the cradle of the palm. That was where the second glove, also black but with white stitching, came into play. This glove fed off the focus of the wielder and it created a kinetic barrier, one that could trap the flame and allow it to build up in ferocity in a small, confined space. Depending on the skill of the user you could manipulate the shape, too, but that was a long way off for me. Point being, if one had the proper motivation and managed to conjure up a strong enough kinetic barrier, you could build one hell of a fireball.

It took Zachariah a year to even hold fire stable and a year longer to be able to cultivate it with enough control that it was weaponizable.

I did it my first try. Luck being a lady and all, it must have just been that in the beginning I was being looked upon favorably. That, or the anger. There was no textbook way this stuff could be done; at the end, it did tend to boil down to willpower. Anger like the kind filling the whole of my soul could feed willpower, just as air will feed fire.

The explosion launched Jackie, throwing her far from Maria. Unfortunately, the revealing of the rune they had used to ruin her skin had been enough to trigger it. An ambient energy flickered to life, its green hue a visual manifestation of Maria's power. Once produced, it swam around her once before gathering at her core and stretching skyward. It made sense to me; Wanderers had a piece of the Beyond inside of them that, unlike the sentient energy, could be manipulated. About twenty feet above her, a small opening started to peel back. The night sky was black; the cloudy forecast gave it a greyish tint, and yet what was opening was different—it was black, but a darker, more insidious kind of black. A living darkness.

The Abyss.

I knew it immediately even though I knew nothing about it or what exactly had transpired to make all this madness possible. When I hit Jackie with the fireball, all hell had broken loose. Two cultists scurried to check on their leader and the other six turned on me. The surge of adrenaline was leaving me quicker than it had come, and hurling the condensed orb of fire exhausted the last of my reserve. I less climbed and more fell to the floor below. One of them swung some kind of crude club at me and instinct allowed me to get my shield arm up in time, though I wasn't able to construct the actual shield in time, so instead I threw it wide. Another hooded figure, spurred on by their fallen leader, vehemently pushed the perceived opening.

Out came the gun, which stopped him cold. I could barely keep the damn thing steady but that didn't matter. I pulled the trigger.

It clicked. Nothing happened.

I laughed, before throwing the thing right into the sneering face of the one who'd been stalled by the sight of it. There was an explosion of blood when it ricocheted off his dome, peeling back the hood to reveal the face of gangly, awkward one I'd met before. I arrested his retreat with my left hand, still smoldering from the fireball, and relished in the agonizing cry he let out. Someone grabbed me from behind—their bear hug managed to rob what little air I still had in me, but before I could fall unconscious, someone else was dead-set on charging me. It was one of the women—a novice witch, if I recalled the breakdown Maria had given me earlier. She had some kind of handheld scythe raised high, looking to come down on my chest and finish me off. Whoever had me wasn't particularly strong, but I was just so sapped of any strength I couldn't extricate myself from the hold.

I got my feet up and absorbed a lot of her momentum with each leg. I was so weak I couldn't even imagine extending to try and kick her off, but fast thinking reminded me of my long-disdained boots.

I released the energy in each boot, catapulting her head over heel into the opposite side of the boat and in turn sending me and my keeper into the other side. I didn't have time to appraise what had happened, but judging from the gout of blood that erupted from out of her neck, I would guess the scythe had turned on her during that short flight.

Behind me, the groaning man was struggling to stand. Since I didn't have the strength to throw a punch, I literally whipped my body around while hoisting up the shield. There was a stomach-churning *crunch*. The telltale sound of a bone breaking.

"Enough!"

The fighting was sloppy, and little did the orator know that whoever came against me next was guaranteed victory. I was treading water when I was in the dead center of an ocean. I didn't even know how I kept my feet beneath me. In hindsight, it wasn't that bad. Out of ten people, I had managed to dispatch about five of them. Maria and I shared a look, and she was so terrified that I could feel her fear reverberating around inside of me. I did my best to try and hold a smile for her, though I know anyone who laid eyes on me right now knew that this fight was over.

Jackie looked downright nauseating. A third of her face was badly burned, taking with it a lot of hair and burning it down to the scalp. There was a blackened tint to her flesh all around the wound and the crazed, primal gleam in her eyes let me know that she was perfectly mad; angry and insane.

"You insignificant *shit*, are you so delusional that you thought you could somehow stop what was written in the stars to come?!"

I was sure I had no idea what she was talking about, but it was giving me a chance to breathe. I'd ignored the lunatic cackling until I saw her finger pointing skyward. That got my attention. The small circle of darkness had grown considerably, now about ten feet across. Captured in the looking-glass to a world beyond our own was a weird cliff. At the bottom were figureless creatures eagerly mulling around. Something about them was familiar, and I would have been able to place it if not for the figure sitting atop the cliff on a stony throne. She was a shapely profile of living shadow, featureless as the boisterous monsters raging below her— but that stare captivated and petrified me. It was otherworldly. The living canvas that depicted this was still growing, rimmed with the green energy being born from Maria.

Desperation was great fuel for a fire, but mine had been snuffed out; now with this living dread, I couldn't even keep my feet. Despair was anchoring me down.

Jackie broke the enthralling stare that had snared me with another heinous burst of maniacal laughter. I could feel the annoyance of the Mistress, and with the spell severed I could at least find my footing again.

With nothing left to give, I kept trying to think of some way I could get a wrench in the mechanics of all this before I fell flat on my face. Most of the followers now looked to the very image that had kept me so rapt, which meant I wasn't going to have to deal with them.

I fingered the half-bat. If I could get it across the threshold with a good enough throw, maybe I could gut the madwoman. At this point I wasn't sure if that would even make a difference.

The entire boat shook, angrily lurching forward when a giant mass of fur and violence leapt out of the portal and landed on the bow just behind Maria and Jackie.

It wrapped those long, malicious fingers around the crazed cult leader. Those black nails dug deeply into her flesh, though judging by the way she kept howling with delight, it was easy to guess she was too far gone to care.

With a horrific jerk the Stalker bashed her against the deck, killing her instantly, before throwing her limp body through the portal he'd just jumped out of. About a dozen others fought over her remains, snapping viciously at one another with their elongated maws and razor-sharp teeth.

Those eyes—those damned reptilian and fascinating eyes—had clued my subconscious into what those things were before my present mind could sift through all the muddled bullshit to figure it out.

Three things dawned on me then: one, coming through the portal prematurely had weakened the gateway; it had shrunk considerably after the beast passed the threshold. Two, this Stalker made the other look like an emaciated pup, with a thicker hide and fuller body that was rippling with a more impressive mass of muscle. It was a foot taller and had to have at least another hundred pounds on it.

And the third was a cold comfort, that even in the face of certain death I'd have enough wherewithal and gumption to make a wisecrack.

"Oh, come the fuck on..."

It leered at me from its elevated station while the cult members scurried to every corner of the boat. Too afraid to stay close, and yet also fearful of trying to flee. Maria managed to sob my name, and even as the monster wound up to dive down on me, I was able to try and ease her with a sincere smile.

"It's okay," I lied to her. "It's all going to be okay, Maria."

I heard the wooden platform whine when the monster launched itself from off of it, like the slip of a guillotine.

CHAPTER 20

SHOWDOWN #2

The thing moved so fast it was hard to track, and by the time it threw itself at me I knew it was too late for me to do anything. What I couldn't have known was that as fast as it was, there was something just as fast and every bit as big that could. A midair collision happened with such savagery that all the scampered cult members let out a chorus of shrieks and screams. Something had hit the Stalker like a living bullet, the force of the impact sending both parties over the side and into the water, and by the time the two untangled I had just gotten to the edge of the boat to look overboard. This creature was less deformed, more natural looking, but definitely some kind of relative to the Stalker. Thicker-armed and -legged, though they weren't as long. The snout was also canine but much more wolfish and not so narrow. There wasn't a patchwork of hair, either; the hide was kept beneath a beautiful field of brown and gold fur. The Stalker was visibly confused, and before it could make sense of what was happening, the other beast set upon it. They fought faster than I could track, and managed to do so in about three feet of water.

Three feet of water.

The boat cracked hard into the shoreline, and with a mighty groan the whole thing rattled before falling silent. I had aimed it at the shore and idled it in hope of this very thing, though I would have wanted to pick my timing a little better if it could have been helped. By now, most of the cult had found themselves a little more brave being that the Stalker was overboard, but with the scrutiny of their Mistress still settled high above them they weren't about to tuck tail and run. They had wizened up enough to know that I didn't have much fight left in me, and coordinated their approach with a series of courage bolstering looks and prods. The Mistress, held aloft, looked perturbed but not yet shaken. That didn't happen until the merry band of confident cultist got scattered to the four corners again by Kaycee. One minute the jackal group was clamoring to finish the fight and quickly closing in on me. The next, Kaycee soundlessly landed between us, except now she not the warm, chiding mother of three. This was the Lioness of the battlefield. Wearing the leaf-inspired armor of her people with a decorative spear, Kaycee, the warrior, made quick work of the first two before the other two thought better of what they had come across and threw themselves overboard. There was a steady soundtrack of feral fighting playing in concert with the panicked screams of surviving cultists trying to escape.

"Friend of yours?" I breathlessly asked while she easily helped me to my shaky feet.

"Xander," she answered.

"Xander?"

A clap of power rumbled the darkening sky above us. The matron of the Abyss was now openly infuriated by all that was transpiring.

"Help Maria, I'll try to hold them off." She instructed, holding my shaking hand in her steady one.

"The—" I started, then fell silent as I saw what was happening above.

The portal quaked again, expanding to let out four shadowy, wisp-thin figures from its yawning mouth. Again, the aftermath of the trespass shrunk the portal. Like everything with magic, there was a balance to factor in, and it didn't take a rocket scientist to figure out that whenever something came through it, it sapped the very bridge binding this world to the Abyss. The four figures looked alien, unnaturally lengthened. Stretched arms above almost feminine waists and spindly legs. Their faces were narrow and their eyes slanted. It didn't take me long to recognize that they were like elves, except they were from the Abyss—they had gotten the misnomer of a dark elf. Their inky flesh was covered in leather like armor, not so thick that it hindered their speedy movements, though. I knew that they had a good grasp of the craft as well as being legendary fighters. Kaycee was a half of their counterpart from the Veil, and there was no way she'd be able to fight off four of them by herself.

Four leapt out of the portal, but only three landed. A shot rang out and it took one of the airborne elves right in the chest and reversed its momentum so fiercely I couldn't even follow where it was flung off to. Given the magical inclination and fabled resilience of the elves, I couldn't even start to imagine what kind of gun could get through all that, but I was hoping one day he'd show me.

Donovan was dumping a spent shell out of a strange looking gun; it seemed to be a much larger musket from a bygone era. Instead of a flintlock mechanism it had some kind of hybrid shotgun working. It was far more decorated than any traditional, man-made gun, and the runework scribed into the shaft of the barrel was illuminated with recently spent energy.

Kaycee was falling into a brutally beautiful dance with two of them, while Donovan was retrieving a single-shot pistol from his hip.

I didn't have time to dawdle or second-guess anything. Xander was locked in a fight with the massive Stalker, Kaycee and Donovan were risking it all to keep the dark elves from finishing me off. I had to get to Maria. I collapsed against the stairwell to the second tier of the bow platform, willing myself up with every bit of effort it was taking my makeshift team to fight off their perspective enemies.

Being so close to the opened rift was usurping in a totally different but equally unnerving way. The crippling despair that enervated every bit of my own will when I locked eyes with the Mistress was back, and there was a biting chill that seemed to sink past my flesh and burrow itself inside of my soul. I wasn't sure when it happened, but I was crawling to Maria, pulling myself up by the contraption she was in.

"Janzen? Janzen!"

I manage a sickly smile for her.

"What's going on? What about... What about what's coming out of the portal, how are you here?"

"A Stalker and some ninja elves?" I made an indignant sound, blending my dismissive snort with a shrug. "That's a warmup."

Despite having her abdomen turned into a Jackson Pollock piece and the fact that she's strung up on some twisted kind of sacrificial altar, she seemed to have a good enough grasp of her facilities to shoot me a perfectly exasperated look.

"We got help."

I was pulling at the straps they'd used to secured her, giving the constraints a vicious tug. The metal binding was cutting into her flesh and I had to steady my breath to keep my head from being clouded with another episode of blinding rage.

"Janzen—"

"—I think I've got something that can—"

"JANZEN!"

The controlled panic in her voice clued me into the fact that I needed to not just turn around, but to do so in a fashion that would move me from where I was. I'd been around enough life-threatening situations to know when it was time to just act. It was one of the biggest mistakes made on a battlefield: inaction.

There was a sharp whisper of something passing by before I heard the break of wood and the whine of warped metal. Something fired at me with enough force that it cut through the deck I was standing on, eating through every layer of the boat before actually exiting out the hull below. There was a blackish residue left over, the acidic quality made apparent by the way it continued to eat through the framework of the boat. I looked around to see about the last two cult members I'd seen on here, the ones who'd helped Jackie when I sent her soaring off with a fireball, but they seemed to still be cowering into one another on the far end.

That's when it dawned on me.

I peeled my head upward, my sluggish movement probably a byproduct of my fatigue, and the fact that if this theory proved to be true, I was doomed. I was out of miracles.

The Mistress was far more visible now, her ashen skin flawlessly stretched over a curvaceous figure. Even as she was readying a spell that would see me dead, I couldn't help but notice how impossibly, twistedly erotic she was; blackened mouth somehow turned a sneer sultry. The fabric that clung to her was a living second skin and left very little to the imagination.

There was another soundless explosion of energy; it was inaudible, and yet with the way it harkened to every other sense, it seemed like you could somehow hear it. It garnered the attention of the mad-eyed Mistress, too, because she turned the spell she'd been preparing for me and actually had to toss it outward to contend with whatever was coming.

I whipped around in time to see Gale, standing on the second story; in her hand was the origin of a lancing shot of blue energy. It met the dark, ichorous spell midway, and when they met headlong, a tumultuous crash roared. It roared with such authority it seemed to resonate in all of us, stalling the fight happening at every corner of the boat. Gale never looked so damn fierce to me than in that moment. She was regal in the simplicity of a green garment, her red hair shimmering with Celtic resplendence. She was every bit as breathtaking as the creature she was defying. I spared her a long, appreciative look; one that even if she could share, I doubted she would have. Appraising the Mistress and the Barkeep, I could tell that it was taking everything in Gale to maintain the stalemate and that the Mistress hadn't even started to overextend herself, though the effort by no mean was a minor one.

I scampered to get back beside Maria, ripping the half-bat off of my hip. "Look, we have to close this damn thing. I'm sorry, this is going to hurt."

Maria initially seemed uncertain, and yet when I lowered the spire of the shard bat down to her midsection she grasped what I had been saying, her understanding didn't steal any of her bravery though and she just gave me a nod. I fit my glove in her mouth for her to bite down before adding to the hideous scar she'd have from all of this. I cut right through the sigil they'd worked into her flesh, hoping to disrupt the magic it's conjured up. I got all the way through, ignoring her muffled wailing and doing my best to hold her steady so the cut was clean.

I pivoted back and did my best to not look long at the mutilated mess of her stomach and instead searched skyward. The portal wasn't lessening; in fact, the pulsing growth was still steadily going. Gale was starting to wane in her effort and when I caught a glimpse of the lower level I could see Donovan retreating under the pressure of a pair of dark elves. At some point, they had traded off. Kaycee didn't look good. She was bloodied in several spots and also outright backpedaling.

"Damnit. Damnit, that should have worked."

"It's bound to me now," Maria said more aloud than to either one of us. "That's what she said would happen. There's no stopping it."

"No, just... Hold on." I took her wrist and wrenched it forward, using the half-bat to cut the ties binding her. I did the same to the other arm. "Take this," I said, handing it over to Maria, who seemed almost impossibly collected. She was the calm at the heart of this storm, so I guessed, at the time, it was fitting. "Cut your feet free. I'm going to get one of these two to tell me how to shut this down."

Maria paused my attempt to leave her side with a clutching hand, one I didn't recall slipping into my own. I was beat and she could see that; the look she leveled at me was one born of respect, gratitude and quiet acceptance. She was so heartbreakingly beautiful in that moment, even now when the macabre grime of blood was washing down the front of her and the whole world was at war all around us. It was only a second but that stare seemed to spirit us away to our own eternity. This isn't a love story, but for the first time I wish I had taken the time to regard her the way she deserved.

She gave my hand a reaffirming squeeze and a nod that spurred me into action. "Watch my back."

"Always."

I got to the pair before they could scramble overboard. Their own nervousness and anxiety turned to outright fear when they saw me locked in on them. I used that trepidation to my advantage, grabbing the one on the left and throwing him down but doing it with the fire-bearing glove so they got a searing bite in the process. Their cry stifled by a courage-stealing glare I hold him in before hoisting the second one up.

"You've got one cha—"

There was a piercing scream, and all the apprehension the pair I had just accosted felt doubled inside of me. Dread gripped me, and worse, I wasn't sure why. I knew everything around me seemed to just stop, though. I couldn't hear the clash of fighting below, the voracious snaps and growls of the beast ceased as well. That awful scream ceased it all.

In the sky, the passage to the Abyss was already waning, that vortex starting to spiral in on itself at its frayed edges. Gale and the Mistress were still locked in a fierce battle, though by now Gale was almost completely pinned back by the wretched attack the dark godling was hurling at her. Even with the prospect of losing that battle she had eyes for only one thing: the altar.

The altar where Maria was sprawled out still held her aloft. Her ghastly face wore a sickly smile—a defiant expression if ever I saw one, and this coming from a man who owned the patent on them. The last vestige of energy being siphoned out of her had completely stalled out, the very energy needed to keep the bridge between this world and the Abyss. It was gone and at first I couldn't figure out why. It took me a minute.

I slipped as I hurriedly tried to get to her, panic flooding every inch of me as the ugly epiphany was set at my clumsy feet. I saw my half-bat, the one gifted with that supernatural sharpness, buried deep inside of her gut. A geyser of blood erupted when the obstinate girl ripped it out of her own body. The gruesome fissure seemed to take a gargled breath before the flood of her own life started to waterfall out of her.

"No!" I just stupidly repeated that over and over again, as if my stubborn refusal of inescapable reality was going to somehow make all of this better. This cut was too wide, the stab so damn deep, that there was nothing I could do even if I had a clear mind and the proper equipment.

"Maria, no-no-no, come on, look at me... Hey, look at me."

Maria, for her part, looked so serene that I had to wonder if this was what real peace must be. An acceptance of a fate you'd designed for yourself, and the power to see it through. The Mistress raging above, speaking a dead dialect, was the polar opposite of the woman below.

"Hey," she said. She was fading, and the dreamy look in those lovely eyes kept me in the present. A fact I was, and am still, thankful for.

"Maria, just, wait—wait, okay? We're going to get you out of here."

My vision blurred. The successive head trauma and tears made sure I wouldn't be seeing straight anytime soon. I was about to leave her side to see if any of them could come up with a solution; on a night of miracle saves, I just needed one more.

Just one more.

Kaycee and Donovan were hustling to get beside Gale; the fight between her and the Mistress was turning too quickly to be kept at an even keel before the portal closed off her ability to hurt all of us. Kaycee was conjuring some kind of shield around all of them while the Tinkerer was letting loose a volley from one of those customized rifles to try and busy the Mistress so she couldn't finish the fight.

Me? Maria had used the last slip of strength she had to grip my hand.

"Stay with me?" Blackish blood crept out of the corner of her mouth, a telling fact that there was no coming back from this; even in a world full of magic, there was a limit to what the body could take. It was a marvel to me that I could so thoroughly get my ass kicked all week and still stand upright, but just one stroke was all it took to take her from me. "Watch my back?"

"Always."

She was cold, and too damn courageous to say anything about it. Maria fought for every breath—not to stay alive and make it through, but to see this fight through. I could tell, and so I spun the altar that those bastards, whom I would chase down to the end of the fucking world when this was through, had strung her up to. I turned her so that she could watch the passage die out. Resolve was written across her fading face. When she couldn't keep her failing body upright, I cradled her in my own weak arms so we could bear witness to what we had done together.

"Makes me wonder... If I wasted all that time... Going to church."

"I think you're going to be all right."

She nestled into the crook of my arm and I drew her to my chest. Death was never clean; people panicked, they fought, there was a crazed resistance to the inevitable—and yet she was doing it so peacefully.

"I knew you were sweet on me," I said softly.

She was almost gone, but she managed a last, melancholic smile for me. It would stay with me forever and break my heart all over again whenever I thought on it. Still, I was grateful; it reminded me that I was alive.

"Please," she said, clutching my jacket. We were both crying, our faces wracked with pain. "You never had a chance with Grove around."

I laughed, and it felt good, even as the last bit of goodness in me lay dying in my own arms. I laid my forehead against hers, and our mingled tears ran down her cheeks.

"Bullshit."

"Bullshit," she echoed with a smile before she was gone.

And then there was an enormous explosion and it all went black.

CHAPTER 21

AFTERMATH

"Janzen! Janzen, oh my God," Kaycee called, sloshing into the water from the shoreline. At some point, the clash between the Mistress and Gale had gotten back to some kind of equal footing and as a parting gift, the dark goddess must have snapped the spell and allowed the one cultivated by our own to implode. It rocked the boat so sharply it tossed most of us overboard before the boat itself banked and tipped sideways. Luckily, I had run us aground, so it wasn't like we were in that deep of water.

Kaycee grabbed my arm and pulled me halfway upright with that shocking strength. She stopped when she realized what it was I had been so desperately holding onto—Maria, now gone from this world, limp and soaked. Donovan was supporting Gale, though the tinkerer stiffened a bit at the sight of me and the girl who'd sacrificed it all to see us safe emerging from the murky water. Kaycee whispered my name with a motherly tenderness.

"Don't," I choked out, pulling Maria close to me.

"Xander." With just an utterance of his name, Gale commanded the warrior into motion. He was barefoot and naked from the waist up, moving toward me and the lifeless body of our modern-day martyr. Maria, a woman who'd had the misfortune of trusting goodness to see her safe at a time when there was none. He reached down and I stopped him with a look.

"Stop," I said. My arm was dislocated again, my body depleted of any energy and sapped of all the strength I once commanded, but this was more important than that. It wasn't graceful, the way I had to wrap her around me. With one good arm I held her, and with shaky legs I got us out of the water. "This isn't for you. This is my job."

They all watched me as I stumbled out of the lake with my dead friend, but I managed. I always did.

We always would.

EPILOGUE

The bar was a dull hole-in-the-wall establishment; the amount of people frequenting it as well as how deep in their drinks they were at this time of the day let me know that I wasn't really all that alone. The smoky haze was going to cling to my jacket for the rest of the day, but that didn't matter. I was exhausted, and judging from my sunken-faced reflection, anyone who spared me more than a look would be able to tell that.

"You ready?" the bartender asked.

He was pissed. My order was a bit unconventional, and I would guess it wasn't the first time he asked if I was ready. I daydreamed, a lot. Even still.

"Yeah," I muttered, fishing out what little cash I had left after this most recent foray. I slapped a twenty down and told him to keep the change.

"You sure you can afford this kind of generosity?" he quipped dryly.

"I can't afford to be magnanimous, but you'll see me around."

The prospect didn't thrill him.

I walked out of the filthy den of forfeited hopes and dead ambitions into the blinding light of midday.

"You ducking the hard stuff again?" Kaycee asked, walking over from her store which was only a few feet down from the underground bar.

"Food." I lifted the to-go bag up for her to see.

"From there? That's brave."

"Bravery is my middle name."

"Well, I appreciate you letting him do all the hard work anyway," she added, lazily grinning. Her toothy expression was like a hungry jungle cat not yet sated.

We both turned our attention across the street to the new storefront under construction. Grove was laboring away, shirtless, trying to get the last bit of framing in place before we opened.

Circle Protection Agency.

"Well, let's go inside and eat, yeah?"

"Yeah."

Kaycee and I roped arms and crossed the road, waving down the hard-working stud. She gave an audible groan when the Adonis slipped into a white shirt.

"You're married, woman," I chided.

"I ain't dead." She laughed, which was contagious.

I gracefully handed Kaycee off to Grove when we arrived at our new joint venture. They halted to look expectantly at me, but I waved them off to go in without me.

They did. Kaycee murmured something while Grove thoughtfully caressed the plaque hung up right beside our entrance—a dedication with the portrait of our friend above it.

The plaque read: *The only thing necessary for the triumph of evil is for good men to do nothing.*

I knew there was a more eloquent turn of phrase, but I felt in that kind of terse simplicity it would be more fitting. This was going to be her legacy. Our legacy. That was why I took a moment to stand outside and take it all in.

We'd worked day and night getting this place put together. The red tape around starting a security firm was a nightmare, but Grove had good credentials once we got him cleared of all criminal charges. Well, once his sister eventually did, after another hard slap to my still-hurting face along with an added warning that we were now on the radar of the local magistrate.

"Circle Protection. Little on the nose, don't you think?" came a male voice from over my shoulder.

"Father Handy." My face tightened when I felt him sidle up beside me, looking at the same thing I was.

"No racy one liner, no sordid quip?" he asked.

"It's no fun when it pretty much writes itself."

We shared a long silence. Inside, I watched Kaycee and Grove set a hasty table with the smattering of furniture we had yet to organize while Max circled like a shark, wagging his tail and shamelessly begging for our food. I didn't pry Father Handy; even though I suspected that he was a cosmic entity, I could tell that he was a bit thrown by my silence.

"Nothing at all, really?" he pressed.

I pointed to the picture of Maria and, more importantly, the quote beneath it.

"Ah, so you think I did nothing?"

"No. I appreciate the marble, and the pep talk at the church, but I've a suspicion that you could have just twinkled your nose and made all this an afterthought. Instead, I got thirty thousand in hospital bills, a dead friend and a whole lot of unanswered questions."

"And you're not going to try and ask me?"

"It's not your play. You're a sideline type, and I don't have the patience to get all vague and mysterious."

"You forgot about Zachariah, too," he said.

That gave me pause. I had started walking away, about to leave him outside to his own devices, but when that last tidbit was offered I couldn't help but follow that line of inquiry. After the boat, I had assumed I was insane, or my brain trauma had gotten the best of me. What didn't follow was that the gloves complied with my use of them so quickly—nothing would ever just fall into sync when it had been used by another person for so long, and I was very confident that Zachariah hadn't crafted those with the thought that they could be universally used.

"Fine, you helped. A little. Is that what you came here for?"

"I very rarely do stuff for me, kid."

The priest had such fascinating eyes. They were like a living thing, moving and expanding. We were not so different in terms of height, though in build we were on opposite ends of the spectrum. Not as severe as it used to be, mind you. Grove and I now had a pretty rigorous diet and workout routine that I followed, mostly.

"Was that really him?" I asked.

The entity hiding in the vessel of a well-mannered priest nodded.

"Weird," I said. Father Handy's hiked eyebrow asked why I thought that was so strange, so I elaborated. "I just didn't think Zachariah was the religious type."

"Ah. Well. Zachariah. I mean, come on. That alone would get him a green light past the pearly gates, you know?"

"So it's in the name?" I asked.

"Marketing and good publicity don't hurt." He was messing with me, and I could tell as much by the tight-lipped smirk we were sharing.

"It was good to see him... Real good."

"He's proud of you," he said.

"I know," I said.

"It's tough to buy that in all this madness there's a God," he offered.

"Like, a God-God, not just a... Like, a big God." Another bout of eloquence helped me convey my point while turning to better regard him.

"You ever entertaining belief is a miracle in and of itself."

"Not saying I do... I mean, with all this madness, plus the grief we bring on ourselves, I can't help but think the one true God thing might be a sham. It's impossible to be all-good, all-knowing and all-powerful, you know."

"Never took you for a philosopher," the priest interjected through a still-rumbling chuckle.

"Intro to philosophy, community college, like four years back... So, I am something of a subject matter expert, if we're being honest."

"Ah," he said, adding nothing after the humored sound, though the smile from all that laughing never ebbed all the way off.

I turned to look at the picture of Maria and felt a pang of guilt again. The choking sadness started to moisten my eyes. "It's just shit that she's not going to enjoy the good afterlife. I know what assholes you are about suicide. Which is bullshit, you kno—"

"Suicide?" He was looking at me as if I were perfectly insane.

"Well, yeah." I looked from him, back to her lovely disposition, the one immortalized at our entrance. We'd cut her father in, too; if this place ever did turn a profit, he would get a piece of it. We figured that would be a nice gesture, and after the initial grieving he seemed more grateful that something good would be carried out in her name.

"Did she take her life, or save all of yours? I didn't see a suicide..."

The reflection in the window pane showed me the contemplative priest, hand in pockets, staring skyward.

Beside him was Maria. Our Maria. My Maria, looking whole and happy. I understood how this thing worked, and knew the second I turned around they'd be gone. The guy couldn't help but work in mysterious ways, and it just fit his modus operandi. I staved off the tears as long as I could, before laying my hand on the glass I was using to look at her.

"She's proud of you, too," he said.

When I turned around they were gone, and even though I was alone, I wasn't. She, like my old mentor, was with me. Like my surrogate family inside.

I walked inside the Circle Protection Agency, turning over the "OPEN" sign for the first time as I did.

ACKNOWLEDGEMENTS

To Karla, my creative partner, the woman with monk-like patience who has helped me not only find my voice but become a better human being. I would have been lost this last year without you and there's no doubt that I would have been one of the twenty-two veterans who take their life daily had you not stuck by me.

My dad for footing a ridiculous bill and yet somehow staying a believer in me and all I could one day do. I do not believe I've met a better man, and I know some greats. Love you Dad, thanks for never giving up on me.

Lynne Davis, the mother that taught me to not only be true to self but to do so fearlessly. You're why I tried to make this a book rich with strong women, because it's all I have ever known.

The writers who helped shape me while we collaborated on such fantastic journeys: Kitt that brought out the best in me and made me the writer I am today. The world is done an injustice until you decide to share your talent with the world and I'll make sure you do just that. Justin Handy for keeping it competitive and for being my brother since thirteen. Casey for nurturing the fun of it all, I love you so big, thanks for quasi-adopting me. Jamie for always having my back and willing to work on (or at least entertain) the endless slew of insane ideas that come out of my mouth. Cake; soul shattering stories made so powerful because of your imagination and passion.

To Nick 'deserving of a better nickname' Hoffman, we're twenty years strong family and here is to another twenty, Michael Condit, Nathan Grove (I'll never pay you back), Aaron Foote, Kerry

Rocks, Anthony Breitfeller, Jason Harrington, Biff, Priscilla, J. Janke, Sirena, Marty, Alex, Dan, Esther, Nina, Aisha and just so many more that hopefully I keep this writing thing going and get an opportunity to better acknowledge, thank and praise them.

A special thanks to Steve Jackson and the unbelievable staff at WildBlue Press, not only am I a first-time author with just a boatload of questions, but I am a complete newcomer to the industry so their patience is appreciated and dedication is second to none.

Last and opposite of least, to Amie Hulme; my partner in all I do and the light of my life.

ALSO AVAILABLE FROM WILDBLUE PRESS!

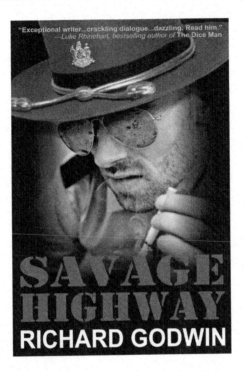

SAVAGE HIGHWAY by RICHARD GODWIN

"The road novel from hell, a scarifying, terrifying tour of a nether world that Godwin convinces us is right beneathrichardgodwin-blog-picture our feet, a surrealist inferno that makes Dante's version look like a Rotary breakfast. By no means for the fainthearted, SAVAGE HIGHWAY has one lesson for any readers who plan a visit to the American Southwest: take the train."– **Castle Freeman Jr.**, author of THE DEVIL IN THE VALLEY

http://wbp.bz/savagehighway

CPSIA information can be obtained
at www.ICGtesting.com
Printed in the USA
LVOW13s1303200318
570342LV00016BB/2156/P

Janzen Robinson is a man torn between two wo[rlds] [li]fe as an apprentice to a group of do-gooding hero[es] [ng] supernatural evils, the once-promising student [s] through the daily grind on the south side of Cleveland, Ohio.

Then fate (or a case of bad timing) brings him face to face with a door that's got hi[s] old life written all over it. From the ancient recesses of unyielding darkness known as the Abyss, a creature has been summoned: a Stalker. It's a bastardization of the natural order, a formidable blend of dark magic and primal tenacity. It[s] single-minded mission? Ending the life of a fiery, emerging young witch.

Thrust into the role of protector, the out-of-practice "Artificer" not only has to return to a life he'd left behind, but must relive that painful past while facing down the greatest threat to come to our world in a century. Janzen will have to journey through the magical underbelly of the city and not only stay one step ahead of an unstoppable monster but figure out why it's been brought to our world in the first place. Past wound[s] are reopened as Janzen looks to old friends, a quiet stranger, and his own questionable wits to see them all to the other side of this nightmare that may cost him his life and, quite possibly, end the world.

ABOUT THE AUTHOR: Lawrence Davis is a decorated U.S. Army infantryman who served three combat tours overseas, including in Iraq. His first book, **BLUNT FORCE MAGIC,** was written in part to help navigate the struggles associated with Post Traumatic Stress Syndrome (personified by The Stalker in his novel). He's a shooting instructor and dog rescue advocate who lives in Florida with his four rescue pitbulls, and extremely patient girlfriend.

FANTASY

WILD BLUE
P R E S S

wildbluepress.com

ISBN 978-1-947290-10-5

90000

9 781947 290105